THE SUBSTITUTE BRIDE

Dorothy Mack

SAPERE
BOOKS

THE SUBSTITUTE BRIDE

Published by Sapere Books.

20 Windermere Drive, Leeds, England, LS17 7UZ,
United Kingdom

saperebooks.com

ISBN: 978-1-913335-37-3

CHAPTER ONE

Into the vibrating silence came the sudden snapping of a log which fell with a small crash, startling one occupant of the comfortable room into starting nervously. The remaining two persons were so engrossed with each other they took no notice of the noise. The gentleman's boyish, good-looking countenance wore an unaccustomed expression of mingled wrath and amazement. Except for a lurking twinkle in the eyes of the lady watching him expectantly, her attitude was one of utter calm and self-possession.

Interpreting that humorous gleam, a reluctant grin appeared briefly, but his voice held nothing but exasperation.

"No, dash it all, Devil, it is out of the question! You shouldn't last a sennight and well you know it. Taking care of other people's brats. It wouldn't suit you at all."

Before the lady addressed by this opprobrious title could respond, the third occupant intervened to protest in a light, sweet voice. "Billy, I do wish you would cease referring to your cousin by that terrible name. It will give people a very odd notion of her indeed."

The speaker was seen to be a young woman, pretty in the typically English style, with a pink and white complexion, fair ringlets and light blue eyes which she raised reproachfully to her husband's suddenly laughing face.

"On the contrary, I think it gives a very fair notion of her character, but there, love, don't tease yourself. I would not think of calling her that in the presence of strangers. Shall I call you Angel instead, Angelica, as your besotted father was used to do?"

The lady thus addressed had unconcernedly returned to her stitchery during this exchange. She looked up now with a hint of a smile. "Do call me anything you like," she invited cordially. "Whatever seems most appropriate." Now both eyes and lips smiled a challenge at him.

Casting an appraising eye over his cousin, the gentleman concluded, not for the first time, that she had been singularly inappropriately named. While there was certainly nothing devilish about her regular but unspectacular assembly of features, a person would be ill judged indeed to assume that her customary serenity of expression betokened an angelic disposition. And those unusual green eyes were distinctly non-angelic witch's eyes, he mused. Not that there was anything devilish in her character either, despite his teasing words. No one knew better than he that there was no harm in the girl. She was warm-hearted and had a generous kindness for the very old or young or ill. With all this, though, marched an independent spirit and a dislike of convention and formality. She had a mighty free tongue, too, he thought worriedly, and none of these traits fitted her to assume an inferior position in someone else's household.

He had cherished a great fondness for her ever since she had arrived with her mother, following the sudden death of her adored father some fourteen years before. From his superior position of eleven years against her mere nine, he had immediately taken the shy, grieving wraith under his protection. She had shared his lessons with his tutor, his horses, his sports and his interests as a brother might have done.

It would have been better if she had been a boy, he could see now with all the clarity of hindsight. Then Charlotte would have had no cause to resent her presence in their home. He could understand that to his very young bride, the self-possessed young woman some three or four years her senior sharing her household on intimate terms with her husband might represent a challenge to her position as undisputed mistress. He was aware that the two girls shared few interests in common, and after four months of enforced association showed no signs that they could exist on any closer terms than polite forbearance.

He sighed inwardly. Angelica had had one season in London while his mother and hers were still living, but had formed no attachment there. Indeed, as he recalled, she had barely tolerated society and had been eager to return to the country. She had no fortune but a small annuity which would cease upon her marriage, and she flatly refused to let him provide her with a dowry. In any case, she was hardly likely to contract an eligible match hidden away at Wroxham Court. Neither were there any relatives she could go to. Her position had not chafed until his recent marriage. Still, there must be some better course than hiring herself out as a governess. He could not see that as an acceptable alternative to continuing here with them.

She had been watching his worried expression while plying her needle industriously and now spoke up briskly.

"Don't look so unencouraging, Billy. I am quite looking forward to beginning an adventure on my own. You know I have a fondness for children, and what is more they attend to me. You will recall when the Moretons visited here last year I was the only one who could deal with that little demon, Cecil. Although I confess to being sadly lacking in musical ability, you will allow that in all other respects I am admirably qualified to instruct the young. By the time I have gained some practical experience, you and Charlotte will have set up your nursery, and I can come back and reign over your children," she finished cheerfully.

Billy still looked unconvinced, but before he could frame a rebuttal, Charlotte had once more intervened.

"When Mrs. Edgerton called this morning, she did mention that Lord Desmond has just lost his governess. Mrs. Edgerton's Miss Pringle is a cousin to the woman who taught Desmond's daughter, and she says her cousin has had to leave to take care of her mother who has been very ill. You are acquainted with Giles Weston, are you not?" she inquired of her husband.

"Yes, of course. Known him for years, though he is quite a bit older than I. Used to be a close friend of m' brother's, but I don't think…"

"Oh, Billy, do you think if you wrote to him Lord Desmond might hire me for the position?" asked Angelica eagerly. "I remember him from that visit he made to Gervaise years and years ago, when we were children. I'm sure he would make an unexceptional employer."

Billy grinned at her. "I'm sure you do remember him, my dear. To the best of my recollection, you followed him around like a Tantony pig after he pulled you out of the lake."

"And whose fault was it that I fell into the lake?" she retorted with spirit. "You would insist that you could handle the boat even with all that wind."

"And you, of course, were always determined to try anything I could do and never paid the least heed to any hints that your company was not desired."

Charlotte's sweet voice interrupted this recital of earlier peccadilloes in which she had no part.

"Will you write to Lord Desmond then, Billy?"

Her husband's expressive countenance sobered suddenly, and he looked long and intently at his cousin before answering reluctantly, "Yes, if she wishes it."

For her part, Angelica met his gaze with her usual equanimity and answered promptly, "Indeed I do wish it."

"Very well, I'll do it tomorrow," Billy said with resignation, and promptly changed the subject by asking his wife about her visit to one of his cottagers who had fallen from his roof while mending it.

Angelica sat quietly, her needle never pausing over her work, but she felt drained of all strength. She was grateful to Billy for turning attention away from her, for she needed time to gather her resources for the next step in her plan to remove herself from her cousin's home without leaving any impression of coercion or ill feeling behind. She bore Charlotte no ill will for her very natural feelings toward her husband's cousin, and was honest enough to admit that she herself had not been happy about relinquishing the reins of management to another. Since her aunt's death two years ago, she had been virtual mistress of Wroxham Court despite the presence of an aged spinster relative for propriety's sake. She suspected ruefully that she must have an odiously managing disposition, a quality very ill-suited to her station in life.

If only she and Charlotte had been of different temperaments, perhaps they could have contrived to rub along more comfortably together. For Billy's sake, she must take some step which would allow him to live happily alone with his bride. Apart from marriage with the widowed incumbent of a nearby parish, which certainly did not appeal, she could think of no other solution than to hire herself out as a governess, the only genteel employment open to a female of her station. Her opinion on the desirability of being born a male exactly coincided with that of her cousin.

She sighed for the opportunities lost through her unfortunate feminine nature, but decided practically to concentrate on preparing herself to become a competent governess. Now that she had made the decision, she was eager to act on it and hoped Billy would soon receive a favourable reply from Lord Desmond. She remembered him with pleasure as a charming man with a friendly smile, who had been kind to his host's younger brother and cousin. They had tagged after him shamelessly following the rescue, she recalled. Wrinkling her brow in concentration, she tried to remember just when the meeting had occurred.

"What's the matter, Devil? Have you changed your mind about seeking a position? A good thing, too, if you have. I still think you totally unfitted for the life of a governess." Her cousin's sharp eyes had noted her furrowed brow.

She chuckled, revealing a solitary dimple at the left corner of her mouth. "No, I am simply trying to recall when we received that visit from Lord Desmond. It was the only occasion when I met him, and I do remember hearing later that same year that he had married."

"Let's see, then it must have been quite ten years ago, because Desmond has been a widower for some six or seven years."

"He is engaged to be married," put in Charlotte unexpectedly.

"Is that so? Now this is a surprise! I run into him occasionally in London, though I've seen little of him since Gervaise died, of course. From what I've heard, he has pretty much forsworn your sex, my love, ever since his wife died."

"Mrs. Edgerton said Miss Pringle's cousin wrote that he was affianced to a very beautiful girl, the Earl of Dorset's elder daughter, I believe."

"He must have an eye for beauty. I remember hearing that his wife was one of the Incomparables of her season. Don't believe I ever met her though. Before my time. Well, as I said, Devil, I'll write to Desmond in the morning, though it will go against the grain with me to play such a trick on an old friend." He grinned wickedly at the affronted expression on his cousin's face and dodged the pillow she threw at him.

"Never mind," he said soothingly, "blood being thicker than water, I'll make you sound like a compilation of all the virtues peculiar to the species governess."

Even Charlotte laughed at that, and the talk turned to more general matters.

A week later, a still bemused Angelica was preparing to bid farewell to her cousin and his wife. The Viscount Desmond had replied with commendable, not to say unnerving promptitude that he would be happy to employ Mr. Wroxham's cousin, and could she come immediately to his house in London as his situation was rather urgent. Puzzling a bit over this, Angelica threw herself into preparations for leaving the only home she remembered, rather relieved that there was no time to ponder the decision. It had been arranged for her to travel in her cousin's carriage with Annie, their former nurse, accompanying her. They would put up overnight at one of the better hotels in London, so Angelica could get a good night's rest and arrive fresh at the viscount's residence in Grosvenor Square the following morning.

The inevitable goodbyes were said, and the carriage rolled smoothly down the avenue of still bare chestnut trees, accompanied by the outrider Billy had insisted upon. Her last glimpse of the Court came as they came through the gates onto the road. When the trees were in full foliage, only the chimneys were visible at this point, Angelica thought, as with misty eyes she watched the grey stone house disappear from view.

She sank back against the corduroy squabs, her face, despite her best efforts, revealing to the woman who knew her intimately some of the desolation she was experiencing at this wrenching apart of her old life. A necessary wrenching, she reminded herself firmly. For Billy's sake, she must go away and make a life for herself apart from his and Charlotte's. It had hurt to see his natural brightness of spirit dimming slightly, as he came slowly to the realization that his two loves could not dwell together in true amity. He was as dear to her as the brother she had never had.

She would find consolation from knowing she was doing the right thing. The faint anxiety that had haunted Billy's eyes this past week would fade as he read the cheerful, happy letters she was determined to write him.

At this point in her reflections, she squared her shoulders and sat up straighter, determined to keep her thoughts on the future.

Neither woman had spoken thus far, but Annie had been covertly studying Angelica, and at this sign that the girl was overcoming her lowness of spirits, she spoke matter-of-factly.

"When you marry, I shall come to you. Mr. Wroxham would be perfectly willing."

Angelica jumped, for she had completely forgotten Annie in her absorption. As the sense of the maid's words penetrated, her lips twitched and her green eyes lit with amusement.

"Come now, Annie," she spoke in a rallying tone, "you speak as if I had only to be seen to be swamped with offers. I have been seen, you must remember, and I was not inundated with proposals of marriage. I am sorry to disappoint you, but at three and twenty I am definitely on the shelf."

"Nonsense!" was the brisk retort. "I know what I know, and that Mr. Linders has been angling after you these two years and more. It's not a manor house, but he has a nice, snug rectory and a private income besides. He may not be a member of the gentry, but he's quality born and a well-educated gentleman. You could go far and do worse."

"Mr. Linders is a very worthy gentleman as you say, Annie, but it is a strange thing — I find myself oppressed by his serious nature. I have always the unworthy desire to say shocking things to rouse him from his gravity. I am sure he secretly believes I have too much levity. In fact, it is my belief that he does not understand me at all, but simply wishes to remarry because he is lonely and a parson needs a wife. Almost any other female would be a better choice than I."

Annie was silenced a moment by the serious tone of her mistress's voice, but eventually she persisted in arguing, "It would be better than working in a nobleman's house."

"No, Annie, believe me: we should not suit at all. At least as a paid employee I will have some independence. There will be times when I am free to do as I please and go where I please. I do not think I have the proper temperament for marriage," she added thoughtfully, her eyes fixed unseeingly on the piece of tatting in Annie's busy hands.

"Nonsense," came the brisk retort. "You will change your tune when the right man comes along."

"Since my non-existent fortune renders me totally ineligible in any case, it is just as well I have never formed the least attachment for any man."

At this prosaic remark, Annie pressed her lips firmly together, but allowed the subject to drop. Her heart misgave her when she thought of what the future might hold for the girl. The prospect seemed as bleak to her as the scene through which they were riding. The damp, grey, cold remains of a frigid winter dish spread before them for mile after mile. Neither woman derived any comfort from the unfolding of the still-fallow landscape, and both were relieved when the villages surrounding the city signalled the end of the tedious journey.

Angelica's pulses were beating in time to her chaotic mental sensations as the sights, sounds and odours of the city drove all coherent thought from her mind. She had forgotten how alive London made one feel. Now her eyes greedily absorbed the passing scene, and she was almost sorry when they swept up to the large hotel.

CHAPTER TWO

Angelica rose very early the next morning, too agitated by the immediate prospect of a fundamental change in her life to remain supine. Her mood hovered between reluctance to cut the last tie to her old existence and eagerness to begin an independent life. Certainly, there must be immense satisfaction in being able to say, "I earn my own living; I owe no one gratitude or humble appreciation for favours bestowed." She resolutely refused to dwell on the ambiguous status of governesses in general, certainly not of the family nor yet of the household. One day at a time would be her motto, and her optimistic nature foresaw a much more interesting pattern of living in a nobleman's town house than the quiet country existence she had been used to since her own brief season.

She was fumbling with the buttons of a demure grey woollen dress made high to the neck, its collar trimmed in the same delicate lace which edged the long tight sleeves, when Annie entered the room to draw back the curtains and stopped, speechless for a second, to see her very much awake.

"Here, let me do that," she said, bustling over to her mistress. "Why didn't you call me, if you must get up at the crack of dawn? Though how a body can sleep with all the noise of this place — carriages and horses going by at all hours — I'm sure I don't know."

"Oh, I don't doubt I'll soon adjust to the bustle of town," Angelica said soothingly. "It never bothered me when I had my come-out, and it is really rather exciting. I would not want to live in town all the year round and miss the changes in flowers and fields in the country, but I am looking forward to seeing all the sights of London. I'll have some free time I suppose," she continued thoughtfully, "and perhaps the viscount will allow me to take the child around a bit."

"Sit down and let me fix your hair," urged Annie, taking the brush from Angelica's unresisting hand. "You never pin it securely enough. And why are you wearing that old rag," she snorted scornfully, "when you have the green morning dress that matches your eyes, or the blue and cream walking dress that is much more stylish. Your hair too is not in the current mode, but there — it does become you better than curls," she amended, cleverly twining the long, honey-coloured mass into a soft, low knot at the back of the head.

Angelica giggled at the affectionate censure in her tirewoman's voice and said primly but with mischief sparkling in the green eyes: "Governesses are not supposed to be stylish, you know. It would call attention to them and remove them from the category of comfortable but unnoticed furniture. As it is, I fear some of my gowns will be thought too — too coming, but," sighing slightly, "I do so enjoy fashioning pretty clothes. Oh, well, my unfashionable hair will dilute any impression that I aspire to unseemly elegance." She folded her hands and walked with eyes modestly downcast to the wardrobe for her bonnet, only to dissolve into mirth again as Annie commented dryly:

"That is coming it much too strong, miss. No one is going to believe you a meek nonentity with those witch's eyes. Oh, I wish I were coming with you to keep you in line. It won't be easy for you to be in a subservient position. Won't you change your mind and come back to the Court?"

Angelica's mood sobered abruptly. "No, Annie. Oh, I could manage to rub along well enough with my cousin's wife if I minded my tongue constantly, but besides the strain of two women in one house, it is really a rather useless existence. After Billy's marriage, I had no real position or responsibility in the running of the house, you know. The small tasks I could do didn't ease the feeling that I was simply a poor relation — a perpetual guest. At least in Lord Desmond's household I will hold a definite position, and I shall feel useful. This will compensate for being in an inferior position."

Annie opened her mouth, then closed it firmly against whatever she had felt tempted to utter.

"Cheer up, Annie. I shall be very sorry to leave you behind, but governesses do not have their own dressers, you know. In any event, it is time I learned to do up my own hair. I fear I have led a very sheltered existence, and believe me, I am looking forward to the experience of being on my own."

"And that's a tarradiddle if I ever heard one," muttered Annie under her breath, but she abandoned the subject in favour of supervising her mistress's breakfast and getting her settled in a hackney cab, after persuading Angelica to leave her baggage at the hotel for the viscount's footman to fetch.

Their parting was slightly tearful on both sides, for Annie had been devoted to Angelica since she had arrived at the Court, a timid nine-year-old, grieving for her father.

Angelica spent the brief time before the cab pulled up to the brick mansion in Grosvenor Square removing all traces of tears and composing herself to greet the viscount in a calm and, hopefully, competent-appearing manner. She could not deny a small tingle of — what? — expectation, perhaps, at meeting him again after ten years. Of course he would not remember her; she had been a mere child when he pulled her out of the lake, but she could still summon up his features in a mental portrait. Very dark hair and eyes, a dark complexion, too, and a sensitive, smiling mouth. He had radiated energy and friendliness, completely charming a young girl. She had begun to wonder if he had changed much over the years when the motion of the cab ceased, and she found herself in front of a massive oak door.

After paying the driver, she summoned up the fleeting remnants of her poise and rapped smartly on the brass knocker. Her earlier mood of excitement had curiously evaporated, leaving only trepidation. This was somewhat dispelled by the friendly, smiling countenance of the porter who opened the door to her, but a glimpse of the stately individual waiting in the hall was less reassuring. Chilham, the viscount's butler, was straighter and more impressive than most generals, and his glance could have quelled a mutiny. It swept impersonally over the face and figure of the unescorted young woman.

"Yes, miss?"

The voice was no warmer than the arctic eye, but by this time Angelica's pride had risen to the rescue. After all, she was expected and perhaps even needed in this household. There was certainly no reason to cower like a beggar at the palace door.

"I am Miss Wayne," she managed, with a fairly creditable assumption of a serenity she was far from feeling. "I believe Lord Desmond is expecting me."

"Oh, yes, the new governess. If you will let Matthew take your wrap," indicating the hovering footman, "I will see if his lordship is free to receive you now."

Angelica barely had time to note with admiration a beautifully curved stairway with a shining mahogany rail surmounting a handsome wrought-iron balustrade, and take an anxious peek in a huge pier glass before the stately Chilham returned.

"If you will follow me, ma'am, his lordship will see you in his study."

Angelica followed him silently, surreptitiously smoothing her clammy palms down the skirt of her gown and running her tongue nervously over her dry lips.

Chilham opened a panelled door, announced, "Miss Wayne, my lord," and withdrew, closing the door silently.

She had a confused impression of hundreds of books and warm dark colours, before her attention was drawn to the man who had risen from behind a handsome desk and come forward to greet her. He was certainly as dark as she remembered, but there all resemblance to her erstwhile saviour ended. He had been gay and laughing, giving an impression of great warmth and friendliness which belied the natural severity of a rather hawkish nose and rocky jaw. This man had the coldest set of features she had ever seen assembled on one visage. As she came rather hesitantly into the area illuminated by pale sunlight venturing in from the window behind the desk, straight black brows snapped together in a fierce scowl which caused her to pause uncertainly, while her heart plummeted uncomfortably to the region of her stomach.

The owner of the black-browed scowl was thinking with extreme annoyance that he could name two lovely women who would not be pleased at the addition to his household of such a young and personable-looking female. He could dismiss the prejudice of his mistress, Mrs. Marberry, but his fiancée, Lady Barbara Darlington, would have to share a roof with this Miss Wayne in the near future, and he would not wager a groat against her making the poor girl's life miserable. As the poor girl in question came forward again, with her chin resolutely raised and the look of alarm which had widened her eyes momentarily at his frown dying out, he decided with a measure of relief that they might console themselves with the knowledge that she possessed no extraordinary degree of beauty, anyway. Not that there was anything specifically wrong with her features, he mused critically, but she was too colourless — insipid was the word — for his taste. Although rather tall for a woman, she was so delicately built as to give the impression of fragility. He wondered uneasily whether she would be able to cope with his high-spirited Jenny. Damn Billy Wroxham, anyway, for presuming on old friendship! The girl was obviously too young and inexperienced for the position.

He was jolted from his unsatisfactory musings by a pleasant, rather husky voice saying politely, "How do you do, my lord?"

One hand held her reticule in a knuckle-whitening grip, but the eyes which met his levelly showed no trace of her earlier trepidation. She was determined not to allow this arrogant-looking man to discover how greatly he had disconcerted her.

The viscount bowed formally and indicated a chair beside the desk, into which she settled herself gracefully. With her head slightly inclined to one side, she questioned him silently with large grave eyes as he returned to his chair.

His first words were abrupt. "You seem very young, Miss Wayne, to have the charge of an eight-year-old child."

Was she to be ignominiously dismissed before even being given a chance? Angelica thought wildly and answered impetuously:

"Too young, sir? Why I am old enough to be the mother of an eight-year-old child."

For the first time since she had entered the room, his expression lightened. Something flickered in his eyes and a muscle quivered in his cheek, but he replied gravely, "Indeed, and how old are you, Miss Wayne?"

"I am three and twenty, sir."

"You must have been very precocious," he commented dryly, and enjoyed the furious blush which sprang to her cheeks. Her eyes sparkled dangerously, but she refused to rise to the bait, saying reasonably:

"I believe I am qualified to instruct a young child, my lord. I have had a rather better education than most young women because I shared lessons with my cousin, Billy, for some years. He was unable to go up to Eton, you know, after suffering a bad attack of rheumatic fever, so was tutored at home while he regained his strength. I have had much Latin and some Greek, as well as mathematics and history." As if to balance this masculine chronicle, she added hastily, "And of course I speak French and Italian, and am considered fairly adept at watercolour painting."

She had been watching him with earnest eyes while she spoke, but now the faintly sardonic gleam in his disconcerted her, and her own gaze dropped to her hands in her lap. She kept them relaxed with concentrated effort.

"And are you equally talented musically?" he asked maliciously.

Unaware of how expressive her countenance was, Angelica failed to realize that her dismay at this question was perfectly apparent to her inquisitor.

"Well no, sir," she confessed apologetically. "I'm afraid I am rather an indifferent performer on the pianoforte, and," deciding to conceal nothing, "much as I love music, I cannot carry a tune at all. In fact, Billy says he'd rather hear the hens cackling."

"How unkind of Billy," he declared solemnly.

"No, he is absolutely right." She was determined not to try to appear under false pretences.

He found such naivete entertaining. "And how are you with your needle?" he questioned, using his own smoothly.

There was relief in the charming voice as she accepted his question at face value. "Oh, I am very skilful at sewing and embroidery, sir, although I have no wish to brag."

For the first time in the interview she smiled, displaying even white teeth and the rather roguish dimple in her left cheek. There was a sudden alert look in the previously lazy gaze which had been quizzing her.

"You see," she continued merrily, unaware of his quickened interest, "whenever Billy and I got into scrapes, which was pretty often, I was sent to the schoolroom to embroider samplers or pillow covers or hem shirts. Sometimes my punishment was for a specific length of time, in which case I dawdled, but Mother discovered, if given a certain number of tasks, I could whip through them very quickly in order to be allowed out-of-doors again. So you see I became very adept at all needlework."

"Then your skill at stitchery is an indication of your naughtiness as a child," he interpreted blandly.

She gave a startled gasp and then a tiny chuckle. "Very true, sir, although it isn't chivalrous of you to phrase it in just that manner."

"I am not noted for my chivalry," he said wryly, and for a moment his brooding gaze dwelt on the flames leaping in the fireplace.

She had the distinct feeling he had forgotten her presence and was in a bleak world of his own. Some instinct of sympathy made her reach out to him.

"I, at least, had cause to be grateful to you for your chivalry on one occasion," she said gently.

His attention was caught. "Have we met before, then? For an instant when you smiled I felt a tug of memory, but ungallant though I may be, I feel certain I could not have forgotten such a charming young woman."

The sardonic look was very much in evidence, and the irony in his tone wasn't lost on Angelica. She was annoyed to think she had given him cause to think she was trying to scrape up an acquaintance, but she kept her voice gaily impersonal.

"I fear I was a very uncharming young hoyden when you pulled me out of the lake, after Billy and I had disobeyed orders and taken the boat out and capsized it, but you were certainly chivalry incarnate to a grateful thirteen-year-old."

"Good Lord, I had completely forgotten that incident! So you were the little green-eyed waif who clung to me so trustingly?" He smiled briefly, but whether at the memory or at Angelica's sudden flush she wasn't to know. For an instant, the smile warmed his countenance so that she almost recognized the man she remembered, but before she could be certain he had sobered again. "Such a long time ago. What a great summer that was, before Gervaise died — before —" He stopped abruptly and, forcing his tone to pleasantness, inquired, "So you, in your innocence, fancied I was a Sir Galahad, did you?"

She was vaguely disquieted by his manner, but strove to remain cool. "Oh, yes, I thought you were wonderful. I remember I wept buckets of tears later that year when I learned you had married. You see, I had expected you would wait for me to grow up."

He drew in his breath sharply, then at her questioning look, said with formal courtesy, "Well, I am happy to renew our acquaintance after all these years, though you are scarcely the same person I rescued, being all grown up and competent to teach children. Only those green eyes and the dimple remain of the little girl."

The dimple was very much in evidence as she smiled confidingly up at him. "I will do my best to teach your daughter, sir. Pray, what is her name?"

"Jennifer, but she is always called Jenny. She is a rare handful, I'm afraid, very spirited and not at all interested in lessons. Her previous governess was too lenient, I fear, and consequently Jenny is too used to getting her own way." His face set in a rather grim expression. "I do not wish her to grow up spoiled, thinking her beauty entitles her to have her every whim gratified." At her startled glance, he nodded. "Yes, already she bids fair to become a beauty like her mother." Abruptly, he changed the subject. "My sister, Lydia, is seventeen and will make her debut this season. My great-aunt who lives with us suffers from an arthritic complaint and is unable to accompany Lydia to parties. After my marriage, of course, Lady Desmond will chaperon her, but I would appreciate it if you could accompany her to some few events before the official start of her season." He grinned ruefully. "She is inclined to be something of a flirt, I fear, so you will undoubtedly have your hands full keeping her in line. Also, I wish her to learn Italian. That was what caused me to accept Billy's recommendation sight unseen. By the way, how does it come about that you speak Italian? I understand you have spent the greater part of your life in the country, though Billy did say you had been presented, I believe."

She nodded rather absently. This increase in her duties to include social events surprised her. "My mother was Italian, but her family cut her off after she married Papa. When he died, she went to live with Billy's mother, who was my father's cousin. They got along famously, and since Aunt Anthea was always invalidish, Mother practically ran the household. She never saw any of her own family again, but she always spoke Italian to me, as it was also my heritage."

"You don't look Italian."

Angelica smiled faintly. "Mother was much fairer than I; in fact, I'm told all the members of her family were blondes. Billy says I have a typical Italian temper, but that is nonsense because Mother had no temper at all. She was an angel."

"She is dead, then?"

She nodded again. "She died the year after I came out. She had a small annuity which comes to me until I should marry, so I am not a pauper, but it is considered improper for a young female to live alone, so I stayed on with Aunt Anthea and Billy. Now my aunt is dead also, and Billy is married. It is time for me to be on my own." She added cheerfully: "I shall be pleased to escort Lydia to her parties for a time, although I should warn you my own come-out was far from a success. I just didn't take. Billy says my wretched habit of saying everything that comes into my head scared off any suitors that my financial ineligibility hadn't. But I am older now and have learned to guard my tongue — most of the time anyway."

"You are very fond of Billy, are you not?" he inquired, watching her through narrowed eyes. "I am surprised you did not marry him."

She gave her throaty gurgle of laughter again. "That would be like marrying one's brother. Billy is just like a brother to me, not a distant cousin. Besides, he says I am completely exasperating and too independent, and therefore destined to remain a spinster. I daresay he is right," she added candidly. "But I do hope I can be of assistance to you, my lord, with Jenny and Lydia."

"I'm sure you will be a great help." He was eyeing the grey dress dubiously; "Er — undoubtedly you will find greater demands will be made on your wardrobe, if you are to go into society with Lydia. Naturally, I will provide the additional clothes necessary in carrying out this unexpected extension of your duties."

Angelica's expression was wry. "Annie was right after all." At his raising an inquiring eyebrow, she explained that her maid hadn't wanted her to wear so unstylish a garment, but that she had thought it better suited to the status of a governess. "I have more fashionable clothes, sir," she concluded, "but I'm afraid the current hairstyles don't become me at all." She raised her firm young chin just a trifle and stared at him challengingly, but his lordship retreated strategically.

"No, no, your hair is fine as it is," he said hastily, a slight tinge of red creeping up over his collar. The new governess might be ingenuous and naive, but she was obviously not meek.

"Well," he said briskly, "it only remains to present you to your charges, and you should meet Mrs. Haskins, the housekeeper." He pulled the rope summoning Chilham and asked him to send Mrs. Haskins to the study.

Angelica sat outwardly serene, but her thoughts were chasing each other around in her head. This had certainly been a strange interview. The viscount was so completely different from her romanticized memories. She slanted a glance at the set face. Could that tight-lipped mouth ever have smiled so freely and boyishly as she remembered?

Intercepting her look, the viscount smiled mockingly. "Well, do you find me much changed in ten years?"

Angelica felt the betraying colour steal over her cheeks again. What could she possibly say that would not sound insulting?

The silence lengthened. The viscount raised an inquiring eyebrow.

"You — you — I look older, my lord," she stammered. To her intense relief, a discreet knock was heard at the door and the viscount called to Mrs. Haskins to enter.

During the viscount's introduction, Angelica was struggling to recover her customary self-possession. Her inability to tell a polite social lie had almost led her to blurt out that he had changed beyond recognition. She took a deep breath and managed to respond politely to the housekeeper's greeting.

Suddenly the doors to the study were thrown open, and a diminutive brunette came impetuously into the room. "I'm so glad you are still here, Giles. Marie and I are going shopping and I need some money. Please may — oh!" she broke off abruptly, catching sight of Angelica, partly hidden behind the ample figure of Mrs. Haskins. "I beg your pardon; I did not realize you were occupied."

She turned to leave the room, but the viscount moved toward her. "Wait, Lydia," he said, taking her hand and leading her up to Angelica. "I want you to meet Jenny's new governess. Miss Wayne, this is my sister, Lydia."

Angelica had been marvelling at how closely the Honourable Miss Weston resembled her brother, while appearing his antithesis in personality. She also had raven dark hair and eyes, but her skin was creamy and the hawkish nose of the brother was a delicate aquiline on the sister. Her pointed little chin, however, looked to be quite as capable of stubbornness as the viscount's. She was smiling now with delight, her face lighting up in response to Angelica's warm greeting.

"Oh, you are quite young!" she exclaimed impetuously, holding out her hand. "It is quite terribly dull in this house, and I am never allowed out without my maid... You will change all that, and Giles tells me you are going to teach me Italian." She clapped her tiny hands enthusiastically. "What fun we shall have together!"

The disappointment Angelica had felt at the coldness of the viscount melted like snow in the sunshine of his sister's warmth. "Thank you for such a marvellous welcome," she said sincerely. "I, too, am looking forward to our lessons together."

Mrs. Haskins, who had watched this exchange complacently, now bustled into action, proposing to show Miss Wayne her rooms. Angelica glanced inquiringly at her employer, who dismissed her formally:

"I shan't see you again until dinner, Miss Wayne. I hope you will find your accommodation satisfactory."

She curtsied slightly, returned Lydia's smile and followed Mrs. Haskins into the hall and up the beautiful staircase, feeling more than slightly drained of energy after the tension of the interview with her employer and the unbounded spirits of his sister. If it were not for Lydia's buoyant friendliness, she would be experiencing a faint dread at being absorbed into a household headed by such a cold man.

Mrs. Haskins paused for breath at the top of the stairs before tackling the next flight. "The saloons and the main bedrooms are here on the first floor. My quarters, the nursery suite and your rooms are on the next, and the servants are above. I'm not so young as I was — these stairs get worse every year."

She saved her breath for the rest of the climb, then began again in a friendly fashion which cheered Angelica immeasurably. "It will be nice for Miss Jenny to have someone young around. Miss Jenkins — she was the governess before you — was getting on and not really lively enough to interest a little girl. Miss Jenny's a rare handful, she is, and if you take my advice, begging your pardon, miss, you'll let her know who's boss right off. There's not an ounce of harm in her, mind you, but with no mother to set the limits, Nurse and the servants let her call the tune so to speak; and as for Lady Orbridge, his lordship's aunt — well, Miss Jenny has her wrapped round her thumb. Miss Lydia's the only one who can make her mind, but she'll soon be too busy with the social round to spend much time with her."

While Angelica was trying to assimilate this spate of information and advice, Mrs. Haskins paused and opened a door leading into a small but attractive sitting room. Up here, the fireplace mantelpiece was of wood rather than marble and the colours in the leaf-and-floral-patterned carpet were muted by time and use, but the small settee with its upholstered seat looked comfortable enough and there were three other chairs in the room, one a charming gilt-and-painted affair with a cane seat. Angelica noted with appreciation a mahogany hanging cabinet inlaid with brass and other woods. So there would be a place for the few lovely Lowestoft pieces that had belonged to her mother.

Mrs. Haskins swept up to a door on the left side wall and indicated the room beyond. Angelica followed her and was equally reassured by her first glimpse of her new bedroom. It might not be large, but the single bed with its carved posts looked attractive with brocaded hangings and coverlet. The blue might be faded to a silvery shade, but the fabric was heavy and in good condition, as were the draperies at the window on the wall opposite. There was a large mirror over the fireplace with a gilt frame, and a small one on a modest dressing table. The washstand was utilitarian, but the china pitcher and bowl were ornamented with dainty blue and yellow flowers. Angelica had no time to study her surroundings further before her attention was claimed by the housekeeper, who was explaining that she was to eat luncheon in company with Jenny and Nurse in the schoolroom. Today they would be joined by Miss Lydia, since his lordship was lunching out. Angelica wasn't too surprised to learn she would dine with the viscount and his sister, in view of his intention that she be a sort of temporary companion to Lydia until she should acquire a new sister-in-law.

A knock on the sitting room door turned out to be the footman, who had been dispatched earlier for her trunk. He had returned with what Angelica realized, with a faintly sinking heart, represented almost all her worldly possessions.

Left alone to settle herself into her new environment, she attempted a sorting out of the blur of impressions she had received since entering this house scarcely an hour ago. She glanced at the pewter clock on the sitting room mantel and was frankly amazed that so little time had passed since she had bade Annie a tearful goodbye and turned to face her future.

As she unpacked her trunk and disposed her belongings in the commodious wardrobe in the bedroom, her thoughts were anywhere but on what her busy hands were accomplishing. Her expression was faintly troubled. Despite the obvious friendliness of Mrs. Haskins and the effervescent Lydia, she was not completely reassured that her coming to this house was after all such a wise decision. All her doubts revolved around the unfathomable, and, she suspected, difficult personage of her employer. She must admit that her imagination had certainly been inadequate to the task of picturing possible changes in the man who had made a brief but lasting impression on a thirteen-year-old child. Heavens! She would have passed him in the street without a glimmer of recognition. How could anyone have altered so basically in ten years? Indeed, this cynical individual appeared considerably older than his years. Surely he must be near her cousin Gervaise's age, having been up at Oxford together. She did a hasty mental calculation; Gervaise, had he lived, would now be three and thirty. Billy had said the viscount had been widowered some six years or more. Could grief for his lovely wife (Billy said she was an acclaimed beauty) have so warped his life as to leave his eyes granite hard and bitter lines around his mouth?

In the ordinary way of things, a governess for such a young child would seldom come in the way of the master of the house, but as she was also to bear Lydia company, she must necessarily dine with the family and come under that sardonic regard. The thought chilled her blood, but she chided herself briskly for cowardice and resolved to do her best to carry out her duties. At least she would enjoy exploring London with the vivacious Lydia.

At this point in her reflections, a knock sounded on the sitting room door. She had scarcely time to call out permission to enter when a quick light step was behind her and she turned, barely suppressing a gasp at the sight of her charge hovering in the doorway.

CHAPTER THREE

Jenny was quite frankly the loveliest child Angelica had ever seen. A good height for her age, she was delicately made and coloured, with thick pale hair seeming more in the Scandinavian than the English style. Her fair skin was healthily tinged with pink on the cheeks and adorable mouth, and her short, straight nose would be a decided asset to any budding beauty. Two large, deep blue eyes were candidly appraising as the little girl returned Angelica's stare with complete assurance. The child spoke first.

"How do you do?" she said politely. "I know you are Miss Wayne. I am Jennifer Louise Minerva Weston. The Louise is for my grandmother and the Minerva," here the little nose wrinkled in distaste, "is for Papa's aunt who lives with us to lend countenance to Lydia." Angelica suppressed a smile as the little girl continued: "I am always called Jenny except when Papa is displeased with me, but I mean to be called Jennifer when I am presented. It is much more grown-up, don't you agree?"

"I think Jennifer is a beautiful name," Angelica answered truthfully, "and, yes, more grown-up than Jenny. Would you prefer that I call you Jennifer now so you may become accustomed to the sound of it?"

The child considered this thoughtfully and repeated it twice before laughing merrily. "No, thank you, it sounds strange to me yet. You may call me Jenny for now. I will let you know when I wish to be called Jennifer," she added graciously. "Pray, what is your given name?"

"Angelica," said Angelica.

"That is a very pretty name. Papa gave Lydia a lovely fan painted by Angelica Kauffmann, but I do not know of anyone else by that name."

"I am named that because I am half Italian."

"Really? I don't know anyone at all who is Italian, but my cousin Fanny has a French governess." She clapped her hands delightedly. "This is ever so much better. I can't wait to tell Fanny. You do speak Italian, don't you?" she asked anxiously.

"Yes," Angelica answered, and then remembering that her father had said Jenny disliked lessons, added casually, "if you do very well with your other lessons, I will teach you some Italian phrases with which you may dazzle Fanny." She gave her attention to shaking the wrinkles out of a dress, but managed to study the little girl's reaction out of the corner of her eye.

Jenny's expression, which had clouded at the mention of lessons, was now thoughtful, and Angelica, deciding she had ventured far enough, refrained from pursuing the topic. Instead, she continued to arrange her belongings, humming softly to herself.

Jenny broke the short silence, and there was no mistaking the challenge in her voice. "I feel I should tell you that I do not like above half having lessons all day long. Girls do not need to study like boys, and Aunt Lydia says nothing could be more shocking than to be thought *blue*."

"I quite agree," Angelica said calmly. "A lady must know how to conduct herself in all situations, however, and if she finds herself unable to converse intelligently with her dinner partner because she has been remiss in learning the use of the globe, for example, when he is discussing Napoleons route into Russia or the duke's campaign in Portugal or Spain — well, you must see that he will soon abandon her for a more responsive companion."

Jenny looked quite struck by this dreadful possibility, but pursued her course undaunted. "Yes, but you must know that I find mathematics a dead bore."

"So do I," replied her governess promptly. "In fact, any lesson that is too long is a dead bore. With your help, we shall try to find the easiest and shortest way to learn those things a lady must know."

"With my help?" Jenny asked, diverted.

"Oh, yes, a slow, inattentive pupil takes so long to finish a task that there is never time to go on to more interesting matters."

Jenny was nothing if not persistent. "What more interesting matters?"

For a palpitating moment Angelica's mind was blank, then she grasped at her earlier straw. "Things like learning Italian phrases and — and setting up battle plans for the armies in the peninsula." Gracious, where had that thought come from, she wondered frantically, while continuing to unfold gowns and casting a surreptitious glance at Jenny to see how that young lady had taken it.

"Could we really plan battles and study how the duke beat Napoleon at Waterloo?" this utterly feminine little girl asked delightedly. "How I should like that! And of course it would be nice to learn some Italian, too. Fanny is insufferably proud because her French is much better than mine. I am going to like having you here, Miss Wayne. Of course, you aren't as beautiful as my mama was, but I like your face and you have a very pretty voice." She added quickly, as if afraid Angelica's feelings might have been wounded, "No one could be as beautiful as Mama, you know. I have her portrait in my room; would you like to see it?"

Her governess's smile was quick and warm. "Of course I should. I'm told your mother was indeed very beautiful."

"Who told you — Papa? He never talks about Mama to me. Nurse and Miss Jenkins said I mustn't try to talk about her because it upsets him. No one mentions Mama, and I do not remember her at all." The lovely little face looked strangely forlorn, and Angelica was wrung by a swift compassion. How heartless to deny the child the comfort of hearing about her mother.

She answered Jenny's question. "My cousin told me that your mama was very beautiful, and your papa said you were going to be just like her."

The child's face glowed with pleasure. "Papa said that? He has never told me so, indeed."

Angelica hastened to repair damages. "Well you know, Jenny, it doesn't really matter if a person looks beautiful if she is not beautiful inside as well. Your papa wants to be sure you learn that it is much more important to be kind and generous and helpful than merely to be lovely on the outside."

Jenny considered this with a furrowed brow, but remained unconvinced. "Yes, so Nurse says, but if a lady is very lovely on the inside and plain on the outside, she may not have anyone offer for her, while if she is beautiful to look at, she will have many suitors even if she is not at all beautiful inside."

Angelica felt herself in deep waters, but struggled gamely on. "It is certainly true, unfortunately, that gentleman are — are attracted to beauty of face and form, and may overlook for a time a lady of shining virtue who does not happen to possess such a happy arrangement of features, but in the end, you know, true worth must always be appreciated, and many a proud beauty has seen her circle of admirers dwindle when her, shall we say, less amiable traits became known."

"I think gentlemen must always prefer ladies who are beautiful," Jenny said very firmly. "My papa does."

A giggle from the doorway saved Angelica from ignominious defeat, for she knew not how to answer Jenny without perjuring herself. Her relieved eyes flew to Lydia's face, alight with amusement.

"Well, Jenny, Nurse sent you to bring Miss Wayne to the schoolroom for lunch and has been waiting this half hour and more."

The rest of the day passed smoothly and pleasantly. Nurse, who was so seldom called by her name that Lydia had to scramble around in her mind to dredge up Mrs. Priddy for Angelica's benefit, seemed at first slightly suspicious of the new governess, who although she looked mild enough, might take it into her head to try to undermine her own important position in Jenny's life. When the conversation at lunch revealed that Lydia would be requiring a great deal of Angelica's time, leaving only the morning free for Jenny's lessons, she allowed her feathers to be smoothed by Angelica's deferential manner and, in a subsequent conversation with Murdock, his lordship's valet, was judged by that individual to be well-disposed toward the new teacher.

Immediately after lunch, Angelica was led by Jenny to view her mother's portrait. She was perfectly willing to praise the late Lady Alicia Weston to her eager daughter, but was feminine enough to have to suppress an uncharitable pang of envy at sight of such beauty. For reputation hadn't exceeded truth in this case. Angelica had seen several Incomparables during her season, but all had been as nothing compared with Alicia Weston.

Her hair was of the same spectacular blondness as Jenny's, and her eyes large and of an incredible blue. Her brows were perfectly arched and much darker than her hair. Well-shaped lips were parted in a slight smile above a delicate chin. The portrait was a half-length; Lady Desmond wore a low-necked gown of sapphire blue velvet, revealing lovely shoulders and a long graceful neck adorned with a fabulous necklace of sapphires and diamonds. One shapely hand with tapering fingers held a single white rose in a graceful attitude against her breast.

Feeling positively drab, Angelica repressed a sigh of sheer envy and managed to praise the portrait with sufficient warmth to please Jenny. In all honesty, no one could fail to find such exquisite loveliness pleasing to the eye. Only the most captious of critics would have said that perhaps the Lady Alicia's expression held a touch of pride and lacked something of the sweetness of her daughter's. It was very lowering to reflect that she was just such a critic, Angelica mused. She was grateful to be able to retire to her room to finish unpacking and directing the maids to press the travel wrinkles from her garments, but her thoughts remained on the woman whose portrait she had admired.

It was little wonder the viscount had felt his loss too keenly to place another woman in the position of his late wife. After such perfection, all other females must strike him as plain. Angelica began to experience a strong desire to meet Lady Barbara Darlington, to whom he was now betrothed. She owed this certain knowledge to Lydia, who had shown a slight reluctance to discuss her future sister-in-law beyond stating that she had enjoyed a great success at her debut the previous year and had refused several offers before accepting the viscount.

Tea was an agreeable break, served again in the schoolroom as Lydia had no afternoon engagement and his lordship's aunt, Lady Orbridge, had not felt well enough to leave her quarters that day. The late winter damp was thought to aggravate her ladyship's arthritic complaint.

Angelica had felt a trifle nervous about dining with the family and gratefully accepted Lydia's proffered escort to the main saloon. The younger girl was dressed in a demure Jonquil muslin, which enhanced her vibrant brunette colouring. Her shining tresses were charmingly arranged *à la Tite*. Angelica herself had chosen a gown of heavy amber silk trimmed in matching lace, to counteract the dowdy impression she had made in the morning interview. With this she was wearing the exquisite topaz set which had belonged to her mother, consisting of a flower made of topaz petals on a fine gold chain, a bracelet of similar but smaller flowers linked together and tiny earrings with a dangling teardrop topaz. There were hair ornaments included in the set, but thanks to Annie's skilful hands, Angelica had not needed to redo her hair, so she left them in their case for a more formal hairstyle.

Lydia was all admiration (and was there a shade of relief as well?) at the appearance of her companion. She chatted happily as they descended the stairs.

"How I wish I were old enough to wear a gown in that ravishing style. One gets so bored with sprigged muslin. However, I am determined to wear something really dramatic for the ball Giles is giving to present me to the ton." She glanced at Angelica and sighed. "I wish I were tall, like you, so I could aspire to elegance. No matter how costly my gowns and jewels may be, I'll never look like a queen."

Angelica chuckled at her mournful tone. "Well, I don't look like a queen either, and being tall has its disadvantages as well. Many gentlemen, especially those of moderate height, object to lanky females as dancing partners, you know. You will have your choice of all the gentlemen. As for your first complaint, nothing is surer than that you will grow older. Enjoy being seventeen, my dear Miss Weston. You will have a marvellous time this season. When is your ball to be?"

"In five weeks' time if I can contain myself. Giles says patience is not my strongest virtue," she chuckled, "and that is certainly true, but very like Giles to be guilty of understatement."

They entered the saloon together, Angelica's eyes flying anxiously to her employer, standing before the fireplace, to see whether some of the disapproval she had felt in their morning interview had been mitigated by her more fashionable attire. Since she was in the habit of making all her gowns, thus saving a dressmaker's fee, she felt entitled to select the fine fabrics she enjoyed working on, and the amber silk was indeed rich looking. However, if she hoped for admiration or approval, she was doomed to disappointment, for no emotion at all was discernible in the viscount's face as he greeted them suavely.

He himself was most impressive in ordinary evening attire, his powerful shoulders encased in a beautifully fitting coat of blue superfine. He wore a white waistcoat, black pantaloons and highly polished shoes. His snowy neckcloth was faultlessly arranged, but his shirt points were not so high as to impede his movements, and she noticed that, unlike many of the beaux she had met, he did not favour a quantity of jewellery, contenting himself with a single black pearl in his cravat and a gold signet ring on one brown hand.

She became aware that the viscount was presenting her to the only other occupant of the room, and turned to acknowledge the greeting of the old woman with a curtsy. Lady Orbridge was rather a surprise, but after a day of surprises Angelica took this one in her stride, merely rearranging her mental image of an invalid to include alert, near-black eyes and a ramrod stiffness of posture. Lady Orbridge, seated in a nest of dove-grey taffeta, clung to the fuller dress styles of her youth, refusing to dispense with her petticoats. She rustled gently as she extended her hand, eyeing Angelica with outright disapproval.

"What can you have been thinking of, Desmond, hiring a mere chit of a girl to oversee Jenny? Why a moderate breeze could blow this one away. Jenny will make mincemeat of her in a sennight."

Angelica gasped at the directness of the attack, but managed to answer calmly enough, "I am really much stronger than I look, Lady Orbridge, and I assure you I can be quite as firm as the occasion demands."

Her ladyship raised black eyebrows almost to her elaborate black transformation in an expression eloquent of scepticism.

"Well, time will have the proving of that, but at least you are not a simpering miss. I can't abide 'em with their mealy-mouthed, fluttery manners, fainting away or having vapours at the drop of a hat. Well, what are we waiting for, Desmond? We are all here, are we not?" She scowled at her nephew, who had been listening with a faint smile to the exchange with Angelica.

"Not quite, Aunt. Robert is to join us tonight. We are going on to White's later." He raised his head. "Ah, I believe I hear him now."

At that moment, Chilham announced in his sonorous voice: "Lord Robert Hoxley."

A handsome man of some twenty-eight or -nine summers came into the room in a rush of apologies. "I am so sorry to have kept you from your dinner, ma'am," he said, bending gallantly over Lady Orbridge's hand, "but that curst man of mine ruined no fewer than five cravats, on my honour, before he managed to tie this." This, as all eyes in the room turned to the person of the speaker, was seen to be a complex arrangement of neckcloth, which, in combination with extremely high starched shirt points, almost imprisoned the wearer's head in a vice.

"You are nothing but a graceless jackanapes, Robert," Lady Orbridge said sternly, but her expression betrayed her fondness for the young man thus apostrophized.

The viscount again performed the introductions, and Angelica found herself smiling at a face dominated by a fine pair of frank blue eyes.

Lydia explained that Miss Wayne was to be Jenny's governess.

"Lucky Jenny," said Lord Robert, lingeringly releasing the hand Angelica had offered. His glance was patently admiring.

"Lucky me also," said Lydia. "Angelica — you don't mind if I call you that, do you?" glancing at the other girl. "Formality is so nonsensical when we are to spend so much time together." Turning again to Lord Robert, she continued without waiting for an answer: "Angelica is going to teach me Italian and accompany me on the social round. I am delighted."

Lord Robert murmured something civil, which was drowned out by Lady Orbridge's repeated demand that they go in to dinner. She allowed Robert to assist her from her chair, telling him he must entertain her as atonement for keeping her from her dinner. The other three followed slowly in their wake.

41

Angelica paused just inside the spacious apartment and turned impulsively to the viscount.

"Oh, what a perfectly lovely room. I have never seen anything half so beautiful as that Chinese wallpaper." Indeed the well-proportioned room was greatly enhanced by the scenic paper featuring a Chinese garden scene done in clear pastels. Lovely fruit trees and exotic, highly coloured birds lent excitement to the overall effect. The ceiling was simply ornamented in the later Adam style, and the plain carpet in a deep gold colour echoed in the draperies allowed the wallpaper to be of central interest.

"I am glad it pleases you," said the viscount, seating her on his left. "My mother had this room redone shortly before her death ten years ago. I have always found it charming, and must hope the future Lady Desmond agrees with you and won't desire to change it."

Angelica spoke quickly. "Surely you would not allow — oh, I do beg your pardon!" Aghast at her temerity, she could have bitten her unruly tongue clear through. Her embarrassed glance implored the viscount's forgiveness. "It is none of my affair, of course. And there I was, boasting to you this morning that I had learned to control my wretched habit of speaking my thoughts directly. Perhaps you will not wish after all to entrust Lydia to my care."

He surprised himself as well as Angelica by answering quietly, "I hope you will continue to speak your thoughts directly to me, Miss Wayne. I prefer honesty in those with whom I deal." Her searching eyes could detect no mockery in his sombre expression and she relaxed slightly, but sought desperately for a change of topic.

"I understand from Lydia that you are giving a ball for her in about five weeks' time. Tell me, when is your marriage to take place?"

"In five weeks."

She blinked at this, then ventured, "Directly after Lydia's ball, perhaps?"

"No, three days before the ball." His face was as noncommittal as the bland voice.

Confusion overcame her, but something must be replied; he was looking at her, one eyebrow slightly raised. "You — you will be here for the ball?" she uttered hesitantly.

"Oh, yes." He put an end to her confusion. "We have decided to postpone any wedding trip until after the season. After all, a major reason for my marriage is to provide Lydia with a chaperone during her come-out. Besides, Lady Barbara would not wish to miss any of the festivities either." There was no deciphering his carefully blank expression.

This prosaic account of his coming nuptials understandably struck Angelica dumb, and she turned with relief to answer a question put to her by Lord Robert on her left.

This first dinner which she had so dreaded passed most pleasantly. Angelica was amused and entertained by Lady Orbridge's astringent wit. It was easy to see why Lydia was not the usual meek debutante one met with at Almack's. With Lady Orbridge as mentor, she had grown up alert and with a poise and confidence that only comes through exposure to the company of adults. She was completely at ease with her brother's handsome friend, but Angelica detected no tendency on her part to play the coquette. Perhaps she was too accustomed to his society to consider him fair game. Angelica smiled to herself, noting that they squabbled amicably like brother and sister.

The dinner was a delight from a culinary standpoint, too. Turtle soup was removed and replaced with filets of turbot in a delectable sauce. Tender squabs were flanked by a dish of asparagus melting in butter and another of broiled mushrooms. Angelica, despite her slenderness, had a healthy appetite and happily partook of these and other dishes as they appeared.

After dinner, the ladies adjourned to a private drawing room, leaving the gentlemen to their port. Lady Orbridge leaned heavily on Lydia's arm. Except when it was necessary to walk, she exhibited no signs that her health was not good. Her air of alertness and upright carriage contrived to fool the world, but Angelica suspected she endured great discomfort in order to preserve this image before her family and the many old friends who came to call, keeping her supplied with the latest *on-dits* in the polite world. Her hands were too stiff to engage in the fancy needlework that was a lady's chief occupation, but her eyesight remained unimpaired, and she was content to read aloud to the two young women working on their embroidery, the branch of working candles flickering on a nearby candlestand.

She was reading from an unpretentious novel by a young woman named Jane Austen, pausing now and then to chuckle or comment on the author's ability to reveal the hypocrisies of social behaviour. They were thus pleasantly entertained until the arrival of the tea tray at ten o'clock.

It had seemed a very long day to Angelica, and quite the most eventful in years. She was ready for her bed, and despite the new impressions teeming in her mind, succumbed to sleep within minutes.

CHAPTER FOUR

The following week marked the beginning of a busy pattern to Angelica's days. Mornings were spent with Jenny, perhaps not with great profit to that young lady's education, but always with enjoyment on the part of both amicable contestants. For contest it was, with Jenny employing all her seemingly endless store of cunning to divert her hapless teacher's attention from study. She was an alert, curious child, older than her years, probably due to overexposure to adult company, but for all that, full of childish energy and enthusiasm for almost all activities — the sole exception being lessons. She asked endless questions about Angelica's life at Wroxham Court, especially delighting in stories of her childhood as the faithful slave and companion of an adventurous boy cousin. Angelica learned that she preferred to live in the country, where she had been permitted to roam about quite freely in the company of the children of the parson whose living had been bestowed by the viscount. She missed the companionship of this lively brother and sister team and felt confined in London, where her opportunities for outdoor activities were sadly curtailed by the damp weather and the disinclination of Nurse to venture farther afield than the gardens in the square.

She gladly welcomed Angelica's company and was grateful for the attention shown her, although this gratitude stopped short of outright cooperation in the schoolroom unless the subject under discussion happened to be wars or battles. It had not taken very long to establish that Jenny read well and had an extensive vocabulary. She doggedly resisted all tutoring in mathematics, until Angelica hit upon the happy notion of including her in the afternoon shopping expeditions with Lydia. They left the disbursement of moneys in Jenny's hands. Delighted with the responsibility, she proved her innate shrewdness and managed quite well, to the astonishment of her aunt.

In a remarkably short time, there sprang up a deep mutual affection between governess and pupil, both of whom were homesick for the country.

London was still rather thin of company since the season wasn't officially underway. Lydia's ball was scheduled for mid-April, but there was time to spare before the invitations must be sent out. Of course her wardrobe needed replenishing before the influx of invitations to breakfasts, teas, luncheons, routs, outings, assemblies and balls which made up the usual round of the debutante and necessitated several changes of clothing a day. After critically surveying Angelica at dinner for several evenings and commenting favourably on a particularly flattering bonnet with a single, curling, green ostrich feather which greatly enhanced her eyes, the viscount entrusted the governess with the awesome responsibility of satisfying Lydia's all too dashing taste, while still dressing her within the bounds of propriety for a very young girl.

Though they had not yet seen anything exciting enough for her own ball, Lydia had several charming muslins made up, as well as a delightful primrose silk ball gown with full sleeves worn over a deeper yellow slip of satin. There were also walking dresses and pelisses to order, not to mention bonnets.

Jenny did not care to accompany them to these sessions, where she must wait patiently while Lydia was fitted, prodded and poked, but she delighted in accompanying them on their trips to the Pantheon Bazaar which brought out the bargain hunter in any female. Angelica succumbed to the lure of some exotic, blue-green Italian silk and bought a length for an evening dress. It was Jenny who found just the right pale pink rosettes to trim it. A pair of long kid gloves in a matching pink were impossible to resist, but put a fearful dent in Angelica's funds.

Fortunately for the budding friendship between the two young women, Lydia had conceived a strong admiration for Angelica which survived being told firmly that she would be considered fast in a purple velvet hat with a huge, upstanding poke, three pink plumes and lilac satin ribbons which had violently taken her fancy when seen in a window on Conduit Street. Lydia reluctantly gave the hat back to the disappointed saleswoman, and giving it a final wistful look, sighed and followed Angelica into the street.

"You know, Lydia, that hat was not at all the thing for a young girl — in fact, I would not wish to be seen in it, myself."

Lydia giggled suddenly. "Are you afraid you would be taken for someone's *chère amie* in something that noteworthy?"

Angelica was slightly taken aback. "Frankly, yes, but you shouldn't know anything about that class of female at your age."

"Oh, pooh. Aunt Minerva does not believe in girls being brought up in ignorance of the ways of the world."

"And the ways of men?" asked Angelica dryly.

"Exactly." In a reasonable tone Lydia added, "How will I know whether or not I am being imposed upon if I do not know how gentlemen act?"

"Lydia," gasped Angelica, "you don't suppose girls of your class are treated in the same manner as such women, do you? Your brother would never allow you to become acquainted with anyone who would not keep the line."

"Well," said Lydia reasonably, "Giles has a *chère amie* himself, and I am very well acquainted with him."

For some inexplicable reason Angelica had difficulty swallowing a sudden lump in her throat, but after a slight hesitation she replied in an expressionless voice, "Surely you do not expect me to believe that your aunt or your brother told you such a thing. It is not very likely when he expects to be married very shortly."

"Of course they didn't tell me but, nevertheless, it is true. I overheard Giles's valet talking to Chilham one day, and I know who it is also."

"Who?" Angelica regretted the improper question instantly. "No," she added hastily, "please don't tell me. This is not something I should know — it is none of my affair."

"I'll tell you anyway. It is Mrs. Marberry. She is a widow and she is received everywhere. I know because I contrived to ask Aunt Minerva, though she did not know why I was asking, of course. I have seen her at Hookam's when I was there with Aunt Minerva's abigail. She is very handsome with dark red hair, and it is my belief she paints her face."

"Lydia, this is a most improper conversation. I beg you will not continue."

Lydia giggled mischievously. "I do believe I've put you to the blush, Angelica. I sometimes think you are younger than I. I am not the one doing anything improper; that is Mrs. Marberry — and Giles, of course," she added calmly.

Angelica was in a quandary. Certainly she should change the subject to some unexceptionable topic, but she could not allow Lydia to judge her brother too harshly. She took a deep breath and began carefully, "You know, my dear, after a man has grown accustomed to the constant company and — and the affection of a wife, it is very hard to remain alone. Gentlemen have appetites which women find difficult to understand. Once your brother is married to Lady Barbara, I am sure he will cut the connection, if one does exist, with this Mrs. Marberry and treat Lady Barbara with every consideration. You must not think him a libertine."

"Oh, I don't blame him. Women have been setting their caps for him, and matchmaking mamas have been pitchforking their daughters at his head these five years and more. I would not be surprised if it has given him a disgust of our sex. He had no intention of marrying until the question of my come-out arose. It being so awkward that I have no close female relative to sponsor my entrance into society with Aunt Minerva really unable to go the pace, he decided that it had to be marriage." She added thoughtfully, a little crease appearing between her brows, "It is my belief that he is not in the least in love with Lady Barbara."

"You must not say that. If he wanted to marry simply to provide you with a chaperone, he could have done it anytime this past year or two. You, yourself, told me Lady Barbara had a great success at her come-out. She must be very lovely, and the viscount, no less than other men, fell a victim to her beauty and charm. It is much more likely that he is head over ears in love with her."

"You would not think so if you could see them together," answered Lydia sceptically. "They don't act in the least like lovers. Giles is punctiliously polite, and Lady Barbara flirts with every man in the room."

"Well, you know it wouldn't do for her to sit in his pocket all evening. That is not considered the thing either."

"You may give over, my dear," said Lydia dryly, "for you won't convince me this is a love match. Reserve judgment until you see them together. I wish he were marrying for love. I'd like to see Giles happy again. He was such a wonderful brother when I was a little girl, so gay and laughing. I absolutely adored him. He has changed out of reason since Alicia died. I'd give anything to see him his old self again," she finished on a hint of a sob.

Angelica gave her hand a quick squeeze, and said as they crossed the street, carefully lifting their skirts, "He seemed greatly changed to me also."

Lydia was astonished. "You knew Giles before? I thought he engaged you on your cousin's recommendation."

Angelica bit her lip again, cursing her wayward tongue. "I can't really claim acquaintance. We met once ten years ago, when he came to visit my cousin Gervaise. But he is much altered from my memory of him."

"Ten years ago you must have been no more than a child. How old are you, Angel?"

"Angel?" queried Angelica with raised brows.

"Yes, the name suits you with your silky hair and calm face," said Lydia with determination. "Do you object violently?"

"No, not in private." Angelica chuckled reminiscently. "It has been a long time since I heard that. My father was used to call me Angel all the time, and Billy called me Devil."

"Well, that was too bad of him, for I am quite convinced you never acted the least devilish in your life; you are much too kind."

Angelica laughed again. "How little you know me, Lydia. Billy and I were forever in a scrape when we were younger, which is why I understand Jenny so well."

"Well I am going to call you Angel, anyway," said Lydia, tossing her curls saucily as she climbed up into the barouche which had come to meet them.

***

Lydia's words had given Angelica much food for thought, and if the slight scowl on her face was any indication, these thoughts weren't exactly pleasant as she absently brushed her hair before retiring that night. As usual, after enduring the viscount's company at dinner, she found herself unable to rid her mind of his image. To give the thing the right name, she was becoming obsessed with the man, she fumed, pulling the brush roughly through a tangle and causing her eyes to smart with the sudden pain.

Again he had been courteous and civil to her, but always with that air of indifference that she found so maddening. Yet, despite this seeming indifference, she felt herself to be always under observation. She tried not to attract his attention because, it must be confessed, that sardonic regard upset her. Why should she care what he thought of her personally, as long as he was satisfied with the way she performed the tasks for which she was hired?

Lydia had described the purple hat at dinner tonight, and he had unexpectedly turned to Angelica, saying dryly, "Accept my devout thanks for your intervention, Miss Wayne," causing Lydia to pout prettily and bringing an amused gleam to Angelica's eyes, though for Lydia's sake she tried to keep her mouth prim. For an instant, she thought there was an answering gleam in his dark eyes, but as on several other occasions it was too fleeting for her to be sure.

Somehow, his cold reserve struck her as more embittered than sad, but perhaps that was how grief took some people. Only with Jenny did he seem human. It must be apparent to the meanest intelligence that he bore a deep affection for his adorable daughter, but even with Jenny this reserve never entirely deserted him. Remembering her own gay, laughing father, always ready to gather her up in his arms, Angelica was moved, not for the first time, by a deep compassion for Jenny. The child had not only lost her mother, but something of her father, too. Thank heavens for Jenny's basically sunny nature. Another child in such circumstances might not have been able to benefit from the affection of servants and teachers, but Jenny welcomed the world gladly.

Angelica's thoughts turned toward the unknown Lady Barbara. Hopefully, she would make the viscount so happy that he would once again resemble the lively young man who had rescued her from the lake. Surely Jenny could not fail to benefit from such a change in the atmosphere. Unbidden, Lydia's pronouncements on the state of affairs between her brother and his fiancée came to mind. One must hope she was mistaken. The giddy Lydia might naturally expect public displays of affection which would be repugnant to persons of greater reserve. She sighed and removed her dressing gown before climbing into bed.

"I'll know better when I see Lady Barbara," she murmured sleepily and blew out the candle on her bedside table.

Angelica's desire to meet Lord Desmond's betrothed was to be gratified much sooner than she knew. His lordship had already breakfasted and was on the point of leaving the morning room when she entered the following morning. He greeted her formally and seated her, indicating a note beside her plate. She noticed that a similar missive reposed at Lydia's place and raised questioning eyes to his lordship's as she broke the wafer.

"It's an invitation to tea with Lady Barbara," he said smoothly. "She feels Lydia has been neglecting her lately, and professes herself all eager anticipation to make the acquaintance of one who has, in such a short time, become a valued member of my household." The words were complimentary to herself, but as usual his lordship's tone left one in doubt.

To cover her confusion and resentment, she dropped her eyes and slowly read the contents of the pretty little note begging Miss Wayne's company for tea that afternoon. His fiancée must have given the notes to the viscount sometime last evening, she thought irrelevantly.

"Well?" There was a tinge of impatience in the suave voice. "Will it be convenient for you and Lydia to visit Lady Barbara today? I will do myself the honour of escorting you."

Angelica accepted gracefully and was spared the necessity of speaking for Lydia by the impetuous entrance into the breakfast parlour at that instant of the young lady in question. Lydia never merely entered a room, Angelica thought with affection. She erupted into it, enlivening the dullest gathering with her infectious high spirits.

"Oh, are you off, Giles? Do have another cup of coffee," she coaxed, dimpling roguishly at her brother while she attacked her breakfast with enthusiasm. "I am persuaded that Angelica would find the exhibition at Somerset House a most educational experience. Do please say you will escort us there this afternoon, dearest Giles."

Seventeen years' intimate knowledge of the workings of his sister's mind left him in no doubt as to her motives in proposing this worthy expedition.

"Made an assignation have you, Lydia?" queried his lordship dryly, while Angelica turned startled eyes toward her. "I've never known you so eager to look at paintings before."

"Well, I am not precisely eager," she admitted, "but you must see that it is necessary for Angelica to see them. Simply everyone is talking about them."

"Try another cast, Lydia," advised her sceptical brother.

"Well," she confessed meekly, "when we met Priscilla Epworth in Bond Street yesterday, she did mention that her brother was escorting her to the exhibition this afternoon. That does not alter the fact that it will be very instructive for Angelica. I daresay she would enjoy it excessively, would you not, Angel?"

Perceiving the viscount's lowering stare, Angelica hastily agreed that she would indeed enjoy the exhibition.

"Do please lend us your escort, Giles," wheedled his unscrupulous sister.

"It grieves me to disappoint Miss Wayne," said the viscount firmly, "but if you will open the letter at your plate, you will see that it contains an invitation to tea with Barbara."

Lydia looked at him mutinously for a moment, but as she had not really counted on gulling Giles about the exhibition anyway, she acquiesced with reasonable grace, only adding coaxingly, "If I go and do the polite today, will you take us to Somerset House tomorrow?"

He eyed her thoughtfully. "If you can manage to conduct yourself in a well-bred manner this afternoon, I will be delighted to be your guide to the exhibition tomorrow." He bade Angelica good morning, tweaked his sister's hair and left the room.

"Well," his astonished sister exclaimed on his departure, "that was much easier than I imagined. You must have a mellowing influence on him, Angel."

Angelica, disclaiming any influence over the viscount, betook herself to the schoolroom where Jenny took full advantage of her abstraction to work on a drawing of one of her dolls instead of the scheduled history lesson.

When the viscount presented himself in the saloon that afternoon, he was greeted by two correct young ladies, delightfully gowned and hatted, but if they felt any great anticipation at the treat in store for them, they managed to conceal it behind polite society faces. Lydia indeed felt none — she had confided to Angelica that Lady Barbara's conversation consisted of descriptions of the newest additions to her extensive wardrobe and a list of the invitations she received. Angelica, herself, was anxious to meet her future employer, for she would in all probability deal more with Lady Barbara than Lord Desmond in the near future. At the same time, she was experiencing an uncomfortable and quite unfathomable reluctance actually to come face to face with one who would soon be of extreme significance to Lord Desmond — indeed, she assured herself, was already of central importance to the viscount. No doubt this was because, after Lydia's pronouncement, she feared lest these two should turn out not to be a well-suited couple, which situation would not improve Jenny's lot. Certainly she had been conscious of a slight heaviness of mood all day.

The weather was deceptively mild for March, and the girls acquiesced willingly to the viscount's suggestion that they walk the short distance to the Earl of Dorset's town residence. He offered an arm to each and complimented them on their charming appearance. Indeed, by the time they had arrived at the imposing facade of the earl's house, the breeze had whipped up the lovely colour in Lydia's cheeks and had even given a healthy tinge to Angelica's normally pale countenance. Without Annie's clever fingers to discipline her heavy hair, Angelica found it necessary to redo her knot several times a day. Although she had waited until just before joining Lydia in the saloon to smooth and re-pin the honey-coloured mass, the playful wind had roughened its appearance and she felt quite dishevelled. She was totally unaware of the appreciative expression in the viscount's eyes as they noted the heightened colour and lingered on a curling tendril which had escaped its confinement. He waited patiently while she and Lydia removed their pelisses and restored their hair in the room provided, and presently ushered them up the stairs to the countess's drawing room.

This was a large square apartment with heavy crimson hangings and carpet, providing a perfect foil for the dramatic dark beauty of the young woman engaging in a conversation with a man of polished good looks. An older woman came forward on hearing their steps, but so deeply engrossed was Lady Barbara that she didn't look up until the butler began to announce them; then, startled, she rose gracefully and went to the viscount with extended hands. He raised them fleetingly to his lips, then performed the introductions. The countess welcomed Angelica politely and smiled upon Lydia, bringing her into the room to meet the other guest who had risen to his feet.

Angelica had been prepared to discover that Lady Barbara was beautiful, nor was she disappointed. Only two years older than Lydia, she possessed in full the assurance that comes with having been feted and toasted as an Incomparable. Exquisitely gowned in deep rose colour, which clung lovingly to a really marvellous figure and set off to perfection her dark brown eyes and darker hair arranged in a *dégagée* style, she would stand out in any gathering. She greeted Giles in a rather languid manner, then turned the full force of those magnificent eyes on Angelica in a deep scrutiny while he made them known to one another. Angelica bore this with her usual equanimity and took the proffered hand, saying politely, "How do you do? I am happy to meet you, Lady Barbara."

Lady Barbara smiled dazzlingly and said in a slow drawl which Angelica thought privately was the one flaw in her person:

"I have been looking forward to making your acquaintance, Miss Wayne. Giles has told me how invaluable you have become in taking over Jenny's education, and, I for one, must thank you for seeing to dear Lydia's wardrobe for her come-out. I would have been delighted to be of assistance to her if it were not for the circumstance of my own wedding taking place at precisely the same time, necessitating countless shopping trips and fitting sessions."

Angelica made some polite rejoinder, while wondering what would prevent Lady Barbara from bringing Lydia with her on these shopping expeditions.

"She does you credit, anyway, Miss Wayne," Lady Barbara continued, smiling sweetly at Lydia who was chattering gaily to the other gentleman in the room. "How sweet and girlish she appears in that charming dress."

The object of this praise looked anything but gratified to hear herself so described, but after one fulminating glance at her brother, firmly pressed her lips together and remained silent.

"Oh, how gauche of me to have embarrassed you with my compliments, Lydia; pray forgive me," trilled Lady Barbara. "Miss Wayne, may I present Sir Anthony Haring. Lord Desmond, my fiancé, Sir Anthony."

The gentlemen bowed, and Sir Anthony expressed his pleasure at making Miss Wayne's acquaintance.

Here, the countess interposed to explain that Sir Anthony was the son of an old friend of the earl's and had just returned to England from Brussels after selling out. The two men began to discuss the present situation in France, while the countess poured the tea which had been borne in on a truly beautiful silver tray. Lady Barbara prettily saw to their needs, pressing them to sample a particularly delicious plum cake which, she said gaily, she had exhorted Cook to bake, knowing what a schoolgirl appetite Lydia possessed. Whether it was the result of this infelicitous remark or a rather large luncheon, Lydia refused politely to try any of the delicacies offered, contenting herself with tea.

Noting the slightly stubborn set to her friend's mouth, Angelica mendaciously professed herself delighted to sample the cook's efforts and turned the subject toward some unexceptional commonplace to divert Lady Barbara, who seemed inclined to pursue the topic of Lydia's lack of appetite.

The viscount, sitting totally at ease, was wearing his most sardonic expression as he watched the byplay.

Lydia seized the opportunity to break away and asked Sir Anthony if he had as yet seen the exhibition at Somerset House. He replied in the negative, explaining that he had been back but long enough to outfit himself and purchase a matched pair of chestnuts for the high perch phaeton he was having built, but declared himself all eagerness to remedy the deficiency.

"Giles is to escort us there tomorrow," Lydia said naively.

"Then I shall count on you to tell me which paintings I should most admire," Sir Anthony put in smoothly, causing Lydia's dimples to appear as she giggled.

Lady Barbara, who seemed able to keep track of more than one conversation at a time, interposed here in her slow drawl:

"Why don't we all go to the exhibition together? I have been most eager to see it."

Sir Anthony jumped into the little silence that followed, declaring, with a warm look at Lady Barbara, that he would be thrilled to have the pleasure of escorting her, and the countess, of course, to view the paintings. The countess thanked him but declined politely due to a prior engagement.

"You have forgotten, my love, that we had planned to go to Wimbledon to visit your grandmother." On seeing a slight pout forming on her daughter's lovely face, she declared herself unwilling to spoil Barbara's pleasure and promised to take her sister in her stead.

Lady Barbara's expression become all sunshine again. "Then it is settled — we shall all go together to Somerset House." She engaged Sir Anthony in a discussion of the plans, calling on Giles to agree to a time for meeting. The countess asked Lydia about the plans for her ball, and the young girl, who had not appeared thrilled at the augmentation of the party, brightened and chatted happily away with her hostess.

Lady Barbara was engrossed in conversation with Sir Anthony. The viscount watched them pensively through slightly narrowed eyes for a moment, then turned to Angelica and said with a smile:

"Should you object if I asked Robert Hoxley to go with us to round out the numbers?"

She smiled gratefully at him and agreed at once to the inclusion of Lord Robert. Truth to tell, she had not looked forward to being the extra female in the party. It was one thing to chaperon Lydia to small private parties as part of her job and quite another to find herself the odd female in a gay outing such as the one proposed by Lady Barbara.

The rest of the visit passed smoothly, with the viscount exchanging desultory remarks with Angelica while Lady Barbara continued to engage Sir Anthony's attention and Lydia entertained the countess with her enthusiasm.

Suddenly Sir Anthony, recollecting the time, apologized for overextending his visit and began to make his adieux to the countess. This served as a signal to the others to rise and follow suit. As Angelica rose gracefully from her chair, Lady Barbara said, smiling:

"Heavens! I had not realized before how very tall you are. How I envy you! I have always considered myself lamentably lacking in inches from a fashionable point of view, and have had to console myself with the realization that at least I do not have to rule out a great number of gentlemen as dancing partners. Did you find this a problem when you made your debut?"

The effect of this artless speech upon her audience was varied to put it mildly. The countess frowned reprovingly at her daughter. Sir Anthony was heard to protest warmly that Lady Barbara was exactly the perfect height for a woman. Lydia's bosom swelled with indignation at the implied slight to her friend, and she replied rather heatedly that Miss Wayne was so slender and graceful as to lend distinction to everything she wore and pointed out that standing beside the viscount, they made a perfectly matched pair.

Angelica herself seemed not in the least perturbed. Giving her hostess back smile for honeyed smile, she agreed that she had considered her height to be a problem when she was a green girl, but that it no longer bothered her in the least. An appreciative smile twitched at the corners of the viscount's mouth and the usually cold eyes had a distinct gleam of amusement, but Angelica avoided looking at him.

Lady Barbara laughed gaily and apologized prettily for her awkwardness. "Of course Miss Wayne is not too tall. She is in the fortunate position of being able to wear anything and look well in it."

The leave-taking was accomplished in perfect civility on all sides, and the viscount led his fair charges back to Grosvenor Square. It was a rather silent walk this time. Angelica, noting the storm signals on Lydia's face, did, it is true, attempt some conversational sorties, but beyond agreeing with her that tomorrow's expedition should indeed prove enjoyable, the viscount initiated no conversation, seeming lost in thought. Lacking his cooperation, Angelica contented herself with murmuring a few commonplace observations on the passing scene to cover Lydia's silence. The viscount left them at the door, telling them curtly that he would be dining out.

As they went slowly upstairs, a side glance at Lydia revealed that she was barely containing herself until they were out of earshot of the servants. Angelica would have liked some privacy to sort out her impressions of the afternoon, but saw that this solace was not to be granted her. Lydia followed her up to the sitting room, her diminutive person fairly radiating fury.

Angelica sighed. "Come in and unburden yourself before you burst," she advised the younger girl.

"Well," snapped Lydia, stripping off her gloves and flinging them onto a chair, to be followed almost immediately by the charming confection that had adorned her head. "Now do you see why I say this isn't a love match? That wretched girl is incapable of the more tender emotions. Do not try to tell me she loves anyone but herself — certainly not Giles. Did you notice the way she manoeuvred herself and Sir Anthony into our party?"

Here Angelica interrupted mildly. "Perhaps she felt a bit left out, my dear. After all, she is engaged to the viscount; she has every right to expect his attentions, and since Sir Anthony was aware of the expedition also, it was only gracious to include him."

"Fustian!" declared Lydia roundly. "You may try to wrap it up in clean linen, Angel, but it is perfectly clear to me that she had every intention of spoiling our outing while providing herself with a golden opportunity to further her flirtation with Sir Anthony. Certainly you could not have failed to notice how he looked at her like a mooncalf. And she gave him plenty of encouragement right in front of Giles. I am sorry I ever mentioned the wretched exhibition."

"That is obvious," replied Angelica dryly. "You are well served for letting your tongue run away with you."

A rueful smile quirked Lydia's lips briefly. "If you are hinting that I am not yet up to snuff, Angel, your point is well taken. I'll know better another time. But all my pleasure in the trip is quite at an end thanks to my sweet sister-in-law-to-be. How shall I endure having her around all the time?" she moaned.

Angelica's thoughts had been running along similar lines, but she stifled them and tried to comfort Lydia.

"Surely you will manage to get along tolerably well when you know each other better. She will be chaperoning you during your season, and you will be grateful for that."

"Shall I?" asked Lydia quietly. "I cannot see her ceasing her efforts to captivate every man in the room simply because Giles has put another ring on her finger. She certainly does not regard the one she is now wearing as a curb to her flirting."

Angelica had not failed to remark the beautiful ruby and diamond ring which adorned Lady Barbara's left hand, but Lydia was going on, "She will continue to try to make me seem no more than a child while she annexes any potential suitors."

"Well," said Angelica reasonably, "you are too young to be thinking of marriage in any case, and nothing Lady Barbara can do will prevent you from being besieged with partners at every ball. You are much too pretty to be a wallflower, my dear."

"She will try," Lydia persisted stubbornly. "And of all the ill-bred remarks to make, that one about your height takes the prize. And Giles told me to conduct myself with propriety. He might better instruct his betrothed in the art of polite conversation."

"You must not mention it to him. Believe me, Lydia, it will not do for you to criticize your brother's fiancée. You must accept the fact that he wishes her to be his wife and try to get along with her. Once her position as Lord Desmond's wife is established, it is my belief she will be glad to have your company and will treat you kindly."

Lydia was patently unconvinced, but shrugged in resignation.

"There is nothing I can do in any event. If Giles is blinded by her beauty, he would certainly pay no heed to a sister fifteen years his junior. Oh, well, if life becomes too difficult here, I can always marry the first man who offers for me. I am not exactly a pauper. I will see you at dinner, Angel."

Turning, she gathered her belongings together and walked swiftly from the room, leaving Angelica deeply troubled by this cynical little speech. Her own impressions of the viscount's fiancée had not been favourable. She tried to tell herself she was being too critical, that the vanity and flirtatiousness she had glimpsed would fade when Barbara knew the security of marriage, but she felt this to be a forlorn hope. No more than Lydia did Angelica believe the girl was in love with Lord Desmond, but she wondered why she had accepted him. An earl's daughter would be unlikely to marry for the sake of a lesser title, and Lydia had said she had refused several other offers. The unkind thought flicked across her mind that Lady Barbara might have been intrigued by the viscount's reputation for immunity to feminine lures. Lydia had said women had been on the catch for him ever since his wife died. Was she the type who would consider this a challenge? Angelica rather thought Barbara would enjoy flaunting her conquest in the eyes of Society. But even if her motive had been less calculating, after watching them together, Angelica felt it was inconceivable that love had entered into her decision. Lady Barbara's attitude toward her betrothed was not only cool but rather callous in exposing him to the sight of her responding to the attentions of another man.

She was less sure of the viscount's feelings. This afternoon he had behaved no differently toward his fiancée than toward his sister or his employee — indifferently polite to all. Certainly there was no special observation, no distinguishing attention to Lady Barbara. Perhaps that was the crux of the matter, Angelica thought suddenly. Maybe Barbara was resentful of his lack of ardour and was punishing him in this way. Perhaps she did love him and was hurt by his coolness.

This thought, which if true might be a better omen for the couple's future happiness, somehow failed to lighten Angelica's sense of depression.

Two things were abundantly clear — Angelica Wayne had no idea of the state of Lord Desmond's affections, and also it was absolutely none of her affair. She turned resolutely to the task of changing for dinner, bemoaning as usual the loss of Annie whose skilful hands could tame the long fall of honey-coloured hair. If she did not become more adept at managing soon, she must seriously consider having it cropped in the prevailing mode, although the vision of curl papers and hot irons was not comforting. Perhaps if she were just to cut several inches from the waist-length fall, the shorter length would be easier to keep pinned securely. Certainly the tedious task of nightly brushing would be somewhat lightened. Proceeding on the theory that it was best to strike while the iron is hot, she moved into the sitting room for the scissors in her workbasket, when, glancing at the pewter clock, she realized there was not sufficient time and hastily re-pinned the shining mass into its customary style, again however without the lamented Annie's neat result.

CHAPTER FIVE

If Angelica had found that the uncomfortable tea party provided insufficient evidence to come to a conclusion about the state of affairs existing between her employer and his beautiful fiancée, the same could not be said of the following day's expedition to Somerset House.

She could not look forward to any outing in the company of Lady Barbara and Lydia in her present mood of rebellion without inner qualms, but she intended to take full advantage of what might well be her last opportunity to study the viscount and his betrothed before the latter became her mistress. She resolutely refused to dwell on the faint chill the very thought of this state induced in her bones, and set about trying to cajole Lydia into a more receptive humour.

To this end she consented to pass under review every item of that young lady's extensive wardrobe which might be suitable both for viewing an exposition of artworks and proving to a certain haughty but nameless young woman that the wearer was no longer a child to be dismissed with a condescending pat on the head. It required all of Angelica's considerable store of tact to dissuade Lydia from donning a far-too-dashing black fur hat purchased under the undiscriminating eye of the late, unlamented Miss Jenkins, but never, as yet, worn. This not inconsiderable feat was accomplished by laying stress on the unfortunate circumstance that the hat did not go with the charming, wine-coloured pelisse trimmed in sable that both damsels agreed not only best suited Lydia's vibrant colouring, but also served to add several years to her age. Angelica, suppressing a shudder at thought of the viscount's probable reaction to the huge black bonnet, thoughtfully inspected the other hats proposed for her consideration and opted for a matching wine-coloured one, demurely trimmed in fur. She overrode Lydia's protest that it was childish by pointing out that the most fashionable ladies of her acquaintance favoured the ensemble look. To complete the costume, Lydia produced a sable muff and insisted that Angelica take the black fur one which matched the rejected hat.

At last the ladies were ready. Angelica privately thought Lydia in her charming outfit looked exactly what she was — a very pretty bud just beginning to unfurl her petals, but she naturally refrained from expressing any opinion so exactly calculated to further exacerbate that young lady's already outraged sensibilities. She did, in the interests of peace, drop a gentle hint that if Lady Barbara should chance to pass any remark which might be construed by persons of excessive sensibility as slighting to herself, she would appreciate it if Lydia would forbear to leap to her defence since Angelica herself, not being troubled by a sensitive nature, would be perfectly content to consider the source. Lydia giggled at this but refused to make any such rash promise, saying darkly:

"I know her better than you do, Angel, and it does not do to let such patronizing persons think they can be rude in that odiously sweet way without suffering the consequences. I refuse to be bullied, and I won't allow her to bully you either." The vivacious little face took on a mulish look.

Angelica sighed. Any expectation of pleasure from the forthcoming expedition had faded on hearing of the increased size of the party, but she could now see that to her would fall the unenviable task of keeping Lydia's militant spirit under control in the face of what she strongly suspected were Lady

Barbara's habitual tactics toward females personable enough to be considered rivals.

The viscount came to collect them with Lord Robert in his wake. He greeted both girls impartially with the rather lopsided and extremely rare smile that blurred the harsh lines of his jaw and erased the somewhat mocking expression Angelica had found to be natural in the short time she had dwelt under his roof. For another brief instant, she glimpsed the man he had been ten years before. As usual, she experienced a small pang as his smile faded and the harsh features re-emerged. Between smiles, one would judge it impossible that such sternness could ever take on warmth.

Lord Robert greeted them, smiling at each in turn. Angelica's first impression of the viscount's friend had been favourable, and further exposure to his friendliness and charm only served to reinforce her original assessment. He and Lydia seemed to be on the easiest of terms. Angelica relaxed and permitted herself a small hope that the afternoon might not, after all, prove the disaster Lydia's earlier mood seemed to portend.

The day was cold but clear, lending a sense of physical well-being as the party climbed into the barouche and set out for the Strand. It had been agreed that they would meet Sir Anthony and Lady Barbara at Somerset House at 2:30, and Angelica noted with satisfaction that they were precisely on time. She said as much to Lydia and was surprised by Lord Robert's chuckle. Glancing at the viscount, she found an expression of cynical amusement on his face.

"My dear girl, if you are expecting to see Lady Barbara and Sir Anthony around the next corner, you are in for a disappointment. Barbara is never on time."

"Lay you a pony, Giles, that they don't turn up in under forty-five minutes," offered Lord Robert.

"I'm not such a gudgeon," replied the viscount. "Let's begin to look around; they'll catch us up in time."

The next hour was spent in wandering around, viewing the various exhibits. Angelica, who had a fair talent at sketching and more than a little at watercolour painting, was extremely pleased at the opportunity to study the techniques of successful artists and found the viscount a knowledgeable guide. Lord Robert, whose interests lay more in the sporting field, finally claimed his eyes were smarting from looking and his ears were ringing from listening to his friend prose on about a lot of dull pictures. He detached Lydia from the absorbed art lovers and led her to a couch of red plush, where they were conversing amiably when Lady Barbara and Sir Anthony swept down on them with profuse apologies for being late.

"Although," Lady Barbara concluded archly, "you two must wish us at Jericho for arriving to disturb your little tête-à-tête." She gave a trill of laughter. "This must be the first time I have ever played duenna. It will be good practice for us before your debut, Lydia dear."

Lord Robert, who had risen at the approach of the latecomers, looked startled and a tinge of red crept up over his cheeks, but before he could utter a remark, Lady Barbara was launched into an introduction making the two men known to each other. Bows were exchanged, and Sir Anthony turned to Lydia, who was still sitting on the couch wearing a glowering expression which she tried to soften as he smiled at her.

"Your very obedient servant, Miss Weston. Remember you promised to tell me which pictures I must most admire." He offered her his arm, and she bounced up laughing:

"I'm afraid you will have to ask Miss Wayne for an expert opinion. She and Giles have been examining and criticizing the pictures for more than an hour now." With a swift glance at

Lady Barbara, "Robert and I were unable to stay the course and came to rest our feet."

"Where are Giles and Miss Wayne?" wondered Lady Barbara, and just at that instant the pair in question came slowly around the corner and then more swiftly as they noticed the recent additions to the party.

Lady Barbara smiled at Angelica, and taking the viscount's arm, scolded him playfully for failing in his duty as Lydia's guardian.

"I did not realize you were quite so gothic in your ideas, my dear," he said smoothly, with his mocking smile. "Surely there can be no need for chaperonage in a public gallery with any number of people milling around."

Lady Barbara laughed, and linking her other arm in Sir Anthony's, declared herself simply perishing for a glimpse of the masterpieces. She smiled kindly at Lydia and added:

"Poor Lydia is tired, but now that Miss Wayne is here, there can be no reason to drag the poor child back over the ground she has already covered."

Lydia, however, declared herself sufficiently rested, and still with her hand on Sir Anthony's arm, strolled off with Lady Barbara and the two gentlemen. Murmuring an apology, the viscount halted abruptly and, detaching his arm from his fiancée's hold, walked back to inquire if Miss Wayne and Lord Robert cared to make another tour.

Angelica decided she was ready for a rest on the inviting red couch, and Lord Robert elected to remain with her.

"I'd do a lot of things for you, Giles, but walking my feet to the bone ain't among 'em."

The viscount bowed slightly to Angelica and followed the retreating trio.

Angelica had been glad of the chance to rest, but in spite of this, she would have pursued her objective of further observation of the engaged pair had not Lady Barbara's dismissal been so evident. She smiled inwardly, recalling Lydia's refusal to be out-manoeuvred. She was learning to hold her own. It was to be devoutly hoped that Lady Barbara would offer no further provocation calculated to cause Lydia to expose her youth and inexperience.

Lord Robert proved an amusing companion, and they were conversing as easily as old friends when the other members of the party reappeared at the end of the long room. The two gentlemen appeared to be in conversation, and the ladies were strolling together.

"Lydia and Lady Barbara make a charming picture together," Angelica said admiringly, "both such sparkling brunettes." Indeed, the two girls, Lydia in her vibrant wine colour and the older girl in palest blue trimmed with black fur, were the objects of admiring glances from strolling art lovers.

"To complete the picture, you should be there in the centre as a lovely fair contrast."

Angelica chuckled. "You are very kind, my lord, but my mirror tells me I am not at all out of the common style."

"Then your mirror lies, Miss Wayne," he answered seriously. "You are definitely not in the common style. It is true that you lack the vivacity which is so much a part of young Lydia's charm, nor do you possess the classic perfection of Lady Barbara's features, but there are many people who prefer your more serene loveliness."

Angelica, who had had very little experience with young men since her unspectacular season four years before, was horrified to think she, who scorned such tactics, might be considered to be angling for compliments; yet she could not suspect Lord

Robert of insincere flattery, so maintained an embarrassed silence. But her eyes, which had been lowered in her confusion, looked up in time to meet the rather narrowed glance of the viscount coming toward them.

Lord Robert noticed the direction of her glance and said thoughtfully, as if continuing his earlier remarks, "Since Alicia, Giles has never really looked at the blonde ones — always seems to favour brunettes. A pity."

Angelica thought this remark rather enigmatic, but had no chance to pursue the topic as the others were nearly upon them.

If the viscount noticed her slightly heightened colour, he made no comment. The others were absorbed in arguing the merits of a painting. Angelica relaxed and rose from her seat. She was conscious of the viscount's intent regard for another few seconds before he proposed that the party adjourn to Grillon's for tea to aid in the recovery from their exertions.

It was an enjoyable interlude. Lydia and Lady Barbara maintained their truce, and conversation flowed easily. Lord Robert, with a mischievous wink at Angelica, devoted himself briefly to Lady Barbara, cleverly edging Sir Anthony aside. That gentleman's manners were too good to exclude the other ladies in any case, but Angelica was faintly troubled by an intuitive guess that he was quite deeply smitten by Lady Barbara's beauty. Certainly he was aware of the engagement between her and the viscount, but Lady Barbara treated her fiancé with a hint of carelessness, which must be considered an encouragement to other men to press their attentions on her. Angelica was aware that, among the leaders of the *haut ton*, flirtations were winked at and outright infidelities often condoned by the injured spouse as long as these were conducted discreetly. The only sin in some exalted circles was to create a scandal. Certainly it was known that some highborn women had foisted other men's children onto their husbands, and many a wealthy gentleman flaunted his mistress in the teeth of society, keeping her in elegant style while the affaire lasted. Even high sticklers among society leaders accepted these men, though the high flyers under their protection were not recognized. Wives closed their eyes to such indiscretions and pretended ignorance of their husbands' activities. Thus the facade of marriage was maintained. Country-bred Angelica had been shocked and revolted at such revelations during her first stay in London, and though no longer shocked was still repulsed by such behaviour. Admittedly, the prevailing custom among the nobility of arranged marriages contributed greatly to this state of affairs, but she considered that simply a greater reason not to marry where one did not love.

She could not believe Lady Barbara bore any tender feeling for Lord Desmond, though it was true she sought to recapture his attention if he spoke for more than a minute or two with his sister's companion. On these occasions he received the same dazzling smile as Sir Anthony or Lord Robert, but the suspicion persisted that the motive underlying the smile was simply a strong desire to retain the attention of every personable male present. Angelica chided herself for pettiness and closely observed the beautiful brunette for any signs of partiality toward her fiancé. She could detect none.

Nor for that matter could she detect the slightest sign of impatience or jealousy in the viscount's manner. Certainly his thoughtful gaze rested often on Lady Barbara's face, but even more often, perhaps, on that of Sir Anthony, who made no attempt to conceal the fact that he was completely bowled out by her loveliness. The viscount, however, betrayed no hint of irritation. He responded politely to all his fiancée's sallies, but initiated no conversation himself. Although aware that she herself was unacquainted with many gentlemen, Angelica felt sure she would be able to discern some shade of hurt in his manner if he loved his fiancée. There was none, but perhaps the man was a consummate actor. Evidently he was enjoying the afternoon, and it was not he but Lord Robert who looked at his watch finally and declared it was getting late. The party broke up on a pleasant note, and presently they returned to Grosvenor Square after setting down Lord Robert at his lodgings.

Angelica sat silent during the trip home, hearing almost nothing of Lydia's prattle, her mind totally occupied with the problem of her employer's relationship with the woman he was to make his wife next month. Whether or not he loved her, Angelica saw nothing but disappointment and disillusionment ahead from such a match. She recalled Lydia's story about her brother's having a mistress. Somehow, there was no comfort in the idea that the viscount was satisfied with this arrangement and expected nothing of personal happiness from his prospective marriage. From her two brief encounters with Lady Barbara, she could see no benefit to Jenny or Lydia from the marriage either.

All in all, she was feeling strangely depressed as they entered the big house. Lydia was already running up the stairs, and Angelica prepared to follow her when the viscount came up behind her and said in a low tone:

"Just a moment please, Miss Wayne. What was Robert saying to you just before we all came up to you in the room at Somerset House?"

Angelica, taken completely by surprise, looked up into the cold-featured face staring steadily down at her.

"Why we … we talked nothing but the merest commonplace to pass the time while waiting for your return."

"I rather doubt the 'merest commonplace' could have caused you to colour up in such confusion. What was he saying to you?"

The man had the eyes of a hawk, Angelica thought distractedly, searching wildly for some noncommittal response. She did not find it, and as usual blurted out the truth: "Lord Robert had just paid me a compliment, my lord. I'm afraid I'm unused to such gallantry." She achieved a deprecating laugh that changed to an indignant gasp as he answered curtly:

"I'm well aware of that." He was frowning thoughtfully into space and failed to see her chagrin at his callousness.

She replied as evenly as the fury which was threatening to choke her would permit. "I have never had any pretensions to beauty, my lord, but I believe it has never been said that I am an antidote either. I'm not quite unacquainted with compliments."

It was his turn to look surprised, and he apologized gruffly. "Good lord, I wasn't implying any insult, you foolish girl. I merely meant that it is obvious you haven't been schooled in the so-called art of elegant dalliance." His unseeing gaze remained thoughtful. "I knew you were too young the moment you entered the library. You are no more up to snuff than Lydia."

Angelica gasped. "Your lordship has apparently forgotten that I am six years older than Lydia and four years older than your fiancée."

He laughed, but it was not a pleasant sound to the indignant girl. "In terms of experience you may be a few months older than Lydia, but you are years younger than Barbara." He directed a challenging look at her mutinous face as if daring her to argue the point. Angelica had to struggle with a deep sense of mortification before she could force any reply through stiff lips. 'I assure you, my lord, you are under a misapprehension. I was not flirting with Lord Robert."

"I know you weren't," he said, still frowning impatiently, "but I am not sure about Robert. He has no thought of marriage, you know. Your welfare is my responsibility while you are under my roof, and I don't want you to get hurt."

"I thank you for your concern, my lord," she snapped in a voice which scarcely conveyed gratification, "but I am well aware that a penniless governess is beyond the pale in the marriage stakes. I promise you I will not set my cap for poor Lord Robert." The bitter words were no sooner uttered than regretted, and Angelica found herself trembling, waiting for certain retribution. It didn't come. The stern face of her employer underwent one of its periodic lightning swift changes. His eyes lit with amusement and he gave a bark of real laughter. "I accept your promise, of course, Miss Wayne, but then you are not penniless, are you? If my memory is correct you have an annuity, which makes you a woman of parts."

For the first time since her childhood, Angelica experienced a strong urge to physical violence. Her fingers itched to slap the mocking face laughing down at her. The silence became tense with foreboding as the green eyes glared wrathfully up into the now almost gently smiling face above hers, and was suddenly broken by the sound of heavy footsteps as Chilham approached from the direction of the kitchens. As if released from a paralysis, Angelica spun on her heel and fled up the stairs as though pursued by all the demons in hell.

***

It took all her resolution to enable Angelica to face the viscount at dinner that night. She seriously considered pleading the headache and requesting a bowl of broth in her room, but fierce pride forbade her to play the coward. The passage of arms on the stairway had been her first real experience with the humiliation of being in a subservient position. Lydia treated her like a sister, Jenny adored her new teacher and until today the viscount had shown an impersonal courtesy, which, if not warming, was certainly acceptable. Until today her sense of personal worth had not been challenged, but now the illusion that she was a person in her own right was shattered by his attack on her in the hall.

Striding restlessly back and forth in the quiet sitting room to the furious pace of her resentment, she told herself fiercely that never would he have spoken so to a woman in his own circle. He looked on her as an inferior being to be kept in her place mentally, even if she must on occasion move physically in his sphere for his convenience. How dare he think she would stoop to flirting with his friends! He had all but accused her of setting her cap for Robert! Humiliation and fury prodded her on until she almost collapsed from fatigue.

It was not until later — when, drained of all emotion, she lay resting on her bed before dressing for dinner — that she allowed herself to see the event from the viscount's point of view. She recalled that he had not actually accused her of flirting with Lord Robert; in fact, he had quickly agreed that she had done no such thing. He had said that he feared she would be hurt. The implication, of course, was that she was so naive she would mistake mere flirting for something more serious. She clenched her teeth at this thought, but in fairness to the viscount, his behaviour indicated the same kind of concern he would have felt if Lydia were in danger of making such a mistake. Not a flattering opinion, of course, but nothing to warrant the excess of indignation which had coursed through her in a flood tide. Puzzled at her own intemperate reaction — she who prided herself on having, in Miss Austen's phrase, more sense than sensibility — she tried to find a reason for her behaviour. At bottom, she came to the unwelcome conclusion that she bitterly resented the implication that the viscount believed any attentions shown to her must necessarily be in the nature of harmless flirtations. Along with this bitter pill was the equally distasteful one that he believed her naive enough to leap immediately to the erroneous conclusion that such attentions were serious attempts to fix her interest.

So he had misjudged her, probably not maliciously. She had already suspected his opinion of women in general was not high. Why should she be so upset to find she was also in the category of women in general? Well, Angelica had never been given to self-delusion, and unpalatable as was the truth, she faced it squarely. It did matter to her what the viscount thought of her. Actually, since he was her employer, she should value his opinion of her, shouldn't she? She was not prepared to delve any further before dinner, but at least this had decided her that she did not wish to appear in his eyes as one who would indulge in a fit of the sullens.

Thus decided, she took extra care over her toilette, again wearing the amber gown, but spending more time on her problem hair. Recalling that Annie sometimes braided the tresses and wound them around her head in a coronet, she patiently began to plait it, but was glad to accept Lydia's help when that young lady came to discuss the afternoon's outing. Lydia was delighted to try her skill and well pleased with her efforts. When Angelica confided that she was planning to cut a few inches in the hope that it would better stay pinned in her customary knot, Lydia protested vociferously.

"Absolutely not! You have the loveliest hair imaginable, so soft and of such a marvellous colour. It would be a crime to cut it. You are most welcome to borrow Marie whenever you need help. She can attend you before she comes to me. This new style is quite elegant, but for my ball you must have something really spectacular — piled up high with curls falling over one shoulder."

"I don't think curls are quite my style," Angelica said laughingly, "but come now, or we shall be late for dinner."

The two girls went cheerfully down to the saloon, with Lydia protesting gaily that for her ball she would decide what her friend should wear and how she should dress her hair. By the time they entered the saloon, she had reduced Angelica to a fit of giggles over a mental picture of herself wearing clouds of puce ruffles and hundreds of curls.

Lady Orbridge and the viscount looked up at the somewhat boisterous entrance of the two girls. Angelica had developed a deep admiration and respect for the old woman in the short time she had been under the viscount's roof. Aunt Minerva bore the almost constant discomfort of her condition like a stoic and scorned to employ any of those stratagems used by other ladies who enjoyed ill health to make themselves the centre of their unfortunate households, controlling the activities of the various members like a puppeteer behind the scenes. She possessed a sparkling wit, a faintly acidulous tongue and very clear-seeing eyes.

Now those eyes were fixed on the two girls as they came toward her laughingly. "Well, you two are certainly in high gig tonight. What is the reason for such outrageous spirits before dinner?" The words were stern but the black eyes twinkled.

"Please, dear ma'am, forgive our sad want of conduct in entering the room like hoydens," said Angelica, seating herself beside Lady Orbridge and smiling warmly upon her. "Your thoroughly outrageous niece has been threatening to have the dressing of me for her ball, and if she were to have her way, I would cut such a deplorable figure as would make you give me the cut direct."

Lydia, still giggling, uttered, "Clouds of puce ruffles and her hair in hundreds of curls, like those ridiculous wigs you used to wear in your youth, Aunt Minerva."

"Try for a little conduct, miss," said her aunt sternly. "In my day, we knew how to create *une grande toilette*. None of these clinging muslins, which leave nothing to the imagination and have no style either. Why, I am told some of the hussies actually dampen their petticoats so their gowns appear pasted on. Sheer vulgarity!" she snorted.

Lydia, her spirits not the least subdued by this scolding, turned to her brother who had been silently observing the scene with a strange little smile on his lips, and demanded impishly, "Giles, don't you agree Angelica must make a really spectacular appearance for my ball?"

The subject under discussion was attempting to frown down the irrepressible girl, but to no avail as Lydia continued to expand on her theme that the family honour demanded a really grand outfitting of all concerned. At this point, Angelica cut in before the viscount could reply: "By the date of your ball, Lydia, Lady Barbara will be the new Lady Desmond, and I have every confidence that you and she together will uphold the family reputation for beauty and elegance."

If she hoped this remark would end the discussion which had become highly embarrassing, she was mistaken. Lydia, it was true, blinked in surprise, having forgotten completely about her prospective sister-in-law, but the viscount now spoke for the first time since the girls had entered the room. Ignoring Angelica's comment, he smilingly addressed himself to Lydia's.

"I quite agree, Lydia, that Miss Wayne must be dressed in the first style of elegance for your ball, but as she is always perfectly attired for every occasion, I think we may forget the puce ruffles and safely leave the selection in her hands. However I must remind you again, Miss Wayne, that since your duties go much beyond the usual requirements for a governess, I insist that it is my responsibility to assume the cost of the additional clothing required to carry out these duties. The bills for the outfit you choose are to be sent to me." The smile had disappeared before he finished this statement and he was looking quite decided.

Coming so soon after their contretemps on the stairs, Angelica was scarcely mollified by his compliment on her good taste and was decidedly provoked by the assumption, or rather command, that she allow him to pay for her clothes. Hot words of denial were trembling on her lips, but the viscount forestalled an answer by walking over to his aunt and assisting her out to the dining room. Perforce Angelica and Lydia followed, and the former had time to reconsider any rash words she might have regretted. However, she was determined to refuse to have him act as her banker and impatiently awaited an opportunity during dinner to make this clear to him. This was not made easy for her because the viscount seemed to be in rare good humour and he dominated the conversation, including the three ladies in all his remarks. Indeed he was so charming and entertaining that Angelica would have enjoyed the meal more than any she had partaken of in his company, had she not been existing in such a state of nervous agitation ever since their return that afternoon as even precluded any appreciation of the marvellous dinner set before them by one of the finest chefs in London.

She ate little, not even tempted by her favourite buttered crab. It was not until she was pretending enjoyment of one of the fancy little pastries that an opportunity arose to speak privately to the viscount, when for the moment Aunt Minerva was plunged into an anecdote about her mother for Lydia's ears alone.

Now that she had his ear, however, she found it extremely difficult to formulate the sentences which would convey gratitude for his thoughtfulness while firmly refusing his offer to buy her clothes for the ball. Disconcerted by the unwavering regard of those cold eyes, she realized she was faltering badly but kept her chin high and her voice low as she ended by saying in a rather pleading tone, "You must see, my lord, that I cannot allow you to purchase my clothes."

"Why not?" Both voice and manner were bland, almost bored, and she was exasperated beyond all bearing.

"Because I am not one of your dependents, my lord. You pay me a generous wage for my services. I cannot accept personal gifts."

"A ball gown would not be a gift; it is a uniform in which you perform your duties as companion to my sister. As such, you can't look like a poor relation."

"You have paid me the compliment of saying that I am always appropriately dressed, my lord. Am I to understand that you did not mean these words?" The green eyes were faintly contemptuous.

"No, my dear, I was not lying to you." The dark eyes were faintly smiling, and his voice was almost gentle as he answered the implication. "The clothes you have are eminently suitable and attractive, but you do not have enough for the life you are now leading. Do not deny it," he said imperatively as her lips parted. "You make your own gowns, I understand?"

"Yes, and I have recently purchased some beautiful Italian silk from which to fashion a gown for Lydia's ball. I promise you it also will be suitable and attractive."

"I'm sure it would be if you had the time to spend on the making, but with Jenny's lessons in the morning and Lydia's activities taking up much of the rest of your time, when do you propose to work on it?"

"Why I ... I often have an odd hour here and there."

"Yes," he cut in brusquely, "I daresay you could manage to finish this particular gown, but what of the others you will need? I have not seen another pelisse than the grey."

Her colour was now high but she answered quietly. "My lord, I think perhaps you forget that my duties with respect to Lydia are only temporary. In less than one month, Lady Barbara will assume the role of companion and chaperone, and I will no longer need a large supply of clothes." She took a deep breath to gather the strength to finish what must be said since he refused to understand her position.

"There is another point which a gentleman might overlook, but I must bring it to your attention." She met his gaze steadily. "A governess — even a governess-companion — is not expected to dress in the same style as her charge. Indeed, to do so would cause a degree of unfavourable comment among those who will be Lydia's hostesses, which I cannot believe you would care to subject me to. Do I make myself clear, my lord?"

There was complete silence for a moment. Her glance did not falter, although his expression was now thunderous.

"Very clear, if you mean to imply that the gossips would have you my mistress living under my own roof." A vein in his forehead twitched and his lips thinned to a dangerous line, but his voice was quite gentle when he added, "I beg your pardon, Miss Wayne. Certainly I have been about the town long enough to have realized that I would indeed be exposing you to the cruel tongues of the so-called cream of society. The fact that I wanted you to outshine them should not have blinded me to the realities. We will speak no more of this for the moment."

She drew a ragged breath of relief and switched the subject to one of the paintings over which they had disagreed that afternoon. He made a polite effort to follow her lead but was rather abstracted for the rest of the meal, scarcely responding to Lydia's sallies.

Angelica was most grateful to find he was not joining the ladies in the sitting room that evening. Although she had thoroughly enjoyed the exhibition, the scenes following their return had been of such a nature as to destroy her usual peace of mind. She felt thoroughly enervated and had no other wish than to retire to bed. Listening to Lady Orbridge's well-modulated voice reading again from Miss Austen's sympathetic story did have a soothing effect on her chaotic thoughts eventually, and when at last they retired for the night, she was calm enough and tired enough to fall asleep immediately, leaving any problems for the future.

CHAPTER SIX

One morning a few days later, the viscount was on his way out of the house, having just left his aunt. It was his custom to call on her briefly each day before beginning his activities. She never came to the breakfast room but was served in her boudoir by her Maggie, who had waited upon her since they were children together.

Chuckling over a particularly pungent comment Aunt Minerva had made about the Duke of York, Giles quietly closed the door to the apartment and made his way toward the front entrance. A whisper of sound caught his attention, and he paused to watch Jenny's teacher come slowly out of the library, her skirts gently rustling as she walked. She failed to see him, engrossed as she was in turning the leaves of a book. He stayed silent, following her graceful passage with eyes which were no longer cold.

Suddenly, near the foot of the stairway, the slim figure stiffened and, to his surprise, she flung a hand over her mouth as if to stifle a cry. Her rigid stance was eloquent of fear, and he started to move toward her when a sound from the upper hall drew his eyes up the stairs. There was a sudden flash of red and white, but before his dazzled brain could make sense of what his eyes were beholding, the colours resolved themselves into the small, laughing form of his daughter careening down the balustrade at a frightening speed. His throat was suddenly dry and his muscles tautened for action, but she was already safely down and enfolded tightly in the arms of her governess, who had dashed the book to the floor and caught the child as she was about to shoot off the newel post. The impact sent them both to the floor, Jenny pink-faced, still laughing excitedly. Angelica's face was remarkable for its pallor, and as he came up to them she was saying in a hoarse voice:

"Jenny, dearest, are you all right? Are you sure nothing hurts? Oh, whatever possessed you to do such a dangerous thing? You must promise me never, never to attempt that again. You might have been badly hurt." She seemed unable to move for the moment. Jenny scrambled nimbly to her feet, regarding the sitting figure in mild puzzlement.

"But, Angel, *you* did… Oh, hello, Papa, did you see me slide down? Did you see how fast I came down?" She was dancing around her father's silent form, tugging at his arm to attract his attention from her governess, whose eyes were closed and whose hand was groping for the post. Finally released from his trance, her father assisted Angelica to rise and, feeling her tremble, kept a sustaining arm about her waist while he frowned at his excited daughter.

"Jennifer," he grated harshly, "if you ever do anything like that again, you will remain all day in your room for one entire month, do you understand me?"

The child's beautiful eyes filled quickly with tears.

"But, Papa," she protested, "it wasn't hard, I wasn't afraid, and besides Angel said —"

"Jennifer, I will speak with you later. You will return to your room immediately and await me. Immediately." His stern voice had its effect. The tears spilled over and an unhappy little girl dashed back up the stairs, sobbing.

Angelica's hand clutched at his sleeve. Her voice was barely above a whisper. "Please, my lord, it was all my fault. Don't be hard on her. She thought — but I never realized — it was said so absently… Oh, the blame is all mine." She was wringing her hands in her distress, and the trembling had increased.

He bent over to retrieve the book and led her unresisting form back to the library. "Do not speak just yet. You've had rather a shock, and you are too upset to make sense. Sit here and don't talk."

She subsided gratefully into the green plush chair he had indicated, since her knees seemed temporarily unable to bear her weight. While she was fighting the waves of faintness that washed over her, the viscount was pouring amber liquid into a glass, which he presently pressed into her shaking hand.

"Drink this," he commanded, then as she took one small sip and shook her head distastefully, "Every drop of it, mind. It will steady you."

He watched her for a moment as she slowly swallowed sips of the fiery liquid, and, satisfied that she had conquered the faintness, walked back to the side table and quickly poured a substantial amount into a second glass for himself. He swallowed it in two gulps, replaced the glass carefully and, still watching her intently, pulled a chair near hers and sat down leaning forward, with his arms on his thighs and his hands linked loosely between his knees.

Angelica was thankful that he had stopped looming above her. In her present guilt-ridden state, his size and air of leashed power frankly terrified her. His shoulders were extremely broad beneath the beautifully cut olive-green coat, and the fawn-coloured knitted breeches hardly concealed the muscular thighs of an athlete. His tasselled Hessians were polished mirror bright. His whole appearance from spotless cravat to equally spotless boots bespoke perfection and neat propriety, although there was nothing of the dandy about him ever. His hair was worn rather shorter than the prevailing mode, kept rather rigidly under control as opposed to the carefully contrived windswept effect achieved by most pinks of the ton.

For once, the harsh features were softened by a look of concern, and Angelica was rather stabbingly aware of his strong masculine aura. Those compelling, night-dark eyes held hers against her will, and she felt the hot colour rise from her throat to her eyebrows. Her breathing quickened painfully.

Fortunately, he misinterpreted the betraying colour. "Thank heavens you are beginning to get some colour back," he said, relieved. "That wretched child of mine frightened you rather badly, I'm afraid."

His matter-of-fact tone succeeded in snapping the spell which his very presence and unusual concern had woven about her but brought her back to a sense of the enormity of the situation. Her voice shook as she said, "Oh, my lord, it was all my fault. I hold myself entirely to blame. Oh, my wretched tongue!"

In her agitation, the fingers of both hands had clutched the stem of the empty goblet she was still holding until the knuckles showed white. He reached over and loosened the cold fingers gently and removed the glass. Her eyes followed the hand that placed the glass on a nearby table then came anxiously back to his face. She was totally unaware that his other hand was grasping one of hers in a firm clasp.

"Why are you to blame, ma'am? Did you give Jenny permission to attempt that rather spectacular feat?" The very blandness of his tone brought an indignant gasp to her lips.

"Of course not! How could you think such a thing?"

"Oh, I don't, I assure you, but you seem so sure that you are to blame for her exploit." One eyebrow lifted.

All her momentary indignation drained away, leaving her contrite once more. "But I am, you see. Jenny was admiring a sampler of mine one day and asked me how old I was when I had embroidered it. I was looking for my scissors at the time and answered absently, and totally stupidly as it turned out, that I had done it when I was ten years old as a punishment for sliding down the balustrade." Her eyes were raised imploringly to his. "I never dreamed that my careless remark could have such a consequence. You can't condemn me more than I blame myself, my lord. I should have realized that such an enterprising child as Jenny would have seen a challenge in my foolish statement."

He laughed in genuine amusement. "If you had known her better, I daresay you might have guessed how she would react, but you have not been here very long, and I understand she has been unusually well-behaved since you arrived. Such an unnatural situation could never long endure. Do not feel too guilty; no harm was done after all." His voice held admiration. "She's pluck to the backbone, my little Jenny. Doesn't know the meaning of the word fear." A teasing smile played about his mouth, quirking up one corner. Angelica dragged her fascinated gaze from the suddenly boyish lips and started as her surprised eyes fell on her hand still imprisoned in his large one. Blushing, she withdrew hers gently, still unable to look at him. At the sound of his laugh, she did look up.

The teasing smile was still there. "You must have been a little devil despite your singularly inappropriate name. Tell me, was it worth the punishment — sliding down the rail, I mean?"

Suddenly, for no apparent reason, she was absurdly happy. The dimple appeared in her left cheek. "Yes, it was," she said frankly. "It was rather like flying, and to be perfectly truthful, I had done it more than once before I was caught." Her expression sobered abruptly. "Do you know, this is the first time I have ever realized how brave parents are. I don't know how my mother bore it, knowing I was running around after Billy, getting up to all sorts of mischief. I never half appreciated the freedom she allowed me. It must have been very difficult for her. I was completely terrified when I looked up and saw Jenny at the top of the stairs and comprehended what she meant to do. I could not move or even call out."

He interrupted her. "Doing nothing was probably what saved her from a nasty accident. If you had startled her, she might easily have lost her balance and fallen."

She shuddered then squared her shoulders and rose from the chair. "In any event, sir, you will not be harsh with her will you, now that it is obvious how she came to do such a foolhardy thing?"

He responded to the entreaty in her voice and eyes. "Of course not, but she must be made to promise that she will not do it again." He rose to his feet and motioned to her to precede him from the room. "Do you think history should repeat itself in the form of punishment also?" His eyes gleamed with humour and hers smiled up into his gaily.

"I'm afraid Jenny is not so handy with her needle as I was, my lord. May I suggest perhaps a handkerchief to be hemmed for her papa? And if she promises not to do it again, you may rely on her not to break her word. Jenny is a very truthful child."

She could not fathom the changing expressions in the dark eyes of the man climbing the stairs at her side. Pain at first, or pride, perhaps. She was mystified but realized intuitively that his thoughts had wandered to another time and place. She had sensed this withdrawal in him as early as that first interview in the room they had just left. Something had scarred this man. It must be related to the death of his beautiful young wife, of course. She was still puzzled, though. Grief was perfectly understandable and a lingering sadness, but could it account for the moody silences and flashes of bitterness? Why would not his memories just as often be pleasant ones? She could not recall ever having seen him in one of his withdrawals wearing a reminiscent smile or even a mildly pleasant expression. His moods seemed all darkness and shadow, pain and regret.

The silence had lengthened when on arriving at the second floor, he put out a hand to detain her as she would have moved toward her own room. She looked at him questioningly. His eyes bored into her face.

"You have a fondness for Jenny, have you not, Miss Wayne?"

Some of the reliefs she felt at his return from his dark vision must have been evident in her voice. "Of course I do, my lord," she replied, smiling warmly. "Jenny is a very lovable child, and I thoroughly enjoy my association with her despite being practically frightened to death earlier."

He did not respond to her light tone but continued to look searchingly at her for some few seconds. He said simply, almost humbly, "Thank you," then left her abruptly and walked rapidly toward the nursery.

Angelica stared after him, bemused by his changing moods until, recalled to the present, she quickly entered her sitting room. She wandered aimlessly around the pleasant little room then sat down on the settee. Her unseeing eyes were on the hanging cabinet, which now displayed the lovely Lowestoft pieces that had been her mother's delight. Never had she expected to see the man she had mentally called arrogant discard his mask of indifference to thank her with what she could only consider humility for her small services to his daughter. She had felt that his affection for Jenny was deep but deplored that reserve which characterized his behaviour even with his adorable daughter. Observing them together before dinner on several occasions, the strange thought had occurred to her that he was actually afraid to reveal his love for the child. Earlier, she had dismissed the thought as the ridiculous fancy of her imagination. But now she wondered again about his relationship with his daughter. Why would he fear to demonstrate his love for the little girl who so obviously adored him? She recalled his grim expression when in their initial interview he had said Jenny must not grow up to think her beauty entitled her to have her every wish gratified. She had been a bit startled at his vehemence at the time. Could it be he really thought natural expressions of paternal affection would prove harmful to the development of Jenny's character? She was reluctant to credit that so intelligent a man might hold such a nonsensical belief but could propose no other explanation to account for his deliberate reserve.

It was not, properly speaking, the place of a governess to criticize a parent's attitude with his child, but where Jenny's welfare was concerned, Angelica was prepared to attempt the impossible. There must be some way to discover if her theory was correct. It would require tact, of course, but she had been pleasantly surprised, in view of the viscount's forbidding exterior, by his patience and attention to herself. Of a certainty he had been kindness personified after Jenny's recent adventure. She had been too upset to question at the time, but now recalling everything that had occurred in the library in the past hour, she realized with a sense of excitement that for the first time there had been no barrier of mockery between them.

She rose swiftly from the settee and gave way to her invariable habit of pacing in time to her thoughts. Why, they had talked together as naturally as old friends! She closed her eyes and visualized his features as he had teased her about her childhood. Why hadn't she realized at the time that he had looked and acted like her erstwhile rescuer? Her heart was beating rather rapidly and her steps were also quick. It had taken a crisis to breach the wall of reserve he had erected around his former self. Could she dare hope that the breach might widen or, with the crisis safely passed, would he revert to his habitual slightly mocking civility? She found that she was extremely eager for their next meeting.

In any event, the next meeting with Jenny at lunch was not difficult. Whatever her father had said to her had swept away the unhappiness Angelica had witnessed. She was slightly subdued but had begged her teacher's pardon for frightening her with such a sweetly anxious air that Angelica had laughed and hugged her lightly. An expression of great relief passed over the little girl's face. Impulsively, she wound her arms around Angelica's neck and shyly kissed her cheek.

"You understand I did not mean to frighten you, Angel, don't you?" she asked once again. "I thought it would be the most exciting thing to do. Papa said he was frightened, too. I never thought Papa was frightened of anything. He takes Rufus over the highest hedges when we are in the country." Her voice was filled with awe at having been responsible for striking fear into the heart of the lion.

Angelica hugged her again. What an essentially sweet child she was. Couldn't her father see there was no danger that a little overt paternal affection would spoil her? Hers was not a selfish nature. She said gravely, "Jenny, even the bravest of people like your papa can be afraid when the ones they love are in danger. You might have been badly hurt, and that would have hurt your father because he loves you very much. It was a great deal too bad of me ever to mention that I did that foolish stunt. I wasn't really thinking about what I was saying, you see, because otherwise I would have remembered how upset my mama and my aunt were when I slid down the rail at the Court."

"Angel?" said Jenny hesitantly. "Did you think it was fun?"

Angelica grinned. "Oh, yes, it was great fun. How about you?"

Jenny's little face glowed. "I felt like I was flying! Is it naughty of me to be glad I did it, even though I am sorry I frightened you and Papa?"

"No, of course not, darling. But now that you know how dangerous it is, you will not try it again, will you?"

"Oh, no, I've already promised Papa I would never do it again."

"Well, then, let us go and join Nurse for lunch. Aunt Lydia is lunching with the Misses Caterham today. They came to call for her half an hour ago."

CHAPTER SEVEN

When Jenny had retired for her rest, Angelica found herself with the time necessary to cut out the gown she had designed for Lydia's ball. The viscount had been right, she thought, with a wry twist to her pretty lips — she would never have sufficient free time to fashion a wardrobe equal to the life she was now leading, but at least she would complete this gown. In any event, once Lady Barbara became Lady Desmond, her own social life would cease as abruptly as it had begun. She acknowledged this with a slight pang of regret. Although she had not expected to go out socially at all when she accepted the post as Jenny's governess, quite a deal of social activity had been included in her duties. She had been very happy in Lydia's company, and it would have been out of character to deny the truth that she was going to find life rather dull when the house had a new mistress. Naturally, she would see much less of Lydia because that young lady would be completely swept up in a round of activity after her presentation.

She enjoyed visiting with Lady Orbridge when the old woman was feeling well enough and she was a reader, too, but life would definitely not be as exciting when the viscount married. No doubt she would see very little of him in the future. There would no longer be a reason to dine with the family. This was the most unwelcome thought of all, and suddenly she could no longer bear the solitude of her sitting room. Rising swiftly from her knees where she had been cutting the cloth, she gathered the fabric together and decided to go down to the library for a book. Lydia was not returning till after tea. Perhaps she would see if Lady Orbridge was alone.

Suiting the action to the thought, Angelica ran swiftly down the stairs and was just about to cross the hall when a commotion sounded at the front door. Chilham made his stately way to the entrance. Angelica was about to enter the library when Chilham's voice, for once losing its imperturbable quality, arrested her motion.

"Why, what has happened, my lord? Here, let me assist you."

Angelica spun around and stared.

The viscount stood on one foot in the hall, looking pale and furious. He was leaning on the arm of a portly gentleman unknown to Angelica and waving Chilham away impatiently with one hand.

"No, I don't need you, Chilham. I can hop all right with an assist from Colonel Revesby."

"Very good, my lord. Shall I have your room prepared?"

"No, no, I have no intention of being rendered bedfast. Call Murdock. If you'll just help me into the library, Revesby. There is a sofa there."

Finally Angelica came to life. She opened the library door, and going in first, snatched the pillows from the green plush sofa.

By the time the viscount had carefully lowered himself to the sofa, sweat was standing out on his forehead and his pallor was even more pronounced.

"What is it, my lord, your foot or your leg?" Angelica asked quietly.

"Ankle," he muttered through clenched teeth.

"Has the doctor been sent for?"

"No, I don't need a doctor; I'll be all right once I get this curst boot off. Where is Murdock? He'll have to cut it off, though it will go sorely against the grain with him to ruin these Hessians."

Angelica had a fair idea of the amount of pain the viscount was suffering but forbore to argue with him in his present state. She held firmly to the belief that the doctor should be summoned, but contented herself for the moment with seeing Colonel Revesby out as her employer requested. Staying just long enough to settle the leg on some pillows, she left the room with the colonel, noting as she did so that the viscount's eyes were closed and he seemed a trifle easier in a horizontal position.

"Are you the new governess?" the colonel asked when they had re-entered the hall.

"Yes."

"Well, I don't mind telling you it is my opinion Desmond needs a doctor, no matter how lightly he treats the injury. Might be broken, after all. Better send to Harley Street."

Angelica murmured polite thanks for the colonel's aid and reassured him everything necessary would be done, but when the outer door had closed, she hesitated for a moment. After all, she had no authority here and the viscount had said he wanted no doctor. On the other hand, she was in complete agreement with the colonel's opinion. Seeing the footman returning, she squared her shoulders and ordered him to take a message to the viscount's doctor.

On returning to the library to inform him of the action, she found him angrily awaiting his valet's arrival. Angelica hastened out again without telling him of the doctor's impending visit and ran up the stairs in search of Murdock. She met Chilham on the nursery floor, but an almost unrecognizable Chilham. Gone was his air of haughty dignity, and his sonorous voice shook slightly as he explained that, unable to find Murdock, he had checked with Nurse, who had told him that since the viscount had not been expected home for dinner the valet had gone to Soho to visit his ailing mother.

"Well, that is unfortunate indeed, but that boot must come off you know, Chilham. You will have to cut it."

At this Chilham turned ashen, and he held out his hands to demonstrate their shakiness. It seemed he had a morbid aversion to illness and tended to faintness at the sight of blood. He was deeply regretful but could not possibly wield a knife under the circumstances.

Angelica, staring at his blanched countenance, experienced an almost hysterical desire to laugh. How the mighty have fallen! Chilham, the intimidating force in the household, reduced to shaking uselessness by the sight of physical injury. Her promise that there was no question of blood failed to stiffen the butler's spine. He suggested that the footman perform the operation, and Angelica had to explain that she had dispatched Matthew with a message for the doctor.

They were descending the last few stairs when the viscount's angry voice was clearly heard through the closed library door.

"Well," said Angelica, shrugging her shoulders fatalistically, "it must be done immediately, so I shall have to do it. Fetch cold cloths, please, Chilham."

Entering the library, she calmly informed the scowling viscount of the situation and asked where she might find a knife.

"You will not do it; you haven't the strength. Get Chilham."

"His hands are shaking too much, my lord. He'd cut your leg and faint away at the sight of the blood. Then there would be two patients." She had been pouring a long drink of brandy while uttering this matter-of-fact statement and now pressed the glass into his hand. "I sent Matthew for the doctor," she explained as he opened his mouth to protest. "This should be done immediately, my lord; it must be dreadfully uncomfortable for you."

At these prosaic words the viscount actually smiled, and uttering a weary sigh, indicated a knife on the long table.

"Very well, my competent Miss Wayne, cut away." He drank the brandy down quickly.

She knelt down beside the sofa, knife in hand. It was a hazardous task and required all her resolution. The knowledge that she was hurting him increased the difficulty tenfold. Sensing that a glimpse of his face while she was cutting would be her undoing, she kept her eyes steadily on her fingers and her lower lip gripped tightly in her teeth. Perspiration beaded her upper lip by the time she had succeeded in easing the heavy boot off, and she was battling tears of emotional weakness. He had not uttered a sound, but the changing rhythms of his breathing and the tensing muscles under her hand were clear indications of the amount of pain she was causing. She sank down abruptly, clutching the boot to her chest, and drew a long ragged breath before she was able to raise her eyes to his.

His pale face was drawn with pain, but the dark eyes glowed with a strange light as he stared intently at the equally pale girl. She could not have broken away from that hypnotic gaze had not Chilham entered the room an instant later with cold cloths. While she laid the cloths on the already swelling ankle, the viscount directed the butler to pour some brandy for her. She protested but was peremptorily overruled. Obediently she sat in the green plush chair (for the second time in one day, her surprised brain reminded her) and slowly sipped the strong liquid. After a moment, it did seem to chase away the weak feeling in her bones and she was more composed.

She smiled, though rather shakily at the viscount who was holding a glass refilled by Chilham. "It seems, my lord, that every time I enter this room I end by drinking brandy. Rather demoralizing."

"Miss Wayne, you are a remarkable woman. I salute you," he said seriously, but his eyes were alight with laughter as he ceremoniously raised his glass to her.

Angelica eyed him calmly. "The combination of pain and brandy is making you utterly nonsensical, my lord."

"What, no blush? My dear Miss Wayne, I thought you always blushed delightfully when a gentleman paid you a compliment." His voice was smooth and he quirked one eyebrow.

Angelica glanced involuntarily at the door where Chilham's tall form seemed to pause momentarily before going out. She could almost fancy that his ears stood out at attention, and now she did colour up in confusion. She bit her lip to keep back a retort. After all, he probably was feeling light-headed. It crossed her mind that this was rather a strange moment to be feeling light-hearted as well.

"Ah, that's better. I would not like to think my compliments are less worthy of blushes than Robert's." As her eyes flashed and her lips parted, he went on smoothly, "Speaking of Robert, I was supposed to dine with him before coming back here to change. I had promised to escort Lady Barbara and her sister to Almack's. When Matthew comes back, would you send him to me?"

"Yes, my lord." Angelica rose from the green chair. "I believe I hear someone now. I hope it is Matthew with the doctor." She crossed the room toward the door, but as she passed the sofa the viscount's hand shot out and seized her right wrist with strong fingers. She managed to stand quietly, looking serenely down at him.

"Thank you, Miss Wayne." He turned her hand over, and to her astonishment, bent his head and pressed his lips to her blue-veined wrist.

The touch was feather light, but its effect on her was as if a red-hot coal had struck her arm, sending painful prickling sensations radiating from the point of contact. This time, she couldn't meet his eyes but was saved by the sound of the door opening. She snatched her hand away and went quickly toward the door as Chilham entered, followed by a stranger whom Angelica correctly identified as the doctor. With a murmured excuse, she left the room and spoke to Matthew. After the footman had entered the library, she stood there in the hall gazing unseeingly at the closed door for several minutes, absently rubbing the spot on her wrist with the fingers of her left hand. She was still standing thusly when the knocker sounded. Recalled to the present, she started to ascend the stairs but paused when she heard Lydia's voice at the door. Running back down, she dismissed Chilham and drew Lydia's arm through hers while she told her the news.

"Oh, poor Giles!" Lydia cried warmly. "Where is he? In the library? I must go to him." She turned toward the library but Angelica held her back, explaining that the doctor was with him still. Instead, she led the younger girl into the small room where Mrs. Haskins interviewed the servants and paid the tradespeople.

"We'll leave the door open so we'll hear the doctor when he leaves the library. He may wish to leave some instructions with you."

"With me?" Lydia's expression of surprise was almost ludicrous. "As if Giles would ever listen to me! When did this happen and how?"

Angelica, looking at the tiny watch pinned to her dress, was surprised to see it was close on six o'clock. "I imagine about an hour ago, if his lordship came home directly. I don't know how it happened or if the ankle is actually broken. It swelled up immediately as I cut the boot off, but I could not tell."

"You cut off his boot? Good gracious, however did you manage? Where was Murdock?"

"Visiting his mother I believe, and Chilham…" Angelica giggled. "You should have seen our stately Chilham with shaking hands, threatening to faint. I shall never be afraid of him again."

Lydia said flatly that she felt she had been denied a high treat if it were indeed true, but she strongly suspected her friend of bamming.

Angelica solemnly held up her right hand. "On my honour."

Just then, hasty footsteps sounded on the stairway, and they went to the door to confront an agitated Jenny and a slightly flustered Nurse.

"Oh, Angel," cried Jenny, flinging her arms around her governess's waist. "What has happened to Papa? I was having my supper when Nurse had to go talk to Chilham. I could hear something about an accident, but Nurse won't tell me what's wrong. Is Papa hurt?" Jenny's beseeching eyes were filled with tears which threatened to spill over.

Nurse said apologetically, "She would not eat, miss, until she knew how her father was."

"That's all right, Mrs. Priddy. Jenny dear," said Angelica, gently disentangling the little girl's arms and retaining a grip on her hands, "your father is not badly injured, but there has been some sort of accident and his ankle is hurt. The doctor is here now. As soon as he leaves, you may go in and see Papa and kiss him goodnight if you will go with Nurse now and finish your supper."

Jenny went reluctantly with Nurse. "You won't forget?" she implored, glancing back over her shoulder as Nurse bustled her up the stairs.

"Of course not." Angelica turned from Jenny to confront Mrs. Haskins, who had puffed her way up from the kitchens where she had been conferring with the chef and had missed all the excitement. So more explanations were made, but Angelica, catching sight of Matthew leaving the library, abandoned Mrs. Haskins to Lydia and walked swiftly toward the footman.

Matthew explained that he had been ordered to deliver a message to Lord Robert Hoxley. He assured her that the doctor had said there were no bones broken, only a bad sprain.

"Well, that is a great relief, although a sprain can mean quite as much discomfort as a break in the beginning." Angelica smiled dismissal at the footman, and Matthew left in his errand.

The door opened again, admitting the doctor and Chilham, whose impassive mask was completely restored.

Angelica liked the doctor's kind face with its network of fine lines surrounding his mouth and raying out from pale blue eyes under shaggy grey brows. The lines sharpened as he smiled at her. "You are Miss Wayne, I believe?"

Angelica confirmed this and returned his smile with interest.

"Lord Desmond told me you very competently cut the boot from his foot. My congratulations; I'm glad there was someone with a cool head in the house."

Angelica avoided Chilham's eye as she hastily asked the doctor about the damage to the viscount's ankle and brought him to Lydia. His manner to the anxious young girl was most reassuring as he explained that, although there was no break, the viscount must keep completely off his feet for at least a sennight.

"There is no problem now, of course, because he is bone weary, but in two or three days when most of the pain is gone, it will be difficult to hold him down. He's always been a bad patient." He gave the housekeeper instructions to have a very light meal prepared for the viscount, and she bustled off toward the kitchens.

"May I see my brother now, Dr. Finlay?" asked Lydia.

"Of course, my dear, but don't stay too long. He is very tired." Lydia departed and the doctor turned to Angelica. "Miss Wayne, I have given Lord Desmond some powders which should ease the pain and help him sleep. He really should not be moved, but he insists on sleeping in his own bed. Certainly he'll be more comfortable there. When the valet returns, he and the footman can carry him upstairs, I should think. That Matthew is a husky lad. Will you see to it that he takes those powders? I will be back tomorrow to check on him."

Angelica assented and saw the doctor to the door. Returning, she saw Jenny, wide-eyed and anxious on the stairs, and tucking the little girl's hand in hers, led her to the library door and knocked. The viscount's voice bade them enter, and Jenny perked up immediately on hearing it.

She ran across the room and flung her arms around her father's neck. He winced perceptibly as she rocked his leg but smiled at her and held her close in one arm, listening gravely to her outpouring of mingled anxiety and relief.

Angelica, who had never seen them in such a natural loving attitude, felt her own eyes mist over. Glancing at Lydia, she saw a happy smile on the young girl's lips. How they both adored him! A feeling of yearning for the parents she had lost swept over her.

The viscount looked up at that moment and smiled at her. She was surprised at how suddenly warm and alive she felt, where only a moment ago she had been experiencing a bitter sense of loneliness and loss.

Jenny kissed her father goodnight and headed upstairs. Lydia departed to inform Aunt Minerva of the viscount's accident. Pausing on her way out, Angelica asked her employer if there was anything he wished.

"Yes," he said with a touch of his former bitterness, "but that does not mean I will be granted it."

This enigmatic reply halted Angelica in her tracks and she raised questioning brows, but a knock on the door prevented a reply, if indeed there were any replies possible.

Lord Robert entered unannounced. He greeted Angelica with a smiling, "Your servant, ma'am," and turned to his friend. "Giles, I know how much you dislike an evening at Almack's, but is not this going a bit far to avoid it?" He indicated the bandaged ankle with a grin. "Tell me, was it all very heroic? Did you rescue a child from under the wheels of a speeding carriage?"

"Damn your eyes, Robert," said the viscount bluntly, but with a reluctant smile. "I stepped on something, wrenching the curst ankle, then fell down the stairs and gave it the coup de grace."

"Cawker!" Lord Robert subsided, laughing, onto the green chair, while Angelica hastily made her exit from the room.

The viscount's eyes followed her flight and lingered on the closed door for a moment. The rueful smile reappeared.

"Damn you, Robert. Now I shall have to apologize for using language unfit for a lady's ears."

"Oh, no, I shouldn't think so. She seems a good sort of girl — not one to take a pet over trifles."

His friend eyed him thoughtfully for a moment then changed the subject. "Robert, will you escort Barbara and Caroline to Almack's tonight?"

There was an exaggerated sigh from the depths of the green chair. "This is what comes of saying I'd do a lot for you, old chap. Right away you set out to test me. What can I say but that I am entirely at your service — or rather at Lady Barbara's." He rose and executed a most elegant bow which deserved a more appreciative audience as the viscount told him dryly:

"Stay and dine if you like. They are sending some pap in to me, but I'm sure Aunt Minerva and the girls would be glad of your company."

"Thank you, but Mrs. Morris has been baking all day in anticipation of your visit, and I'd best provide her with at least one diner if I'm not to be punished with burnt meat for a week. Besides, it will take time to make myself elegant enough to be a fit escort for the beauteous Barbara." He smiled innocently into the viscount's suddenly narrowed gaze and took his leave after warning his friend to obey the doctor.

The occupants of the dining room were rather subdued that evening. Lydia was quieter than usual, and Lady Orbridge was rather concerned for her nephew. By the time she had dressed for dinner and gone to satisfy herself that Giles was being adequately looked after, he had drunk some broth and eaten some ham but appeared drawn and exhausted. On being asked whether the doctor had left anything for the pain, her nephew had replied curtly that he didn't need anything and refused to quack himself. The ensuing argument had done nothing to improve her temper, and she confided to Angelica that men were all totally stupid when it came to their health. She then went on to enumerate at some length the various occasions on which the late Lord Orbridge had failed to follow his doctor's advice. Angelica, who was feeling quite enervated by the onslaught to her emotions of two frightening events in one day, talked to her soothingly and promised to see that the viscount swallowed the powders left by the doctor. After dinner, she took her courage in hand and rapped on the library door.

The viscount had a book in his hands, but one look at his tired, set face told her he was too uncomfortable to concentrate. His "Well, Miss Wayne?" in forbidding accents would have been completely daunting in other circumstances, but she raised her chin just that trifle and looked steadily at her employer while inquiring politely if he had taken the medication.

He replied shortly that he had not, and again took up the book he had lowered at her approach as if that closed the conversation.

"I beg your pardon, my lord, but the doctor specifically delegated to me the responsibility of fixing your medication, so if you will show me the powders, I will prepare them for you now."

"You may prepare anything you choose, Miss Wayne, but I refuse to take drugs I do not need."

"Please, my lord, I don't wish to tease you, but how shall I face the doctor tomorrow and tell him I failed to carry out his orders?"

His lips thinned still further. "You may tell him you take orders from me, and I ordered you to throw the powders out."

From her downcast eyes to the lovely hands clasped together in front of her, she was the picture of meek submission. Her voice was faintly mournful. "Of course, my lord, I realize as your ser— as a member of your household staff it is not my place to make suggestions. I am very sorry."

At his indrawn breath Angelica knew she had gone too far, and she had to fight an almost uncontrollable urge to dash out of the room so she would not have to face the contempt in his eyes. Her heart was thumping madly and the clasped hands were no longer a pose; her knuckles were white.

After an interval that seemed an eternity, the viscount said coldly, "And well you should look terrified. How dare you accuse me of treating you like a servant!" Each word was enunciated clearly and fell like a distinct chip of ice.

Now she did look at him. "I am truly sorry, my lord. I did not mean that." The words tumbled out in her haste to blot out what she had said. "It is just that I would have tried anything to get you to take the medicine. Please, my lord." The strain of the long, emotionally charged day was beginning to tell on Angelica. She kept her head up but her eyelids half closed to conceal the tears that threatened to fall. She could not know the devastating effect of her slim figure taut with fatigue and her proudly carried head on her employer, but he capitulated abruptly.

"Oh, get the curst draught ready if you must. Then get yourself to bed before you collapse."

She could not trust her voice but silently prepared the doctor's prescription and handed it to him with a hand that she willed to steadiness. He drank it in equal silence. The only sounds in the room were the crackling hiss from the fireplace and the suddenly loud ticking of the silver mantel clock.

The viscount handed her the empty glass. "Will you please send Murdock to me?" There was no emotion in the quiet voice, but Angelica longed to smooth the furrowed brow with her hand. She clenched the hand into a fist and replied softly, "Of course, my lord. Goodnight, sleep well."

She went swiftly from the room, grateful that the day would soon be ending, but her steps slowed on the stairs and it was a physical effort to maintain a steady pace. Within five minutes of sending the valet to his master, she was climbing into her bed without even unpinning her hair.

CHAPTER EIGHT

The household settled into a new rhythm with the viscount's injury. Even the day after the accident, when he was still experiencing considerable pain, he insisted on being downstairs, choosing to spend the day in the library. Angelica was relieved that she had not had to witness his descent, leaning heavily on Matthew's strong arm because she had a fair idea of what his stubbornness had cost him. Fortunately for his recovery, there had been no callers that first day and the doctor saw to it that his patient spent most of the day sleeping.

The news of the accident spread among his cronies soon enough, and on the following day his enforced solitude was relieved by visits from several of his friends.

Each day after her rest Jenny would race to visit her father, and Angelica was happy to observe that these visits pleased him immensely. He enjoyed hearing about her lessons, though his black brows escalated on hearing her recapitulation of the Battle of Waterloo. He politely requested to see some evidence of her needlework and sketching, to Angelica's amusement. Jenny, blossoming like a flower in the warmth of his interest, began to apply herself to her lessons with an earnestness that was touching. If her father were working or reading, she would bring some sewing or drawing materials to the library and work contentedly alongside him. His pleasure in her company was genuine, and as father and daughter drew closer together, Angelica became convinced that there was no longer any necessity for her to speak to the viscount about his fear of spoiling the child. It must be apparent to the meanest intelligence that Jenny yearned to please him and eagerly sought his approval. He could not fail to see that she possessed consideration for others also. Jenny was indeed full of energy and high spirits, but any danger of her growing up narcissistic or wilful was remote.

The viscount insisted on dining *en famille* and enjoyed hearing Lydia's accounts of the mild social activities and shopping excursions of her day. To Angelica he was unfailingly courteous, but there was again a slight shade of reserve in his manner. She told herself that this was precisely the tone she wanted in their relationship. She had been acutely uncomfortable on the two or three occasions when he had seemed to forget for the moment that he was her employer. After all, they could never be friends because of the difference in their stations, and since he was soon to be married, it was imperative that they continue on a formal basis. Angelica had no illusions as to her own position when Lady Barbara became the mistress of the viscount's establishment. She would be permanently relegated to the schoolroom. She told herself reasonably that that was exactly the situation she had expected when she had accepted employment in a nobleman's household. It was nonsensical to be sunk in some ridiculous melancholy simply because her horizons had expanded for a brief time. Since she was a reasonable girl, she preserved her air of calm serenity, but it cost her something to do so.

Lord Robert managed to spare his friend some time almost every day. When the viscount had ventured to thank him for acting as escort to Lady Barbara at Almack's, Robert had cheerfully brushed aside his thanks.

"But I *am* grateful, Robert."

"No need to be, old chap, because I did not really act as deputy. That fellow Haring was there already for dinner. I gather he's some sort of connection to the earl — seemed as thick as thieves anyway. Well the long and short of it is, when I explained about your ankle and offered my services, damned if the fellow didn't jump in and insist that he couldn't let me sacrifice my plans for the evening when he was already in knee breeches. Well, he had a point of course. I had stopped off before going home to change."

Giles expressed mild interest in the outcome.

"Well, naturally I was not going to retreat and leave the field to that man-milliner. Told Barbara I'd be back in an hour. And I was," he finished triumphantly. "Never dressed so fast in my life."

Giles sighed and, eyeing his friend's brightly patterned waistcoat, asked what offended Robert about Sir Anthony's style.

"You must know Weston never made his coats, nor Stultz either. All that shoulder padding, waist so tight he could barely breathe, and lord, Giles, the buttons were as big as saucers. Fellow's a curst dandy. Good seat though. Saw him on a nice bit of horseflesh in the park yesterday."

"Alone?"

"No, Barbara and Caroline were with him. Well, stands to reason — family connection and all."

A little smile appeared on the viscount's lips. "Barbara sent me a letter commiserating about the ankle. She was all apologies for not being able to come to see me immediately — the pressure of previous commitments."

Lord Robert eyed him speculatively. "You don't seem particularly worried," he suggested when his friend made no further comment.

"Oh, but I am, Robert." And now there was a rather bleak expression in the dark eyes, but he swiftly changed the subject to the upcoming races.

If Lord Robert had no other plans for the evening, he would stay for dinner and repay his host by losing to him at piquet, but he was usually engaged with friends, and the time after dinner hung rather heavily on the viscount's hands.

One evening almost a sennight after the accident, he joined the ladies in the small drawing room after drinking his port in lonely splendour. Lydia was playing softly on the pianoforte while Angelica worked on a piece of needlepoint. Aunt Minerva had dined in her rooms that evening, not having felt up to the task of manoeuvring herself to and from the dining room and enduring the discomfort of a formal dinner.

He hobbled in, leaning on a stick, and lowered his large frame into a cane-seated chair. When Angelica suggested he would be more comfortable in the deep wing chair by the fireplace, he shook his head, saying he preferred a chair easier to rise from. She looked faintly surprised but continued sewing. He made no attempts at conversation and she assumed he was enjoying the Mozart that Lydia was playing. Glancing up after a time, she was a bit embarrassed to find his eyes fixed on her hands, until she realized his thoughts were elsewhere. She returned her attention to her work, but he had caught her regard, and shaking off his mood of abstraction, asked her abruptly if she played piquet.

"Yes, my lord. Billy taught me."

"Billy Wroxham is the world's worst cardplayer."

"Too true, my lord," she answered serenely. "He owes me in the neighbourhood of two million pounds."

The viscount's face lighted with pure mischief. He laughed and said gaily: "That sounds remarkably like a challenge to me, Miss Wayne. Surely you will not refuse to let me pit my skill against so successful a player?"

"Of course I will play you if you would like it, my lord."

"Why are you studying me so intently? Trying to guess whether or not I shall fleece you? Naturally, we shall play for the same stakes you and Billy play for."

"I beg pardon for staring, my lord. It was just that I suddenly recognized you. Really for the first time."

He looked puzzled. When she realized what she had just blurted out impulsively, she was overcome with embarrassment, and rising quickly, went to get the cards.

She was quite composed when she returned, but as they settled at a table to begin play, he returned to her unfortunate remark. "What did you mean a moment ago, when you said you recognized me for the first time?"

"It was a foolish remark. Please forget it."

"No, I would like an answer and a truthful one, please."

He is quite relentless, she thought resentfully, but answered truthfully as always: "It was just a passing fancy, my lord. Something in your face momentarily — a carefree expression perhaps — put me forcibly in mind of the way you looked when I first met you ten years ago."

He smiled into her eyes. "Do you know, Miss Wayne, that is probably the nicest thing you have ever said to me. Especially since I have it on your own admission that you were madly in love with me ten years ago."

She stared at him in frozen horror. As her lips parted indignantly, he went on in the same teasing voice, "I think one compliment deserves another, so I shall tell you that you are not at all as I remember you ten years ago. Now shall we play cards?"

She was more than willing to abandon any personal discussion, and since she had a fondness for card games, especially piquet, settled down for an enjoyable evening. And despite the fact that it was perfectly evident before the second rubber that the viscount was the superior player, she did enjoy the game. Once when the luck was strongly favouring her, she won a rubber, and on another occasion drew out a rubber to three games, but there was little doubt as to the eventual outcome. Like many women, she gambled on slim odds with the inevitable results. Nor did she possess the ability to read her opponent's hand as the viscount clearly did. It was certainly frustrating to find herself more than once robbed of a pique. She had the true gamester's faith in the swing of fortune moreover, and scarcely noticed when Lydia bade them a laughing goodnight, so intent was she on gaining her revenge. Shortly afterward, she glanced up to find the viscount's eyes fixed on her with amusement and something else she could not define in their dark depths. It brought her out of her gamester's reverie and she raised her brows questioningly.

"My dear Miss Wayne, will you forgive me if we make this our last rubber for the evening? Tomorrow you shall have your revenge, but I must confess I am beginning to feel a bit sleepy."

"Oh, my lord, I beg your pardon for keeping you up so late when your ankle must be giving you pain. I am a typical loser, never knowing when to stop. And I must confess I shall be happy to throw this particular hand in," she said, suiting the action to the words although he protested. "What time is it anyway?"

On being told it was nearly midnight, she gasped with amazement and rapidly gathered the cards together.

He laughed again and put a large hand over hers on the table. "My ankle is fine, my little gamester. It is merely that I am sleepy and you, apparently, are tireless in pursuit of Dame Fortune."

She blushed hotly and withdrew her hand under the pretext of gathering the last of the cards together. Rising too quickly, she failed to notice her skirt caught under a chair leg. She lurched sideways and would have fallen but for the viscount's strong arm immediately around her waist as he jumped up, knocking over his chair. She fell back against his chest, momentarily unable to regain her footing. The hard beating of his heart was instantly apparent, and her own set up a counterrhythm with its hammering.

Fighting an almost overpowering urge to turn in his arms which had tightened about her, she stiffened and tried to move away. His arms loosened instantly but something caught her hair, jerking her head back.

"What on earth?" She tried to move her head to the side but the viscount said abruptly:

"Wait. A pin in your hair is caught in my tiepin I think, but I cannot see where to release it."

However, waiting in such close proximity to him was intolerable to Angelica. A second impatient jerk of her head and she was free, but her hair came loose from its knot and tumbled down her back. Automatically putting up a hand to gather her hair to re-pin it, she encountered his hand in her hair and dropped hers as though burned by the brief contact. Avoiding his eyes, she moved a step away. Again, she gathered the long tresses in her hand but was unable to find any pins.

"Here." His voice was husky, almost harsh. Glancing from under a shield of eyelashes, she saw two of her pins in his extended hand.

"Th... thank you," she said haltingly, accepting first one pin and then the other while she twisted her hair with fumbling fingers and attempted, not too successfully, to secure the mass with the inadequate pins. "I'm afraid I do not possess Annie's skill at arranging my hair. I shall simply have to cut it." She was scarcely aware of what she was saying, prattling for the sole purpose of concealing her nervous agitation at the intimacy of the last few minutes.

At his explosive "No!" she looked up in surprise, meeting his eyes for the first time since her awkward stumble had precipitated the embarrassing scene. His eyes glowed darkly in a strangely pale face. The candles burning low in the chandelier cast flickering shadows that made his mouth appear grimmer than usual.

"I … I beg your pardon?"

"Do not cut your hair. It's very beautiful and it suits you. I… It is very late. Goodnight, Miss Wayne." He turned away abruptly to pick up his stick.

For an instant she stood as though in a daze, then with an almost inaudible, "Goodnight, my lord," turned and walked quietly out of the room. Once on the other side of the door, however, her poise deserted her, and by the time she reached the handsome stairway she was running, trying to escape from the terrible realization which had struck her like a thunderclap when she had looked at the stern, pale face of her employer just a moment before. She loved him! Ten years had not made any difference. She had loved him as a child of thirteen, she still loved him and she had never felt more miserable in her entire life. It was fortunate that she met no one on the stairs or in the halls, because by the time she reached the sanctuary of her room, tears were streaming down her face and her heavy hair had come loose from its two pins and was streaming down her back.

***

The next morning, a pale and heavy-eyed Angelica entered the morning room rather late in the hope that the viscount, who was an early riser, would already have left. In this she was gratified, but Lydia, looking up with a smiling welcome, said immediately, "Good gracious, Angel, you look ghastly. Are you sickening for something?"

"No, of course not. It is just that I did not sleep well last night with a persistent headache. I shall do fine when I have had some coffee." Sitting, Angelica poured coffee from a silver pot and liberally added cream and sugar. The thought of food choked her, but the smell of the coffee was revitalizing. She warmed her cold hands on the cup and took a deep swallow.

Lydia's voice broke in on her reflections. "Giles looked under the weather this morning also, though I must say he nearly took my head off when I mentioned it. He went off to the library to work with nothing more than coffee in him, too. He is trying to rush that foot, that is what it is."

Angelica stirred guiltily. "I'm afraid I kept him up very late playing piquet."

"Did you win?" asked Lydia with a wicked grin.

"Need you ask?"

Lydia giggled. "Not really. If Giles ever lost his fortune, he could set up as a gamester."

"I was not used to think my play contemptible, but the outcome last night was never in doubt. Well, I must be off to the schoolroom. Jenny will wonder what has become of me."

Angelica escaped thankfully to the schoolroom. She could not bear to discuss Giles even with his sister after the revelation of the previous night. How could she have been so stupid, so completely foolish, as to have fallen in love with a man who probably regarded her as an upper servant, moreover a man who was to be married to a spectacularly beautiful woman in less than three weeks? There had been no answer to this agonizing question during the long sleepless night, and she was no closer to a solution now. At least in the schoolroom she could usually manage to keep all personal matters in the background. Today she was not completely successful in banishing the viscount's image from her thoughts, but at least by lunchtime she was feeling more able to cope with life in general. Lydia was to join them for lunch. By way of a greeting, she said ruefully:

"Well, I do hope you are feeling better now, Angel, because I fear I have some news which is enough to ruin anyone's day. Barbara is coming to visit her Dear Giles today, only a little more than a sennight after his injury, and we are to be present to offer her tea."

"Shush, Lydia," said Angelica, with a glance at Jenny who was all big eyes and ears. "Naturally you must play hostess unless Lady Orbridge is feeling well enough to preside over the tea table, but surely there is no necessity for me to intrude on a family gathering."

"Aunt Minerva has met Barbara only once. Giles brought her here shortly after their engagement. To be blunt, they rather took each other in dislike. Aunt Min says she is totally affected. Barbara says nothing, to me at least, but she has never repeated her visit. I went to see Aunt after Giles gave me Barbara's note and asked her to help entertain our guests, but she is feeling a bit knaggy today so I did not persist."

"If you would not object too much, Lydia, I still have the headache a trifle. I had thought a quiet afternoon might banish it completely." She hated to desert Lydia, but Angelica felt totally unable to confront Lady Barbara until she had regained some of her composure. Last night had completely shattered her peace of mind, and so far her only thoughts had been of escape.

Lydia looked at her closely, then said kindly, "I do not blame you for crying off and you do look sadly pulled, my dear. I shall have to do the honours alone. Giles has already made me promise to be the perfect hostess, all sugar and honey." She pulled a wry face which made Jenny laugh.

Angelica achieved a wan smile, but she scarcely listened to the lively chatter between Jenny and Lydia and was only faintly aware of Nurse's deep voice like a minor chord at intervals. She bent her attention to a pretence of eating until she could make her excuses and retire to her rooms.

Solitude, however, did little to restore her spirits. She wished nothing so much as to escape from this house which held everything she loved. How could she stay and witness the arrival of another woman as its mistress? In one sense, it might be easier if Lady Barbara were in love with the viscount. At least then his happiness would be assured, and she hoped she had enough character to want his happiness first. If her reading of the situation were correct, however, this marriage which was so nearly upon them would bring contentment to neither. Nor would there be any benefit to Jenny to have a stepmother who would take away the attention she was beginning to enjoy from her father. Angelica had little doubt that Lady Barbara would be a demanding wife. She was too used to being courted to willingly share her husband with a young daughter. Lydia detested her prospective sister-in-law, but she at least could escape to marriage.

Her own presence would serve to insulate Jenny from some of the disappointment she foresaw. Angelica was aware that the lovely child had rapidly developed a deep affection for her new governess, and she returned it in full measure. But could she remain here even for Jenny when Giles married? Her rebellious heart cried out against such punishment. How could she put him out of her mind and make a new life for herself if she were forced to live under his roof?

She found herself pacing the sitting room floor as she had paced the bedroom floor last night. Suddenly she stopped, revolted by her own submission to misery, and seizing her workbox, began to sew the dress she had cut out for Lydia's ball. The task was vaguely soothing, and she was a good deal calmer when a knock sounded at the door.

It was one of the maids to say that his lordship desired Miss Wayne to bring his daughter to the drawing room to meet his guests. Angelica bit her lower lip fiercely, but maintained a composure that was all pose. She promised to appear with Jenny as soon as possible. Glancing hastily into the mirror, she saw that her hair was coming loose and had to take the time to re-pin it. In an unconscious reflection of her mood, she had worn the grey wool in which she had arrived at Grosvenor Square just a fortnight ago. It was too late to change, and indeed why should she attempt to compete with the beautiful Barbara? She hurried to Jenny's room, where Nurse was helping her charge to don a charming dress of frilled pink muslin with deeper pink ribbons. Jenny was all excited at the prospect of greeting guests and her deep blue eyes sparkled with anticipation.

Angelica praised her appearance, and together they descended the stairs to the main apartment. Jenny was not usually shy, but she had only met Lady Barbara twice before and stood a little in awe of her. As they approached the drawing room, she slipped her hand in Angelica's and smiled trustingly up at her.

It was thus they entered the room from which light voices and laughter drifted. Angelica's eyes instinctively flew to the viscount sitting on a blue sofa, then she glanced away and thereafter avoided looking at him. One glance was sufficient to show her that he was at his most sardonic. His face wore the familiar mocking smile as he listened to something Lady Barbara, seated at his side, was saying. Dressed in a deep red which suited her brunette colouring, she was as vibrant as a deep dark rose. She broke off as the newcomers entered, and holding out both hands, charmingly bade Jenny come and kiss her. The little girl dropped a shy curtsy and pressed her lips to the scented cheek offered her. She smiled at Lady Barbara but nestled into the arm her father had wrapped around her.

"It's so lovely to see you again, Jenny. Please say she may have some tea, Giles. I shall make it for her myself, just as she likes it." Lady Barbara smiled enticingly up at the viscount.

He smiled lazily back. "Of course you may do as you wish, my dear Barbara."

Lydia relinquished the teapot briefly while Lady Barbara prepared Jenny's tea and settled the child on the long sofa on her other side. She resumed her place at the right of the viscount and seemed to see Angelica for the first time.

"How do you do, Miss Wayne? It is nice to see you again, looking charming as always."

Angelica knew she looked anything but charming, but responded quietly and summoned up a social smile. She accepted tea from Lydia and seated herself as far from the sofa as was possible, greeting the other guests. She knew the countess and was introduced to Lady Barbara's sister, a girl of Lydia's age, who although not possessing her sister's beauty was still a very pretty girl. In colouring she was fairer than Lady Barbara, having medium brown hair and hazel eyes. They were about of a size, and the Lady Caroline Darlington was as exquisitely dressed as her sister in a cream-colored gown with a triple flounce on the skirt embroidered in deep green to match the deep green sash. She wore a charming green bonnet on her shining curls and presented a most appealing picture, laughing with Lydia and Sir Anthony Haring.

Angelica was rather surprised to see Sir Anthony among the guests, but imagined he was lending them escort. She took little part in the ensuing discussion, responding politely when the countess included her in her remarks but initiating no conversation herself.

Without appearing to do so, she was observing Lady Barbara and the viscount with no little surprise. On the previous two occasions that the betrothed couple had been together in her presence, Angelica could only have described Barbara's demeanour toward the viscount as careless. Today, that term would have been extraordinarily inappropriate. Indeed, the sparkling brunette was almost hovering over her injured fiancé, urging him to try the delicious plum cake and pouring more sherry into his glass herself. Glancing at Lydia, Angelica had to stifle a smile at that young lady's eloquently raised eyebrow. Having once settled Jenny at her side, Lady Barbara had apparently forgotten her presence. She had eyes for no one else in the room; all her attention was upon her fiancé.

The object of these caressing attentions appeared to be singularly unmoved by such tender ministrations. The lady's intimate smiles were met by bland, cynical quirks of the gentleman's lips, while mocking amusement stared out of his eyes.

Angelica, observing the scene in some surprise, felt a flash of sympathy for Lady Barbara. If Giles were her fiancé and looked at her in such a fashion, she would be sorely tempted to kick him. Lady Barbara, however, seemed to find nothing amiss and did not lessen her efforts to entertain the viscount. She did glance briefly about the room once or twice, but always her attention came back to the man sitting beside her.

On one such occasion, Angelica followed the direction of Barbara's brief glance and her eyes lit on Sir Anthony and lingered, widening with shock. The other three women were gossiping together, and Sir Anthony, ignored for the moment, was gazing at Lady Barbara with a sad, hungry look in his blue eyes and a white line around his tightly compressed lips. Why, he's in love with her, Angelica realized with one of those uncomfortable insights. Her hand rose unconsciously to her throat. She tore her glance from the silently suffering Sir Anthony and turned it toward the viscount, surprising an intent regard directed at herself.

It was the first time he had looked at her since she had entered the room, and the old mocking gleam was clearly apparent in the instant before she lowered her lashes in self-protection. She could not know whether he too had discovered Sir Anthony's secret, but she was desperately determined to conceal her own. Obviously by ignoring her, he sought to correct any false notions she might have entertained following his impetuous declaration the previous evening that he thought her hair beautiful. If she had been so foolish as to read anything personal into the compliment, it would not have been his words so much as the intensity and reluctance with which they had been uttered — as if they had been coerced out of him — that would have been responsible.

But Angelica was not a girl to cherish romantic illusions, and while it would be useless to deny that his words had given her intense pleasure at the time, she did not require subsequent coldness on his part to convince her that they were but the quickly regretted impulse of the moment. They had enjoyed a very companionable evening, and perhaps in the flickering light of several candles she had suddenly reminded him of his dead wife, who had been extremely fair. Whatever the explanation, she had taken a resolve never to allude to it even in her thoughts and to avoid being alone with her employer in the future.

For the first time this day, someone else's concerns had driven her own problems from her conscious mind. She wondered if Lady Barbara was aware that Sir Anthony felt a strong *tendre* for her. The suspicion that she did know and was trying to make him jealous by devoting herself to her fiancé occurred to her only to be dismissed as nonsensical. After all, Barbara had been engaged to the viscount before Sir Anthony even met her. There was no contest: the prize had already been won. It might have been understandable if a girl with Barbara's desire to be courted had engaged in a light flirtation with another man to rouse jealousy in a rather cool fiancé, but nothing else made sense.

She was roused from her reverie by the entrance of Lord Robert Hoxley. His easy manners and genuine friendliness made him a favourite everywhere, and he was greeted with pleasure. After accepting a glass of sherry from Lydia, who dimpled under his teasing praise of her abilities as hostess, he smilingly seated himself near Angelica. She returned his smile warmly.

"I see young Jenny is *aux anges* to be in company," he commented to her after noticing the rapt expression on the little girl's face as she listened to the conversation between her aunt and Lady Caroline.

Angelica looked fondly at her charge. "Yes, she is rather lonely in London, poor child. She is rarely invited anywhere. If her mother were alive, no doubt she would have friends who would call with their children, but alas, Lady Orbridge's callers are mostly elderly; consequently, Jenny sees very few people beyond her immediate family."

"Well," he said, eyeing the engaged couple, "Giles's marriage should improve that situation anyway."

Following his glance to where Lady Barbara was still exercising her charm for the viscount's sole benefit, she had the impression that Lord Robert's expression was one of relief. Recollecting that this was Barbara's first visit to her betrothed since his accident, she could not help wondering if perhaps the girl had been encouraging Sir Anthony's attentions in the absence of her fiancé. She longed to ask Lord Robert, but of course that was impossible. She could not gossip about her employer's fiancée to his friend.

She murmured a conventional response to Lord Robert's remark and changed the subject. It was with a sense of relief that she saw the countess gather her daughters and take her leave, accompanied by Sir Anthony. She wondered if the viscount had noticed the latter's lovelorn expression earlier, but dismissed the thought since his attitude was quite noticeably cordial to the younger man while farewells were said. Somehow, she could not picture the viscount as complacent in the face of a threat to what was his. Her instinct told her he would be a possessive husband.

As Angelica left the room to shepherd Jenny back upstairs, she heard her employer ask Lord Robert to stay for an informal dinner. The door closed behind Lydia, who went off to tell Aunt Minerva about the tea party.

There was a companionable silence in the drawing room as Giles refilled Robert's and his own glass. He eyed his friend thoughtfully for a moment, then said abruptly, "Am I correct in assuming that young Haring has been very attentive to Barbara of late?"

Lord Robert stirred uncomfortably in his chair. "He's a friend of the family," he replied evasively. "Can't refuse him the door, you know."

"Ah, quite. And from something the countess said, I gather that you have given them the pleasure of your company frequently, my dear Robert." The straight black brows rose inquiringly.

Robert looked even more uncomfortable. "Thought you would be glad to have me act as escort for you whenever possible. Very happy to oblige." His eyes fell before the viscount's speculative gaze, and he stared down at the amber liquid he was absentmindedly swirling sluggishly in his glass.

"I am indeed grateful to you for your good intentions, but, Robert..." There was a pause, and Lord Robert looked up and met his friend's eyes inquiringly. The viscount continued in very gentle tones, "If you wish to aid me, Robert, then please cease your present efforts on my behalf."

This time, the quality of the silence in the room was tense with portent. Expressions of blank surprise, doubt and sudden comprehension chased themselves across Lord Robert's pleasant countenance. In contrast, the viscount's face was devoid of expression.

At last Robert spoke. "So that's it, is it?"

"As you say," said the viscount dryly. "Now, shall we have a hand or two of piquet before dinner?"

CHAPTER NINE

The next few days passed without leaving any impression on Angelica, who went through the motions of daily living like a sleepwalker. If challenged, she could not have described what she was wearing without looking down, nor recalled the last mouthful of food she had swallowed. In her state of numbed misery, everything was grey and all food tasted of sawdust. Only in the classroom with Jenny did she come to life, for Jenny's affection soothed away pain like a warm bath. In Jenny's company, her tired brain ceased pondering ways to escape from her present situation. The child's attitude toward her studies had improved somewhat, and this was indeed a source of satisfaction to Angelica because arousing Jenny's interest demanded all her ingenuity and patience. The deepening warmth and intimacy between the viscount and his little daughter since his accident was another cause for gratification. She knew she should remain for Jenny's sake, and during the peaceful hours in the schoolroom, her troubled heart would agree that this was the best course to pursue. Certainly in time she would be able to subdue the wild longing for the warmth of his rare smile directed solely toward herself. Everyone knew that time healed all hurts, and there must come a day when she could face him with a true serenity, not the stiff mask of indifference she had donned desperately to hide her inner turbulence.

Unfortunately, victories achieved in the calm of the schoolroom faltered in the arena that was the dinner table. In the presence of the cool formality the viscount had assumed since their evening of piquet, her hard-won peace of mind disintegrated like a burned-out log at the blow of the poker. The viscount did not suggest another evening of card play. Within two days of his fiancée's visit, he had begun to take up his normal routine, although he carried a walking stick when he left the house.

In her unhappiness, Angelica could not have honestly said whether his frequent absence from the house helped or hindered her own search for tranquillity. She was miserable in his presence where his indifference acted like a whip on an open wound, and she had to exercise her own self-control to the limit to present a picture of like indifference. In his absence, she slipped into a numbed state which demanded almost as great an effort to disguise from the keen eyes of his sister and his aunt. The singular result of either situation was an emotional fatigue which welcomed bedtime while not succumbing to rest.

Lydia, totally immersed in plans for her ball, made no comments on her companion's unusual quietness, but Lady Orbridge had no all-entrancing project to blind her. She told Angelica frankly that she looked like death and asked the reason for the shadows under her eyes. Angelica's stumbling explanation involving headaches from sewing and restless nights resulting from the headaches left her sceptical and watchful.

On Angelica herself, the watchfulness had a salutary effect. She was filled with self-loathing at her own weakness and made a more determined effort to find enjoyment and satisfaction in the ordinary daily contacts. She had reached the nadir, and helped by Lydia's bubbling happiness, she began to take a greater interest in present affairs. Heading for Lydia's room to look through some recent fashion journals, she became aware of the sounds of hammering behind closed doors. She frowned suddenly in concentration. This was not the first time she had been dimly aware of unusual activity going on in the house during the past week, but her self-absorbed state had precluded curiosity. Now she was intrigued, and after being bidden to enter by Lydia, asked frankly, "'What are all these strange sounds on this floor?"

Lydia, curled up on a blue settee in an attitude that would have brought instant wrath upon her head if seen by Lady Orbridge, looked startled. "You cannot mean that you are unaware of the alterations in progress, Angel. Why, the house has been a veritable beehive of activity for a sennight or more." Her eyes widened in frank incredulity as Angelica stood there silently, too embarrassed for the moment to speak.

"I… I must have been too involved with Jenny's lessons of late to have taken much notice," she stammered, rather inadequately to judge by the sudden gleam of speculation in the younger girl's eyes.

"Well, it is simple enough, really," said Lydia carelessly, though her slightly narrowed gaze did not waver from Angelica's face. "Her ladyship's rooms are being prepared."

At first, Angelica missed the implication in the dry tone. "Lady Orbridge?" she questioned with a faint crease between her brows. "But … but I thought … oh!" The realization rippled along her nerves in a shock wave. Lydia sat very still watching her, and Angelica forced a smile, saying with brittle gaiety, "How very stupid of me, to be sure. Lady Barbara's rooms, of course. The wedding must be quite soon now."

Lydia released a little breath and uncoiled gracefully from the settee. "Yes, it's only ten days or so now. Come, I will show you her rooms. Giles said they are practically finished." She stepped toward the door, but Angelica felt almost a physical repugnance at the thought of examining the rooms being readied for another woman. "No," she said sharply, and then regulating her voice with difficulty, continued, "Please, Lydia, it is not my place to be shown Lady Barbara's rooms, especially if she has not seen them herself."

"Nonsense," was the brisk reply. "Why should not you and I look in to see how the alterations are coming along? We have had to put up with the noise and inconvenience, and the rooms are not out of bounds like a seraglio."

"Lydia," breathed Angelica, slightly shocked as she often was by this knowledgeable girl, but she followed her obediently, her initial reluctance overcome by a masochistic need to prove to herself again that she did not belong here.

After the briefest of knocks, Lydia opened the door to a beautifully proportioned apartment furnished as a sitting room. The early afternoon sunshine streaming through two large windows opposite the door dazzled their eyes momentarily, producing the illusion that they had stepped into a golden chamber. Both girls drew in their breath in involuntary admiration. The room they were in was not made of gold, but the pale yellow walls and ceiling, whose simple cornice and dado were painted white, took on golden life from the sun. The effect was heightened by a deep gold carpet patterned with a tracery of acanthus leaves in green. The white marble fireplace was exquisitely inlaid with green and rose marble representing flowers and ivy leaves. The only ornaments on the mantelpiece were two green and white Wedgwood vases, but the French-style mirror of carved gilt and pine-wood above the mantel supported candleholders in its elaborate frame.

Angelica's eyes were still upon the beautiful chimneypiece when Lydia tugged at her sleeve and said almost reverently, "Look, Angel, Giles has had that beautiful fabric which covers the sofas placed on the walls under the dado. Isn't it rich-looking?"

Indeed, Angelica felt no hesitation in agreeing that the cream-colored brocade printed with roses varying in tint from pale yellow to deepest amber gave a sumptuous appearance to the room. The green in the carpet and fireplace ornaments was repeated in the velvet fabric covering two comfortable-looking wing chairs by the fireplace. One was on a smaller scale than the other, and a lovely rosewood worktable nearby proclaimed it a woman's chair. Other chairs of painted and gilt beechwood had cane seats. Filmy yellow curtains at the windows were drawn back with draperies of the same patterned brocade.

Angelica could not suppress a gasp of delight as her eyes followed the sun's rays to a handsome, glass-fronted rosewood cabinet whose shelves were displaying a collection of ivory and jade figures and boxes.

"How exquisitely beautiful," she whispered to Lydia. "They must be worth a fortune."

"They are," said the young girl calmly. "My father and grandfather acquired most of them, but Giles has added several pieces. They will be wasted on Barbara, though. She prefers fans or jewels to ornament her beautiful person."

At the mention of the future mistress of the viscount's establishment, Angelica's delight in the beauty of the sitting room evaporated instantly. "Perhaps we had best leave now," she suggested soberly.

"Not until we have seen the bedroom," said Lydia, scandalized. "Surely you are not so lacking in the feminine trait of curiosity as that, Angel?"

Angelica smiled reluctantly and accompanied Lydia to a door on the fireplace wall from which issued an occasional burst of hammering. They opened it, expecting to see work in progress, and were simultaneously halted in their advance by the beauty of a completed room. Where the sitting room enveloped one in the warmth of its golden glow, the bedroom was all cool, shimmering green and silver. The ceiling and frieze here were slightly more elaborately decorated with lovely oval and circular designs in stucco painted white against a misty green background. This green was echoed in the silk wall covering of the wall behind the bed. The other walls were papered in green and silver stripes. The wainscot below the dado rail was painted white also. Not that the girls realized the details of the composition until later. Their eyes were irresistibly drawn to the large bed with its diaphanous hangings patterned with tiny, rose-coloured flowers.

"Angel, is it actually silver?" Lydia almost gasped at the beautiful shell-shaped canopy from which the hangings draped gracefully, tied to the carved posts at the foot of the bed.

"It can't be," said Angelica as the two girls approached for a closer look at the shining canopy.

"Begging your ladyships' pardon, but it certainly is silver."

The girls spun around at the hoarse voice and discovered its owner to be a burly workman. He had previously been hidden by the huge japanned wardrobe beside which he had just finished hanging a painting.

"His lordship himself told me it's silver, come from France, it has." He smiled proudly at them, accepting their homage personally.

The girls dutifully expressed their admiration as he pointed out the beautifully inlaid dressing table with its sparkling crystal and silver fittings and the silver-framed mirrors. In this room, all the candelabra were also of silver. They gleamed against mahogany tables and atop an elaborately carved rosewood candlestand. Small chairs with rose-coloured velvet seats and oval backs provided the only colour accent other than green. Angelica noticed that the handsome carpet, whose white designs echoed those in the ceiling, also had a rose-coloured background. She wondered idly if the ceiling had originally been painted rose and thought privately that this would surely be a more becoming background for Lady Barbara's brunette beauty. For her own taste, however, she could not imagine a lovelier setting.

Lydia glanced at her friend and said with some surprise, "Do you know, Angel, your eyes exactly match the misty green colour which Giles had used so extensively in this room?"

Angelica's eyes were fixed blindly on the door which she knew must lead to the viscount's rooms. Bruised and tormented by the idea of Lady Barbara occupying this lovely suite, she made no answer, but Lydia had not seemed to expect one. After agreeing with the workman that the charming portrait of Lydia's grandmother elaborately gowned in the style of sixty years past was just at the right height, the two girls took their leave.

"Well," said Lydia the moment the sitting room door had been carefully shut behind them, "I must say I am greatly impressed. Those rooms are sumptuous enough to please even Barbara. Though I am strongly of the opinion that she will immediately remove the long table and install another wardrobe."

"But there are two enormous wardrobes in the room already," protested Angelica faintly.

"I'll wager you a pony on the outcome," Lydia offered, grinning impishly up at her friend.

***

At dinner that evening, Lydia bubbled over with enthusiasm in her description of the rooms to an interested Aunt Minerva. Angelica's normally pale countenance was faintly tinged with pink as she felt the viscount's penetrating gaze upon her, but she feigned absorption in Lydia's remarks and kept her own eyes averted in the dim hope that he would allow the subject to drop. However, this hope, never very strong, died almost at birth as a quiet, deep voice said, "And you, Miss Wayne, do you feel the rooms will be suitable for the use of the future Lady Desmond?"

The mockery in his tone burned her, but she raised her eyes and returned his stare unblinkingly. "I think they are the loveliest rooms I have ever seen, my lord," she answered with quiet dignity, hoping desperately that he would not sense her deep unhappiness. For she had decided that not even for Jenny's sake could she remain in this house bearing daily witness to the fact that her heart's desire was forever unattainable.

"I am happy they meet with your approval," he said, and this time there were no undertones in the grave voice, but there was a questioning look in the almost black eyes that puzzled her. It was with relief that she turned to reply to a remark made by Lady Orbridge.

CHAPTER TEN

Angelica dressed with exceptional care the following morning in the green gown which she knew most flattered her colouring. She took extra time winding her hair and pinning it securely. Unaware that there was a faintly haunted look about her eyes, she merely noted with bleak satisfaction that a good night's sleep had erased the shadows under them. For, surprisingly, once her decision was taken, she had been able to sleep deeply. Now she was preparing to act on this decision and gained confidence from the knowledge that she appeared serene and cool. It was imperative that she present her decision in a reasonable and matter-of-fact manner. Her pride revolted at the thought that the viscount might guess that she was not indifferent to him, and there had been occasions when his penetrating stare had almost put her out of countenance. Faint alarm had tingled through her body at these moments. She was conscious of struggling against an almost hypnotic magnetism. Alternating with periods of brutal indifference on his part, it was not surprising that she was no longer easy in his presence as she had been for a brief, pleasant interval during their acquaintance.

Fortunately, she had had a letter from Billy that week stating that his wife was increasing and feeling most unwell. He had not suggested that Angelica come home, merely mentioning that Charlotte was finding it difficult to carry out her duties in managing the household. Angelica was aware that this was likely to be a temporary situation, but she seized upon it as her reason for leaving the viscount's establishment and was fully prepared to embellish the truth to the degree necessary to convince him of the urgency of her immediate departure.

Casting one last glance in the glass, she gathered her courage in hand and proceeded to breakfast. As she had hoped, the viscount was present and, after wishing him and Lydia good morning, she politely requested a few moments of his time at his convenience.

He studied her thoughtfully and agreed to see her at ten o'clock in the library.

She resumed a pretence of eating with the sinking feeling of one who has burned her bridges behind her. At that moment, Chilham appeared with an envelope on a silver tray which he presented to the viscount, whose eyes narrowed at the sight of the handwriting. He waved Chilham away and opened it with a murmured excuse. Lydia was chattering of a forthcoming shopping spree, but Angelica was only half listening; her attention, though covert, was upon her employer. He read the missive, his face intent and, Angelica thought, slightly anxious. She saw his knuckles whiten as the grip of his fingers on the single sheet of paper tightened convulsively. His eyes surprised her questioning glance, and she wondered at his fleeting expression of relief. Immediately, however, a curtain descended and his face betrayed no emotion at all as he took his leave of the two girls, reminding Angelica that he would see her at ten o'clock.

As the time of the interview crawled slowly forward, Angelica was seized by an agony of nerves. Without conceit, she was aware that the viscount would be reluctant to see her leave for Jenny's sake. She feared herself a poor match for his tongue on any occasion and felt instinctively that her only hope lay in maintaining a calm, detached manner. Only quiet insistence would win her a dignified escape, and she was not convinced of her ability to maintain this attitude, knowing the shattering effect her employer had on her emotions. But she must escape, she must! To stay was unthinkable. It would be constant torture to see him daily with Lady Barbara beside him. It was with the courage of desperation that she rapped smartly on the library door. On being bidden to enter, she opened and closed the door quietly, approaching, with chin up and eyes steady, the desk where he stood.

The viscount smiled at her in the companionable way she had enjoyed briefly. "Sit here, Miss Wayne. I have something to discuss with you also, but ladies first, of course. What may I do for you?"

The smile almost unnerved her, but she plunged into her request and, for a time, managed a creditable calm despite the effect of his expression, which changed rapidly from courteous attention to incredulity to black anger as she finished.

'I'm sorry, my lord," she faltered finally. "Indeed, you have cause to be angry with me for inconveniencing your household at such a busy time, but my cousin needs me." Her eyes pleaded with him, but he rose abruptly from his chair and began pacing the floor, his brow thunderous, never taking his accusing eyes from her pale face.

"He needs you? I need you!" he snapped coldly. "What about Jenny? The child adores you. How can you leave her so abruptly? I thought better of you than this, Miss Wayne."

She lowered her head to hide the pain his words gave her. Because he had every reason to feel incensed, she could not resent his anger. Forcing a calm attitude she said quietly, "I am deeply sorry to leave Jenny, my lord. She is … is fond of me I know, but the relationship between the two of you has improved so greatly of late that she will not miss me for long.

After all, she is to acquire a new mother also, and I feel sure Lady Barbara —"

"No!" It was a short, cold syllable interrupting her.

She blinked. "I beg your pardon, my lord?"

He said very deliberately, "Jenny is not about to acquire a new mother. Barbara was married this morning to Sir Anthony Haring. The letter I received at breakfast bore the glad tidings."

For an instant Angelica was stunned. Then fierce anger for his humiliation chased red flags into her cheeks, and she also sprang up from her chair. "Oh, how could she? Are you sure, my lord? Perhaps there is still time to prevent this." She wrung her hands in agitation, her horrified eyes on his face.

"Yes, I am sure," he answered curtly. "In any case, I have no wish to prevent the marriage; I want no unwilling bride. Here, read this." He took a paper from his desk top and thrust it into her reluctant hands. She looked at him doubtfully.

"Go ahead, read it," he said with an impatient gesture.

She stared at him for another second, sensing his controlled excitement, then lowered her eyes to peruse the short note in her hands.

My Dear Giles,

I am sorry but I cannot marry you. Our engagement was a mistake. I have realized for some time that your feelings for me have not been of such a nature as to ensure a successful marriage. Sir Anthony Haring loves me and by the time you read this I shall be his wife. Please forgive me and wish me well as I wish you.

Barbara

The silence was absolute as Angelica finished reading and looked up. The viscount was staring into the fire and did not move until she cleared her throat hesitantly.

"I am sorry, my lord. I was afraid that Sir Anthony was head over ears in love with Lady Barbara." She could not prevent the question going round in her head. "Is it true that you do not love her?" She caught her breath at her temerity, then blurted out, "Forgive me, I had no right to ask such a question."

"I shall answer you just the same. Yes, it is true." His intent gaze stabbed her, holding her own for what seemed an eternity.

Angelica, hoping her sudden happiness was not revealed in her face, hurried on. "Of course, under the circumstances I will stay on for a while. Will Lydia's ball be cancelled?"

"Certainly not."

"Very well. I shall be glad to lend what assistance I may. Can I be of service in cancelling the wedding invitations and returning any gifts which have been sent here?"

"No, why return them? It seems a shame to cheat people out of a wedding."

Angelica stared at him, wondering if the shock had unhinged his reason temporarily. "My lord," she said gently, "the arrangements must be cancelled as soon as possible to save even more embarrassment."

Suddenly he seized her hands and drew her closer. His eyes were the black of obsidian as they searched hers. "Why cancel them at all? My reasons for marrying remain the same. Jenny needs a mother and Lydia needs a sponsor for her come-out. Both of them hold you in great affection. Would you do me the honour of becoming my wife?"

Angelica's heart gave a terrified lurch and began hammering in her throat. She was afraid he would feel the trembling of her body in the hands he held in such a brutal grip, but her instinctive efforts to remove them resulted in an even more painful grasp.

"No, of course not!" she gasped, all colour gone from her face. "Would you go from one proposed marriage of convenience to another on the instant? The shock has affected your wits, my lord. Do not persist in saying things you will regret. We do not even belong to the same world; we should not suit."

He frowned impatiently, quelling any further, protest on her part. "I have never been more clearheaded in my life, and I should never regret asking you to marry me. As far as your not belonging to my world, I never heard such fustian. You, with your well-bred manners have more right to be called a lady than Barbara for all her airs and undeniable beauty. You are perfectly at ease in society, and I'll hear no more nonsensical talk of this nature." Suddenly he grinned boyishly, and she felt a relaxation in the painful grip on her fingers. "I had no idea you could be so missish," he taunted with a glint in his eyes.

The smile she loved almost undid her fragile composure, but his teasing words stiffened her resolve. "I am not in the least bit missish," she retorted, indignantly aware of another mischievous smile. His change of mood from barely controlled rage at her announced intention of leaving to this present buoyancy utterly confounded her. She strove valiantly for cool composure.

"Be sensible, my lord. It is my opinion that you have had a fortunate escape. Enjoy your freedom. You do not have to marry to obtain a friend for Lydia and a teacher for Jenny. Wait. Someday you will meet a woman you can love wholeheartedly."

"I have —" he started furiously, then proceeded more quietly, "absolutely no expectation of such an impossible event."

The words stung her, and she stood very still with her face averted. They seemed the death knell to her fragile hopes that someday he might come to regard her in such a light. In her misery she missed his next remark, but her attention was caught by the words that followed.

"You do not have to decide this minute. Take time to think it over. I realize this has come as a shock to you, Angelica, but let me repeat your own advice — be sensible. I can offer you wealth and position and provide the background your loveliness demands."

She warmed with pleasure at his use of her name and the graceful compliment. She glanced up at him uncertainly, but his next words froze her completely.

"You will not find me a demanding husband. You will be free to live your own life. All I ask is that you conduct yourself with discretion and do nothing to harm my name."

"So," she said with the calmness of despair, but with an undertone of bitterness edging her quiet words, "as well as a marriage of convenience this would also be a marriage in name only, with each of us free to conduct discreet liaisons. How generous of you to accord to your wife that privilege most men keep to themselves."

"Stop that!" Now he was angrier than she had ever seen him. He dropped her hands and grabbed her shoulders. "You make it seem disgusting. It is, after all, the way of our world to a large extent. Do you wish it otherwise?"

She could not fathom the expression in the dark eyes and dropped her own hastily. She felt hot tears crowding behind her lashes and knew she must escape before disgracing herself. Her voice was shrill. "Of course not; I don't wish it any way. I repeat: I cannot marry you, my lord." She began to struggle in his grasp. For an instant, he held her tighter and actually pulled her up against his lean, hard body, then he released her so abruptly she nearly lost her balance.

"I won't accept that as final. Come to me here tomorrow with your reasoned decision, and I make you my word I shall abide by it."

She opened her lips to protest, but he turned his back on her. The tears crowded closer; she spun about on one foot and fled through the door and up the stairs, blinded by now fast-falling tears. In her room she threw herself on the bed and weakly gave way to the storm raging within her.

Later, sitting up on the bed, she briskly rubbed her palms across the still wet cheeks, more than a little astounded at her own weakness. Even during this last week with the dreaded event of Giles's marriage hanging over her, she had not given way to such a passion of weeping as had just overcome her. In a sense, moreover, the reason for tears no longer existed. Not only was there to be no marriage to Lady Barbara, but Giles had asked her to marry him. Certainly she could ask no more of life than to become the wife of the man she loved, so why had she instinctively recoiled and refused his offer so bluntly? Why had she not seized the opportunity to marry him? The bitter answer came from her heart. It would be an empty farce. He had decided to marry for reasons wholly unrelated to the state of his affections, and there could be no happiness for her in such an arrangement. He had said he wanted no unwilling bride. Her sensitive lips curved in an uncharacteristic sneer. Well, she wanted no unloving husband. Married to him, she would be in constant trepidation lest she betray her longing for his affection. Her fair skin burned at the thought of having her love coldly rejected. But it would be infinitely worse if he pitied her and pretended.

She leaped off the bed and began pacing furiously. With icy certainty she knew she would be unable to bear his pity. Something inside her would shrivel up and die. So her tears were for what might have been and for the unhappiness of a future without him. She could not stay now. Not even for the sake of his daughter would a proud man like the viscount wish to keep around as a constant source of annoyance a woman who had refused to marry him. She would stay until Lydia was fully launched then seek employment elsewhere.

Wearily, she began to repair the ravages her emotional lapse had wrought in complexion and hairstyle. When Lydia knocked to ask if she would be free to go shopping after lunch, she agreed with composure and hastened up the stairs to apologize to Jenny for not appearing earlier for lessons. She found her young charge engaged in sketching a bowl of fruit which she had undoubtedly wheedled from Cook. Looking at it critically, she realized once again that the little girl possessed talent. She must speak to Giles about a drawing master for her before she left. She sighed impatiently and decided to refuse admittance to any thoughts of the future. One day at a time would be her creed for the rest of her stay under this roof.

Hours later, on returning to the house after a lengthy shopping expedition with Lydia, Angelica was surprised to receive a royal command in the guise of a politely worded invitation to take tea with Lady Orbridge in her rooms. A moment's reflection convinced her that undoubtedly Aunt Minerva wished to enlist her aid in cancelling wedding plans. During their outing together, she had realized that Lydia did not yet know of Lady Barbara's marriage, but had not thought it her task to inform her.

After greeting Angelica affectionately, Lady Orbridge lapsed into silence until Maggie had laid the huge silver tray upon a fragile-looking table and fussed about the fire which seemed perfectly adequate to Angelica.

"Never mind that, woman. Go on, we shan't need you any longer," said Lady Orbridge impatiently.

Angelica glanced at her hostess from under her lashes as she prepared her tea, for the old woman's swollen knuckles rendered such small actions painful. She smiled in sympathy, recognizing the suppressed excitement her ladyship was imperfectly concealing. Barbara had been no favourite of hers. Even in the face of the scandalous talk which was no doubt already circulating among members of the ton, she must be relieved to see her beloved great-nephew out of a bad bargain. She sat patiently, preparing herself for a pungent description of Lady Barbara's character. Her ladyship's first words, however, rocked her off her heels figuratively speaking and left her gasping with embarrassment.

"My nephew gives me to understand that he has made you an offer and that you have refused him. Will you object to enumerating your reasons for my benefit?"

Angelica's colour fluctuated deliciously and her slight figure stiffened. "I ... I hardly know what to say, ma'am. I'm taken aback to find Lord Desmond has confided such a private matter to anyone, even you." She paused and seemed unable to resume. After a moment Lady Orbridge said bluntly:

"I would rather not engage in roundaboutation. Tell me directly, is Desmond personally repugnant to you?"

Angelica's colour deepened. "Of course not, ma'am," she blurted hastily.

"Then how can you be so foolish as to whistle such a catch down the wind? A young woman in your position can scarcely hope to make a more advantageous match."

A flash of anger lit Angelica's green eyes at these caustic words, and she lowered her head to conceal it. Her voice was expressionless as she answered, "I quite realize this, ma'am."

"Is there anyone else for whom you have a *tendre*?"

"Oh, no."

"Then why have you refused Desmond? I thought you have been happy here. I know Lydia and Jenny hold you in affection, and I would be perfectly satisfied with the match."

"Why, ma'am?" inquired Angelica with an arrested look in her eyes. "One would have to go a long way to find a more unequal match in the eyes of the world."

"I have lived too long to care a ha'penny for the world's opinion. I approve because I think you would make Desmond an unexceptionable wife. You are a lady to your fingertips and you have a kind heart. You would not let him down."

"But Lord Desmond does not really want a wife, be she ever so unexceptionable. He has rather a contempt for our sex. I do not think I could live with such coldness, no matter what the material advantages."

"I have said nothing of material advantages," retorted Lady Orbridge with a touch of hauteur.

"I beg your pardon, ma'am, but Lord Desmond did stress the advantages of wealth and position which would accrue to me from such a marriage."

Lady Orbridge eyed her shrewdly. "And these made no appeal to you?"

Angelica made a hopeless little gesture with her hands but said nothing.

"Many a successful marriage started off with no more than mutual respect and liking. And many a so-called love match has floundered under the unromantic stresses of daily living."

As Angelica still made no response, she abandoned generalities. "Are you in love with my nephew?"

Knowing it was useless to lie with those shrewd black eyes intimidating her, Angelica answered truthfully in a voice that barely reached across the small table dividing them.

"Yes, but he does not love me." There was a sad finality in her tone.

"Good grief, girl, have you no backbone? Is it not worth the gamble that in time his affections will animate toward you? I know he is disposed to like you very well indeed. I have watched you together, and you can make him laugh like he has not done in years. All men are flattered to know a lovely woman has a *tendre* for them."

"Ma'am, you wouldn't! He must not know! I could not bear it if he pitied me. Please, you must promise me not to disclose this to him. I could not bear it," she repeated in agonized tones, extending one hand in a supplicating gesture.

Lady Orbridge was not proof against such appeal.

"There, there," she said briskly, patting the young girl's hand. "Of course I won't meddle. Though it's all pride, you know, and when you get to my age you will realize that there is no room for pride in love." Her expression became abstracted. "I could cite you dozens, nay scores of instances where people let themselves be ruled by their pride instead of by their heart and thereby lost the affection of someone dear to them." She sighed. "But there, if there is one thing I have learned it is that the young refuse to profit by the experience of those who have lived longer."

There was a slight pause while Lady Orbridge seemed to be making up her mind whether or not to say something else, then she went on, "Giles has too much pride, too. That is why this second humiliation is going to make a recluse out of him unless you rescue him, my dear."

"Second humiliation? What do you mean, ma'am? I don't understand."

"What do you know about Giles's marriage?"

"Why, nothing except that his wife died over six years ago. I have seen her portrait. She was exceedingly beautiful. He must have loved her very much to have grieved so long."

"Fiddle!" snapped her ladyship inelegantly. "It is not grief but bitterness and regret that have turned him into the cynic you now see. Alicia was incapable of loving anyone, but Giles was young and he could not see past her beautiful face. Like dozens of others, he dangled after her. The Lord only knows why she chose him when there were at least two matrimonial prizes she could have had for the taking, but choose him she did. Right from the start she led him a merry dance. It did not take him long to discover how complete was her indifference to anyone else's wishes or feelings. She was furious when she realized she was expecting Jenny, and she flatly refused to have more children. Giles was thoroughly disenchanted by the time she ran off with another man when Jenny was about two years old."

"What?" Angelica had listened in growing astonishment, and now the single faint syllable escaped her lips.

The old woman continued relentlessly. "She eloped with a poet who wrote rhymes to her eyebrows and worshiped her in verse. Giles found out within hours and set off after them. They evidently became aware of the pursuit, and the poet sprang his horses on a bad stretch of road. He was a cow-handed driver under the best of circumstances and the vehicle overturned. They were both killed. Giles has never been able to rid himself of a feeling of guilt because of the way the accident happened, although he was in no way to blame. You can imagine the scandal broth the whole episode provided. Naturally we tried to hush it up, but they had been seen on the road and in one or two inns. There was no way to keep the story from becoming one of the *on-dits* of the year. Something like this never ends either. It's likely someone will eventually tell Jenny the truth about her mother, and then the misery will start all over again. So you see, my dear, there is indeed a reason why Desmond is distrustful of women. He has already lived through one humiliating episode, and now it has happened again."

"Poor Giles," Angelica breathed softly, almost to herself. "It is small wonder he is no longer the man I remember."

"You knew my nephew before he was married?" queried Lady Orbridge sharply. "You could have been no more than a child at the time."

"He came to the Court with Billy's elder brother the summer I was thirteen. He was so handsome and friendly, always smiling, and he never fobbed Billy and me off as Gervaise was wont to do. We both admired him and tagged after him shamelessly." She came back to the present and her expression hardened. "Tell me, does Lady Barbara know the story of Giles's marriage?"

"Of course she does."

"Then how could she act with such cruelty? Surely Giles would have released her from the engagement, and she could have married Sir Anthony after a decent interval. I cannot understand deliberate cruelty. She must have known he would be made to look ridiculous."

"I can understand it very well indeed," Lady Orbridge snorted. She went on acidly as Angelica raised questioning brows. "Desmond has failed to prostrate himself at the Incomparable's feet. He has conducted himself just as he ought, but it must have been evident to the meanest intelligence that he was not enslaved by her beauty. If the engagement had been broken by mutual consent, there may have been those who refused to believe Barbara did the jilting, and that the chit could not abide. She is as vain and heartless as Alicia was. The boy is a fool when it comes to women!"

This last was said in such exasperation that Angelica could not forbear to smile, though her heart ached for her love.

Lady Orbridge pounced on her. "You have it in your power to spare him the greater part of the scandalmongering this wicked elopement will cause."

"I?" Angelica's mind had been far from her own problem during the recounting of the tragedy of Giles's marriage, and for a moment she gazed blankly at the old woman.

"If he were to marry someone else almost immediately, especially an attractive young woman like yourself, it would be rather ridiculous to speculate about his broken heart, would it not? And it would certainly take the wind out of Barbara's sails."

"People would be bound to recognize it for the face-saving gesture it would be. No one is going to believe Giles could prefer me to Lady Barbara."

"Nonsense, it would be up to the two of you to convince them otherwise." She glanced at Angelica's downcast eyes and clasped hands and continued in an almost gentle tone. "Giles was a loyal husband to a faithless wife. Surely you can expect the same loyalty. He would never allow you to be embarrassed or ill-treated."

Angelica gnawed her lip and thought with some bitterness that Giles had evidently omitted to mention to his aunt his promise to ignore any discreet infidelities on his wife's part in exchange for a similar tolerance. She had a lowering suspicion that, if she mentioned this to Lady Orbridge, the latter would dismiss her instinctive objection to such a state of affairs as unrealistic and give her a lecture on marriage among members of the polite world into the bargain. She sighed with resignation. Obviously the problem lay within herself. It seemed she alone saw mutual love and private satisfaction as the proper basis for marriage. Obviously she expected too much. But her parents' union had been just such a love match. Evidently such good fortune was not to be hers. At this point in her musings, she jerked herself erect. She was reasoning as if it were a foregone conclusion that she would marry the viscount. When had she changed her mind? Was she motivated by a desire to spare her beloved public humiliation, or was there still some foolish faint hope that refused to be extinguished that eventually she might win his love?

Lady Orbridge had been silent, darting an occasional glance at the troubled girl. Now she leaned forward and spoke softly. "My dear, it is only in the past year since Lydia has left the schoolroom that Desmond has begun to go out into society again. Until then, he stayed buried in the country, contenting himself with male companionship and sport. His visits to London were for business or duty calls on me. Oh, he would act as escort if I requested him to, but always he remained completely remote. Until recently, he did not betray the slightest interest in a personable female of marriageable age, no matter the lures that were cast out for him."

Here, Angelica interrupted dryly, "Yet I seem to have heard of a certain Mrs. Marberry, ma'am, with whom his lordship is believed to have a very warm relationship indeed."

"I was not speaking of the muslin company or that loose woman. Good God, girl, you must realize they do not matter in the least. Desmond is not a monk. I was used to think you a young woman of superior sense, but now I vow your head is more stuffed with romantical nonsense than Lydia's."

Angelica smiled wryly at Lady Orbridge's exasperated expression. She would have thought it a practical, not romantic notion that successful marriages have mutual fidelity as their firm basis, but it seemed she and Lady Orbridge probably could not agree on what constituted a successful marriage. Nevertheless, the old woman had a deep affection for her nephew and was concerned lest he again suffer from being the object of scandalous gossip and speculation. She was sincere in her belief, however mistaken, that this proposed alliance would be beneficial to Giles. Having heard the story of his disastrous first marriage, Angelica was reluctantly inclined to agree that perhaps a conventional marriage of convenience which would pass as a success in the eyes of the world was all he really desired. Loving him as she did, would she not be the fool Lady Orbridge clearly thought her to let some other woman take what had been offered to her? She who was so close to Jenny and Lydia would suit his purpose better than another flighty young socialite in Barbara's image. His aunt was quite correct, she thought, with unwonted cynicism; Giles had execrable taste in women.

She smiled fondly at the old woman regarding her rather anxiously and said gently, "You win, ma'am. I shall give his lordship a favourable answer tomorrow."

Lady Orbridge's face showed her relief at Angelica's decision, but when the latter asked if Lord Desmond had requested that his aunt play the role of advocate with her, she hastily declaimed.

"Oh, no, my dear, and I beg you will not enlighten him about our little talk. Desmond has the devil's own pride, and no more than you could he bear to be the object of pity. I am convinced he would infinitely prefer to think you married him for those material advantages he stressed than because you felt sorry for him."

Knowing that she must at all costs conceal from him the humiliating fact that she was marrying him solely because she loved him, Angelica felt it mattered little if he considered her reasons to be purely mercenary. That way, the obligation would not be all on his side, which should salvage his pride. She chose not to dwell on the unflattering light in which her action would appear in the eyes of society. Time enough to be concerned about the awkwardness of her situation when she was forced to meet his acquaintances. It was punishment enough for one day to contemplate the awkwardness that must attend any meeting where a prospective bride retracts her initial refusal and substitutes a formal acceptance of a proposal of marriage.

CHAPTER ELEVEN

In the event she was proved wrong on both counts. There was very little awkwardness attending the meeting between the viscount and herself the next morning, and practically no time in which to bring her courage to the sticking point before meeting his acquaintances.

She entered the library and greeted him rather shyly. He was wearing his polite social expression, but she thought she detected a hint of anxiety in the dark eyes which met her own steadily. She hesitated briefly, trying to form the sentences which would convey her change of heart, but he rescued her with one of his rare and warming smiles, though his eyes remained serious.

"I am fervently clinging to the hope that you have reconsidered your refusal of yesterday," he said quietly.

"Yes, my lord, I have." She was equally calm. "If you still wish it, I will marry you."

"I wish it very much indeed. Thank you, my dear. I shall do my best to see that you do not regret your decision." He raised her hand briefly to his lips and then retained it in his while he led her to the sofa and sat down beside her. "I do not wish to press you, but unless you dislike it excessively, I really think it would be best if we were to continue with the wedding plans already established. There is no way to wrap it up in clean linen. There will be a lot of talk, but if we delay announcing our engagement for weeks or even months, there will still be talk now, and then it will start again when we do proceed. Meanwhile, I shall be without a hostess for Lydia's ball and your own position as her chaperone will be less unassailable."

Angelica sat with downcast eyes, curiously still and remote. She was fully aware of the sensation their betrothal and immediate marriage would create, and there was no denying that she shrank from the ordeal, but like the viscount, she felt delay would spare them little while making Lydia's situation extremely difficult. In the absence of Aunt Minerva or another close relative, only Giles's wife could perfectly fulfil the position of chaperone.

She managed a shaky smile and answered frankly, "Well I shall dislike it excessively, of course, but there is really no alternative if Lydia's ball is to go as scheduled. I will do whatever you think best, my lord." She was completely unaware that her wistful but gallant smile had gone straight to his heart and imbued him with a fierce resolve to protect her from gossiping tongues.

He squeezed her hand gratefully. "The very first thing to be done is to acquaint Lydia with the change in brides. I know just how fervently she wished to have Barbara as a sister-in-law, but I am sure we can count on her good manners to conceal her chagrin."

This dry comment startled a gurgle of laughter from Angelica. "Oh, yes," she said, raising dancing eyes to his, "we may trust Lydia to say all that is polite and proper."

He grinned at her then and rang the bell. After Chilham had departed to fetch Lydia, he took her left hand and drew her gently to her feet while reaching into his waistcoat pocket with his own left hand. As she glanced at him questioningly, he produced a ring and placed it on her fourth finger, bending his head to brush his lips against her fingers after doing so.

"This will help convince Lydia that she is not dreaming," he said with a faint smile.

Angelica raised the hand he had released and stared at the perfect emerald with the halo of small diamonds which was adorning it. She gasped in delight. "It is the most magnificent ring I have ever seen, utterly beautiful." She raised eyes green with challenge. "You were very sure of me, my lord. Or did you have another candidate in mind if I persisted in my refusal?" Immediately she could have bitten out her tongue for assisting in that petty remark. His eyes, which had been friendly, grew cold.

"No other candidate," he said coolly, "but it was agreed that the ring would go back if it did not suit."

Impulsively she laid her hand on his sleeve. "Please forget I said that, my lord. It was most unbecoming of me." For a moment there was an uncomfortable silence, then he placed his hand over hers.

"It is forgotten in return for your forgetting 'my lord.' It will give me pleasure to hear you use my name, Angelica."

She smiled into his eyes. "Of course, Giles." She coloured under his intent regard, and slowly his eyes warmed. Her colour remained high as his eyes lingered disturbingly on her mouth. She lowered her long lashes to veil her own eyes, totally unable to meet his demanding glance any longer. He bent his head, bringing his lips within inches of her own. She knew he was going to kiss her and was conscious of her heart pounding as if to break out of her body, but suddenly a light knock sounded at the door. Giles raised his head but tightened his grip on her hand as she pulled hers away from his arm.

Lydia came dancing in. "You wanted me, Giles? Good morning, Angel, I missed you at breakfast this..." Catching sight of her friend's hand held firmly in her brother's, she broke off her words and turned inquiring eyes to his face.

"I called you here, Lydia, because it is time you knew that there has been a change in the wedding plans. Miss Wayne has just consented to become my wife."

His smooth voice implied that this was of the same magnitude of importance as a change in the menu for the evening. Angelica was lost in admiration for his aplomb, but Lydia's manner matched his in casualness. She dimpled mischievously.

"Well, I am absolutely delighted, of course. May one inquire what you have done with the body?"

Giles raised one eyebrow.

"Barbara's, of course. You do not expect me to believe she simply stepped aside for Angelica?"

"Barbara was married yesterday to Sir Anthony Haring."

"Well, if that isn't the outside of enough!" Lydia exclaimed indignantly. "That wicked girl — not but what this is about the only good turn she is ever likely to do another human being if she lives to be one hundred."

She ran to Angelica and hugged her impetuously. "Oh, Angel, I am so happy that you are to be my sister. What fun we shall have!"

The viscount watched them indulgently. "You did assure me our Lydia would say all that was civil and proper to the occasion, did you not, my dear?"

"No, did you, Angel? How very brave of you when you must have known I'd make you look all nohow." Spinning about, she placed her hands on her brother's shoulders and went up on tiptoe to plant a kiss on his cheek. "I do hope I am the first to wish you happy, Giles."

"You are indeed, my dear sister. I shall send a notice to the Gazette, of course, but it won't appear until tomorrow.

Meanwhile, I propose to escort you both to the theatre tonight to assist in spreading the news."

Lydia clapped her hands in anticipation. He glanced at Angelica, who was suddenly rather pale, and added quietly, "The sooner the news is abroad, you know, the more likely the astonishment will be over and done before the wedding."

"Good heavens, I'd forgotten about the wedding!" exclaimed Lydia. "Do you mean to go through with the original plans, then?"

"Yes, why not?" answered the viscount calmly. His sister gazed at him in admiration, but Angelica barely repressed a shudder. How alike they were, this brother and sister — each of them so ready to take up a challenge and high-handedly carry through with an action before the outraged eyes of the ton.

Just then, Chilham entered with a message that Lady Ebbington-Smythe and Miss Ebbington-Smythe were awaiting Miss Lydia in the small drawing room.

"Well, I see half the news is abroad already," said the viscount with his sardonic smile.

Angelica looked questioningly at him, but it was Lydia who answered. "Lady Ebbington-Smythe is a veritable tattlemonger, and that horrid daughter is becoming her image. Do I have your permission to break the news of your marriage plans, Giles? I promise you I shall greatly enjoy the telling."

"Yes, you have my permission, but, Lydia, I won't tolerate incivility, and guard your tongue with respect to Barbara."

Lydia paused at the door to say reproachfully, "You have spoiled all my fun, but I shall conduct myself with perfect propriety. Do you come with me, Angel? It should prove most diverting."

This time Angelica couldn't repress the shudder, which did not escape the viscount's attention. "No, Lydia, you handle this alone. Angelica and I have certain matters to settle yet."

After Lydia had left, Angelica found the relief which had welled up in her at being rescued from Lady Ebbington-Smythe's malignant tongue slowly oozing away as she met the viscount's long, measuring look, but she continued to meet it with outward serenity until he spoke.

"We have things to discuss, but I am unsure how best to broach the subject. You have rather a lot of uncomfortable pride, my dear."

"Which you are about to demolish?" Angelica guessed with a faint, rueful smile.

There was an answering gleam in his own eyes as he motioned her to sit down and absently seated himself opposite her in a cane-seated chair. From the depths of a wing chair, Angelica had the nervous impression that he loomed over her.

"I think I can understand what a trial this next week is going to be to someone with your sensitivity and independent spirit. Some people will undoubtedly think Barbara has broken my heart and I have seized upon you as a weapon with which to strike her in retribution. Others will assume you have made a dead set at a wealthy man. The fact that you have been living in my house will not go unnoticed either. This has to be faced," he said with a touch of impatience as he regarded her pale, set face and downcast eyes. "It will not please me at all to see you meek and deprecating and dressed like a dowdy governess so that the gossips may add pity to their other judgments of us."

At that, her eyes did raise to his face and he was pleased to see they sparked with anger. "Would you prefer to see me dressed as a … a pet of the fancy and exhibiting the manners of a substitute female living under your protection?" She was appalled at her own words but still too angry to apologize. His amused look did nothing whatsoever to mollify her.

"Billy has a lot to answer for," he drawled and smiled again at the blush that overspread her cheeks. Abruptly he grasped her hands and compelled her attention. "My dear, I am sorry to be so clumsy. No one looking at those honest eyes could think you other than a lady. But I believe the best way to carry this off is for you to hold your head high, and to be dressed in the first style of elegance."

"Thus adding envy to their feelings against me," she could not resist adding.

He ignored this thrust and continued implacably. "I insist on providing you with a suitable wardrobe, Angelica." She looked mutinous and opened her mouth to protest, but he placed a finger against her lips. "Hear me out. I know how this suggestion offends your sensibilities and especially that independent spirit, but in a week you will be my wife and naturally there will be a settlement —"

"No!" she interrupted almost violently, jerking her head away from his hand. "Let us leave money out of this. Of course you will buy my clothes after we are married, but let us have no talk of settlements."

"I do not intend to talk to you but to Billy when I write to him today," he answered calmly.

"Billy? What has he to do with any of this?" She was taken aback, having had no time to consider the practical aspects of her change in status.

"As your only relative, it is to him I must apply for consent to our marriage."

"But I am of age."

"Oh, the application for consent is mere form, of course, but the settlement is another matter. We won't discuss it if it

160

distresses you. But we shall discuss the matter of your wardrobe. I will have you outshine those whose tongues will be gloating over this elopement. If you prefer, you may send the bills to Lady Orbridge, who will be most happy to supply your trousseau."

She preferred nothing of the kind, but Angelica had no trouble assessing the stubborn line of his jaw. He meant to have his way at all costs. Obviously the cost would be to her pride, but she loved him enough to do whatever he wished to see him through this wretched situation. It was that or remove herself from his life completely, and the persistent small ray of hope that he might come to love her would not permit this.

She rose from her chair and regarded him sombrely. "It shall be as you wish, my lord. Lydia and I will begin to select clothes this very day."

"What will you wear tonight?"

"Well, I have finished the gown I intended to wear at Lydia's ball. As it is not too elaborate, it should do nicely for the theatre. May I go now? There is a lot to plan. A week is not overlong to arrange to have a wedding gown made."

"I trust to your customary efficiency, my dear. Would you like me to ask Robert to accompany us tonight?"

"Oh, yes, please. Lord Robert is always so at ease in every situation. He will help dispel any awkwardness."

"Just don't let him hear you 'my lording' me," he said dryly.

"Of course not, my Giles," she amended hastily.

"I am, you know."

Angelica did not know what to make of this enigmatic reply so elected to leave the room on a fleeting smile.

***

161

Lydia knocked on Angelica's door before lunch, eager to relate her experience with her morning callers. Angelica felt an equal reluctance to learn what had transpired, but Lydia was not to be contained.

"And, Angel, when she said in that honeyed voice she affects how deeply she sympathized with Giles, I longed to call her a liar to her face, but I took a deep breath and told her with equally spurious sweetness that we could not accept her sympathy under false pretences because we were so relieved that now Giles was free to marry the woman he loved. Angel, you should have seen her face. She was absolutely put out of countenance, and that insipid daughter of hers sat gaping like a fish with its mouth open."

"I suppose it is too much to hope that she went away without asking the identity of this paragon?"

"Naturally, and I was only too happy to convey the information to her. Without doing it up too brown, I managed to imply love at first sight and noble renunciation until Barbara's elopement made your marriage possible."

Angelica squirmed inwardly. "Lydia, please, I beg of you, do not tell your brother precisely what was said during this interview. Men do not care for gossip."

"Oh, but I have told him already. I went straightaway to the library on their departure. He was writing a letter, and he was most interested to know in detail what occurred. He laughed when I told him and said he regretted not being present to see Lady Ebbington-Smythe discomfited by a schoolgirl, which I am not," she added indignantly.

Angelica knew an instant's impulse to physical violence but whether directed against the viscount or his mischievous sister she could not have said. However, the moment passed and she was soon able with tolerably good grace to fall in with Lydia's plans for shopping.

Despite her scruples, Angelica was female enough to enjoy every moment of the many shopping expeditions she and Lydia undertook in the next few days. From many years of sewing, she knew well what suited her style best and quickly selected a design for her wedding gown that very afternoon. It was sheer joy to order gowns, morning dresses, afternoon dresses, pelisses and hats, plus the attendant accessories to compliment the various costumes.

The two girls were pleasantly tired on their return to Grosvenor Square, but tea and the prospect of an evening at the play revived them sufficiently to take pains over their toilettes.

Lydia, who was enjoying the whole situation enormously, insisted on sending Marie up to Angelica to dress her hair in a more formal style than her usual soft knot. Marie was delighted to have the opportunity to work with such long, luxuriant tresses and applied herself eagerly to the task. She swept the hair to the top of Angelica's head and pinned it there in sections which she crossed in an almost plaited effect, allowing some curls to fall free, not over the ears in the prevailing fashion, but down her back. She was so patently pleased with her efforts that Angelica forbore to state her own fears that it was rather too elaborate.

About her dress she had no doubts at all. The rich greeny-blue Italian silk had made up delightfully, and the pale pink of her long gloves made an unusual and dramatic contrast. By a stroke of good fortune, they had spotted a lovely stole of Albany gauze in the same ravishing pink shot through with silver. She allowed Marie to help her drape it becomingly about her creamy shoulders later in Lydia's bedroom.

"Miss Wayne, you look *très ravissante*. No one will believe this so *jolie* gown was made by other than a Frenchwoman," she declared seriously.

Angelica realized this was the highest praise of which Marie was capable, and a little glow of pleasure heightened her normally pale skin as she admired the total effect before the long mirror. The knowledge that she in no way resembled anyone's picture of a governess gave her confidence that she would not disappoint the viscount. She resolutely refused to dwell on the coming ordeal of her first public appearance as the second fiancée of the Viscount Desmond in one week.

Lydia, adorable in a youthfully styled gown of ivory silk with coffee-coloured ruffles, caught up a matching scarf and urged her to make haste downstairs. For once, there was no mischief in her eyes as she said seriously, "It won't do to delay until all your courage oozes away, Angel. You look absolutely lovely, and Giles will be very proud of you."

Angelica's lips trembled into a grateful smile for her young friend's thoughtfulness, and for the first time she felt a slight sense of anticipation rising at the thought of being seen with the viscount, knowing she was to be his wife. He came forward unsmilingly at their entrance, and she held her breath momentarily in her fear that she would disappoint him. However he raised her hand to his lips and said just for her ears, "You look beautiful, my dear. I shall be greatly envied tonight."

It was nonsense, of course, but she was deeply grateful and smiled up at him warmly as he led her over to Lady Orbridge for her inspection.

Aunt Minerva, having settled matters to her satisfaction, was in a mellow mood, even allowing that some of the newer fashions did achieve a certain unstressed elegance. She admired

Angelica's ring and patted her cheek fondly before demanding to know why that foolish dandy, Robert, was never on time. However, Lord Robert had entered the room while she was inspecting Angelica, and spoke indignantly in his own defence.

The dinner party that night was a very merry one, consisting entirely of persons who liked each other — a generally unattainable dream for most hostesses. Consequently, the comfortable mood thus engendered still enveloped them when they later entered their box at the theatre. Angelica had had no leisure in which to become anxious, because Giles had been very attentive and Robert and Lydia were in their usual high spirits. If Angelica had had any doubts about Lord Robert's acceptance of her as a suitable wife for his friend, the warmth and sincerity of his felicitations had dispelled them at once.

During the first act of the play, she remained relaxed and even managed to enjoy the excellent performances. They had come in a bare moment before the curtain went up, so she did not become conscious of curious eyes on their box until the interval. They were then besieged with callers, most of whom came to be presented to the viscount's new fiancée. At one point, Lydia leaned over and whispered in Angelica's ear that their current popularity was certainly a tribute to the speed and efficiency of Lady Ebbington-Smythe's news-carrying tongue.

Angelica gave a gurgle of laughter, which caused two gentlemen who were waiting to be presented to revise hastily their opinions of her physical charms. By Gad, when the wench smiled, revealing that unexpected dimple, she lit up like a candle. Maybe that sly dog Desmond knew what he was doing after all.

Colonel Revesby was among the callers during the second interval. He expressed pleasure at the chance to renew his acquaintance with Angelica and heartily congratulated his friend on his good fortune. A sharp-eyed matron of uncertain age, elaborately dressed in violet satin and diamonds, who had professed herself all eagerness to meet the viscount's fiancée, said abruptly, "But what is this, Colonel? Surely I understood that this is Miss Wayne's first appearance as Desmond's fiancée; after all, it is only two days since — That is, I believe the engagement is of very recent date, so how is it you have stolen a march on the rest of us and made Miss Wayne's acquaintance previously?"

"The engagement is a surprise to me also, Lady Scourby," the colonel explained smoothly. "I met Miss Wayne before she became engaged to our discerning friend, Desmond."

Angelica waited without breathing for Lady Scourby to give way to her obvious desire to question the colonel further on the circumstances surrounding his meeting with a girl who seemed to have been prestidigitated overnight into the beau monde, but something in the colonel's bland gaze silenced that lady's curiosity, and she quickly took her leave. Angelica unobtrusively released the breath she had been holding. She slanted a look at the viscount. He was perfectly at his ease talking with a party of friends. She supposed the awkward moment must have escaped his attention completely and knew a brief jab of irritation that he should be so unconcernedly enjoying himself while she was undergoing the not always kind scrutiny of the ton. However, when his friends left after being presented to Angelica, he lowered his voice and said, laughing:

"It seems the good colonel is more than a match for Lady Scourby's acid tongue."

"So you heard?"

"Of course I heard, but you already had one champion, and did not require my aid. In any case, it must come out that you were employed by me as a governess. Barbara will see to that," he said with a calm that infuriated her for no fathomable reason.

"What do you mean 'were employed'? I am still Jenny's governess." Her voice was soft, but there was a decidedly militant tilt to her small chin. She knew she was behaving badly, but some demon of mischief goaded her on.

He gazed at her thoughtfully for a moment, then said with quiet determination, "You ceased to be Jenny's governess yesterday morning. This week you are her friend, and after next week you will be her mother."

Her defiance dropped from her like a discarded cloak, and she put out her hand in mute apology. He grasped it firmly and retained it in his until the next caller arrived at the box.

Only one other awkward moment occurred to blur the general happiness of the evening. The middle-aged wife of one of Giles's acquaintances, after archly congratulating him on his good fortune in winning such an attractive fiancée, turned to Angelica with a bright smile.

"And when is the wedding to be, my dear?"

Before Angelica could reply, Giles said blandly, "Have you forgotten that you have already received an invitation to a wedding, Mrs. Anson?" As the lady in question blinked in surprise, he calmly added the information that the arrangements for time and place were as previously scheduled.

Then before Angelica's bemused eyes, Mrs. Anson shed her arch manner and smiled with real warmth at the viscount while patting his hand. "Good for you, my dear boy." Then turning to include Angelica in her remarks, "I wish you both happiness and a long life together."

Despite her embarrassment, Angelica felt she had made one friend that evening.

CHAPTER TWELVE

The week before her wedding was crammed with shopping excursions and social events. Angelica patiently endured the tedium of long hours of fittings for the wardrobe with which Giles was so determined to provide her. No one could have guessed from her calm demeanour that she writhed under the pricks to her pride which these sessions inevitably unleashed. Being a level-headed girl, she did not underrate her own attractiveness, but she accepted without rancour the knowledge that she was no dramatic beauty like Lady Barbara. By presenting her exquisitely gowned on all occasions and paying her assiduous attention, she knew the viscount hoped to create the impression with his friends that she was his true choice for a wife, and this knowledge she also accepted, but with a slight bitterness. Though he might succeed in fooling some among his acquaintance, which might ease his sense of humiliation at being jilted, she was of the opinion that many were watching this performance with amusement and scepticism. If his attentions had been motivated by love, she could have endured being a cynosure for the eyes of the polite world with true equanimity, so happy would she have been privately. Knowing this was not true, it cost her dearly to present an unruffled appearance in society. It seemed every hostess of his acquaintance was desirous of entertaining the viscount and his bride-to-be.

At least her odious pride enabled her to keep smiling, she thought ruefully one evening as Marie helped her into a jade-green gown of softest velvet. Her sandals and gloves had been dyed to match, and she would wear a cloak of the same velvet.

Giles had gifted her with a charming necklace and earring set of jade the day following their engagement and had requested her to have an outfit made up in the same colour. As she critically surveyed the monochromatic ensemble, she was amazed again at the viscount's unerring taste. He had planned the decoration of the beautiful suite she was soon to occupy, and he took an unusual interest in what she wore. Billy had not the least knowledge of women's fashions and took no notice of his surroundings at all. As he was the only male close to her, she had not unnaturally assumed that gentlemen paid little attention to the details of women's dress. And she greatly preferred them unobservant, she thought wrathfully later as Giles's critical eye ran over her knowledgeably, for all the world as if he were appraising a painting he was considering purchasing. As he finished his inventory, he became aware of a deep green gaze and the slightly aggressive tilt to her chin.

"There is a faintly martial air about you that belies your really soft and lovely appearance in that gown. Green is your colour, my dear. Your eyes rival the jade."

Angelica struggled to maintain her annoyance in the face of his praise.

"I feel like a slave on the auction block," she muttered ungraciously.

Giles threw back his head and gave a boyish shout of laughter, putting her forcibly in mind of her childhood saviour.

"I'll buy it," he chuckled, wickedly enjoying the faint colour which crept into her cheeks at his bold gaze.

This new, carefree Giles had the most paralyzing effect on her breathing, Angelica thought indignantly, but her lips curved upward in a reluctant smile as she allowed him to assist with her cloak. Indeed, in the privacy of his home Giles had become a friendly, undemanding companion in whose company she could relax and almost forget her situation. It was only when he adopted that spurious lover-like air in public that she was mercilessly reminded that she had lost her heart to a man who was marrying her to save his face and provide his sister with a chaperone.

She sighed slightly and squared her shoulders for yet another public appearance. Thankfully, these were becoming easier, for by now she had renewed acquaintance with a few women with whom she had been upon friendly terms during her own season. They were now young matrons, secure in their positions, and she was grateful for their support. The assembly that evening was rather more enjoyable than most because she felt less of a curiosity now and there were several of her friends present, including Mrs. Anson. Angelica had taken a liking to this kind, outspoken lady and enjoyed a comfortable cose with her while Giles played cards with friends. The furious activity of the past week was beginning to wear her down though, so she was grateful when Giles collected her rather early. They chatted unselfconsciously in the carriage on the way home. She was ready to bid him goodnight at the stairs when he stopped her with a hand on her arm.

"Wait, I have something to say to you, Angelica. Come into the library. I know you are tired, but I won't keep you more than a minute or two."

Preceding him into the book-lined room, Angelica thought fleetingly that all the important moments in her eventful few weeks in Giles's home had occurred in this room. Her first nervous meeting with a prospective employer had taken place here. Here, Giles had put forth his startling proposal, and it was here she had first refused and then later agreed to marry him. A brief quirk of her lips lightened her sober expression as she recalled the day of Jenny's slide and Giles's accident. For a while, it had seemed every time she crossed the threshold she finished by drinking brandy.

Giles was watching her face. "What memory has made you smile?"

"I was wondering if you were going to ply me with brandy again," she said with an impish smile.

His answering smile was quick to comprehend her meaning.

"Not this time. You are so tired it would probably knock you out. I just wanted to tell you that Billy and his wife will be arriving tomorrow in the late afternoon. They will stay here for the two days remaining before the wedding. And they are bringing a surprise for you."

He watched her smile fade and the sparkle die out of the green eyes at the mention of the wedding: she expressed polite appreciation for his hospitality to her cousin, but his voice was curt and he brushed aside her thanks as he bade her goodnight. After she had quietly left the room, however, his rigid composure slipped and his shoulders sagged slightly as he stared for a long moment at the closed door with a bleak face.

It was a slightly nervous Angelica who sat with Lady Orbridge and Lydia in the drawing room the following afternoon, awaiting the arrival of her relatives. A strong affection existed between the cousins, and Billy had an uncanny knack of sensing her mood. The constant strain of pretending for his benefit to be fond of his Charlotte, a pretty widgeon with more hair than wit and jealous into the bargain, had been largely responsible for her decision to take up a position as a governess. She had no worries on that score now that she no longer had to endure Charlotte's daily proximity, but she quite dreaded to have Billy discern the true state of affairs between Giles and herself. He had married for love and would wish nothing less for her. To ask Giles to pretend to Billy that he loved her was unthinkable. She could only hope he would not abandon for the duration of her cousin's visit his public role of devoted suitor which had previously offended her. It was of the utmost importance that Billy should think her a happy bride.

Consequently, it was with less than her customary composure that she rose to greet the party when at last Chilham announced them, but her first sight of her cousin's smiling face banished all trace of nervousness. His light brown hair was brushed in a Brutus, and for once he had taken pains with his dress. The olive-green coat of fine wool fit beautifully over his strongly moulded shoulders, and his neckcloth was more intricately arranged than was his custom. Only the twinkling brown eyes were unchanged.

"Oh, Billy, it is so good to see you." She went hurriedly toward him with hands outstretched.

He grasped them briefly then hugged her impulsively, planting a smacking kiss on her cheek. "I must say you are looking as fine as five pence, love. Being affianced agrees with you."

She laughed up at him, then the smile stiffened slightly as she glimpsed Giles over his shoulder. He had entered the room behind Billy and Charlotte, and his arctic expression both startled and disturbed her. She kept her voice gay, but there was a look of unconscious pleading in her eyes as she hastily freed herself from Billy's embrace.

"Oh, Giles, do come in. I am persuaded I have no need to present you to my cousin, but I think you have not yet met Charlotte." She performed the introduction and noted with relief that his features had relaxed into a friendly smile as he bowed gracefully over Charlotte's hand and made her welcome. He was still smiling as he turned toward her husband, extending his right hand while with his left he encircled Angelica's shoulders and gently drew her close to his side.

"I am glad we agree that Angelica looks charming. If being engaged is responsible, I am looking forward to seeing what marriage will do for her," he murmured, enjoying her suddenly scarlet cheeks and the bronze-tipped lashes shadowing them.

"Oh, Lord, Devil, have you not yet outgrown that schoolgirl trick of blushing?" demanded Billy with mock outrage.

"Devil?" Giles raised one black brow slightly.

Angelica intervened hastily. "My father was used to call me Angel, and Billy felt I needed to be put in my proper place, so adopted that foolish name for me."

"Now I wonder which is more apt?" Giles said silkily, then led their guests forward to be presented to his sister and aunt, thus thankfully rendering any answer to this question unnecessary.

Dinner was a very gay affair that night. Even Charlotte, generally suffering from the extreme fatigue which often accompanies an interesting condition in its early stages, was able to participate wholeheartedly, having been persuaded to retire to her room for a therapeutic nap after tea. She declared the excitement of being in London again, especially for such a happy occasion, was better than any powders prescribed by her doctor.

Angelica, on entering her room to dress for dinner, had paused in amazement on the threshold, then dashed across the room to enfold in a crushing embrace the large woman laying out her gown. "Annie, Annie! Charlotte didn't tell me she was bringing you. How happy I am to see you!"

"There, there, Miss Angelica. No need to act like a hoyden," declared the old nurse sternly, but her eyes looked suspiciously moist. "It's that glad I am to see you, though, and looking very bonny, too." She held her erstwhile nursling at arm's length and surveyed her through critical but loving eyes. "You still don't pin your hair up neatly. Look at those wisps trailing down. Well, I'll fix that after you have had your bath."

Angelica chuckled. "It's lovely to have you here scolding me. I have missed you terribly. Perhaps Charlotte will allow you to dress my hair for the wedding?"

"What, don't you know yet that I'm to stay here with you as your dresser? His lordship wrote to Mr. Wroxham and asked him if he could spare me because he thought you would prefer it to having strangers around you."

"Oh, Annie, did Giles really do that for me? How kind of him! He told me Billy and Charlotte were bringing a surprise with them, but I thought it was a wedding gift, which of course it is, but from him, not them." She hugged Annie again.

"There now, Miss Angelica, stop dancing around, do, and let me get you ready for dinner."

Angelica subsided and allowed Annie to take charge. She felt foolishly happy, and the only time a slight shadow passed across her face was when Annie assumed complacently that the viscount must be very much in love with her. Annie had made the viscount's acquaintance on entering the house and had obviously been won over by his charm and consideration. Angelica felt a deceitful wretch by her silence, but this is what Giles wished people to think. She banished thoughts of the future from her mind and went down to dinner happier than she had been since discovering she loved a man who probably was no longer capable of returning any woman's love.

On entering the saloon, her eyes flew to Giles, who was standing before the fireplace looking magnificent in his severe black and white evening attire chatting with Charlotte and Lady Orbridge. He came forward immediately and asked teasingly if the surprise had met with her approval.

"Oh, yes, Giles. Indeed I do not know how to thank you." She smiled radiantly up at him.

"May I suggest an eminently suitable method of expressing your appreciation, my love?" he said softly, with a gleam of laughter in his eyes. As he had wrapped an arm of iron around her waist and tightened his grip at her instinctive recoil, she accepted the inevitable and, reaching up, kissed him shyly on the cheek. He released her immediately and led her over to Lady Orbridge who had been indulgently watching the byplay from a sofa.

The time remaining before the wedding passed swiftly. Angelica saw almost nothing of Giles who went off with Billy each day, nor did either disclose what passed between them on the subject of the marriage and settlement. Lydia was very helpful in keeping Charlotte entertained and assisting with the listing of wedding gifts, which were arriving in quantities. Angelica had been secretly appalled at the number of guests expected; even with the subtraction of Lady Barbara's relatives it would be a large affair. She had promised Giles she would not think about the day at all, but it was not a promise she could entirely honour. It would be such a relief to have it behind her, so she could concentrate on making Lydia's ball a memorable occasion for the young girl who had been her first friend in the house and would soon be in truth her sister.

Fittings for the new wardrobe had taken up so many of her daytime hours that Angelica had scarcely seen Jenny alone for a sennight or more. Schoolroom luncheons had perforce been abandoned. Now, on the day of her wedding, she entered Jenny's room to visit the child before beginning to dress.

Nurse rose to her feet out of respect for her new mistress, but Jenny remained at a table where she was engaged in painting, a rather sulky expression on her lovely little face. She barely returned Angelica's cheerful greeting.

Angelica glanced at Nurse and raised a questioning eyebrow. That worthy lady merely shrugged in real or pretended ignorance, and obeying an absentminded gesture from Angelica, took herself out of the room.

"Well, Jenny love, are you going to tell me what's amiss?" She smiled coaxingly at the pale blonde head stubbornly bent over her painting.

"Nothing is wrong," came the uncompromising reply.

"Oh, I see. That has me in a puzzle because if something were troubling you, I could try to make it right, but if nothing is wrong, how can I help?"

There was a deepening silence from the table.

Angelica moved over to the tense little figure and put a finger under her chin. Jenny resisted efforts to raise her face, continuing doggedly to slap paint on a sketch that was rapidly assuming the aspect of an explosion of colour. Angelica sighed and said gently, "I have not really seen you for several days, but you do know this state of affairs is only temporary, don't you, Jenny?" She watched the small fingers pause over their daubing for an instant, and encouraged by this sign of attention, continued softly, "It was necessary you know, dearest. Your papa wanted me to have all the clothes I would need to take Aunt Lydia into society and, of course, I had to become acquainted with his friends. After the wedding, we will have much more time together."

The bright silver head jerked up. "I thought it was a good idea for you to marry Papa, because then you would stay here always. Nurse says you won't be my governess anymore now." Jenny's eyes and voice held accusation and her paintbrush was still — waiting.

It was a relief to have her suspicion as to the reason for Jenny's fit of the sullens confirmed, and Angelica sought for the right words to comfort her.

"No, I won't be able to teach you your lessons every day, dearest, but I shall be so happy to be your mother instead. Now you may come to my room to have chocolate with me in the mornings, and when Lydia and I have lunch at home, you shall join us." She noted that Jenny's deep blue eyes had brightened considerably, though her mouth remained stubborn.

"Shall I be able to come to your room every morning?" she demanded, staring intently at Angelica.

"Every morning," was the prompt reply.

Jenny gave a shuddering sigh, flung her paintbrush down and burst into tears. She wrapped her arms around Angelica and sobbed out her fears that she had been abandoned by her father and her teacher. Angelica soothed and petted her, reminding her gently, after she had calmed down, that she must not look all red-eyed for the wedding.

When she left to begin her own toilette, it was with a devout prayer of thankfulness that she had gone to see the child on impulse. Now if only if she could manage to convince herself that this marriage would be the best thing for everyone, including herself. She entered her own room slowly, unaware how faithfully her face reflected her troubled thoughts.

Annie, after glancing keenly at her mistress, closed her lips firmly on the impatient words she had been about to utter. She urged Angelica into a chair before the small dressing table and proceeded to unpin the heavy hair. During the ensuing brushing she talked in a calm, monotonous tone of the comings and goings below stairs. She knew her mistress did not half listen to servants' gossip, but noted with satisfaction the lessening of tension in her face and felt the relaxation of the slim shoulders under her soothing hands. It was difficult to accept that her nursling was now a grown woman and no longer confided her troubles to one who was, after all, merely a servant, but at least she had the power to ease her spirits. Annie's clever fingers brushed, braided and coiled the honey-coloured mass into a more elaborate style than the usual soft knot, even weaving a rope of pearls into the arrangement. She kept it all to the back, though, because for her wedding Angelica would wear an exquisite diamond and pearl tiara, which had belonged to the viscount's mother.

By the time an excited Lydia had entered to inspect her new sister, Angelica was completely composed. If there was a hint of wistfulness in the green eyes, Lydia, at least, was unaware. She exclaimed over the simply cut gown of magnificent French lace sewn with thousands of tiny pearls, noting with a little pang that Angelica had the height to carry the court train with grace.

"But you are too pale, Angel. Wait just a moment."

She was gone on the words and back before Annie had tucked a sheer handkerchief into one of the long, tight-fitting sleeves.

"This will give you a just touch of colour," the younger girl declared, rubbing something lightly into Angelica's colourless cheeks and over her lips.

"Lydia, you little hussy, where did you get that paint?" her victim demanded laughingly.

Lydia observed the new sparkle in her friend's eyes and called upon an indulgent Annie to admire her efforts. "There, now you look healthier. It isn't in the least artificial, is it, Annie? I used the tiniest bit, Angel, and what you don't know won't worry you."

Angelica shook her head in mock despair. "I can see that I have as yet no real inkling of the task I have undertaken in presenting you, miss. I shall need as many eyes as Argus to see you do not ruin yourself."

Lydia, totally unabashed by this stricture, hugged Angelica warmly and helped her to enter the carriage which was to take Billy and his cousin to the cathedral.

Never afterward was Angelica able to describe her wedding in any detail. For the most part, she went through the motions like a sleepwalker, but apparently she made the correct responses as the moment demanded. There were, however, a few images which impressed themselves on her memory. Billy, unnaturally quiet in the carriage, looking at her steadily with deep affection. They spoke little, but just before handing her over to Giles he had said, "He's a lucky man, but so are you lucky, Devil. Be happy, my dear." He had bent and kissed her quickly, then led her down the aisle to Giles.

Neither would she forget Aunt Minerva's warm embrace after the ceremony. "You have made me very happy, Angelica," she said in the rich voice which belied her fragile physical condition. "Be good to her, my boy." The snapping black eyes held her nephew's equally dark ones for an instant.

But the image which was most deeply seared into her memory was that of Giles himself, waiting to receive her from Billy's care. He was so tall and vitally masculine that her heart had begun a rapid hammering before she was close enough to see his features. What would his expression be on this occasion? She knew a sudden stab of pure fear. Oh, please don't let it be his customary sardonic regard. She knew with frightening clarity that she would be unable to bear that cynical quirk of lips and brow. It would shrivel the tiny seed of hope which never quite died. As they drew closer she searched his face closely, her own eyes desperately serious, her soft mouth not quite steady. Some of the tension left her as she noted his unsmiling countenance. His eyes were darkly serious and held her gaze for a long, heart-stopping moment. His mouth was tightened in a line of repression, but she was so relieved at the absence of any mockery that she softly released an indrawn breath, and her lips trembled into a slightly uncertain but incredibly sweet smile of welcome. Something flamed suddenly in the dark eyes looking down at her, and his mouth softened at the same time that his fingers tightened painfully around hers.

Angelica listened intently to the bishop's sonorous voice reading the beautiful words of the marriage service, knowing that she, at least, believed each one. For an instant, while Giles repeated the vows in a strong voice, she had the oddest little feeling that he could not have said these words binding her to him forever if he did not mean them. Something in his eyes questioned her, but she could not think straight; her mind was full of the sense of the vows they were exchanging. Her own voice, though soft, never faltered when her turn came, and again he held her gaze imprisoned in the fathomless depths of those eyes. They disturbed her concentration until she realized suddenly that the ceremony was over and Giles had been exhorted to kiss his bride. She glanced uncertainly at the bishop and gave a slight start as she felt Giles's hand on her shoulder. He turned her slowly, his hands sliding up to encircle her neck, and he pushed up her chin with both thumbs.

"Hullo, Angel." His voice was a husky, throbbing whisper.

As her wondering eyes flew to his, he bent his head and his lips descended on hers. It was a deliberate kiss, gentle but searching, and after the initial shock Angelica's lips warmed and came alive under his. Careful chaperonage had effectively curtailed any inclinations she might have had toward flirtation back in her salad days. This first instance of a man's lips on her own was therefore an unnerving experience. If his brief kiss on her wrist had once caused a burning sensation along her arm, this one sent flames shooting through her whole body, and she was trembling slightly when at last he drew back and tucked her shaking hand firmly under his arm. The sound of his soft, triumphant laugh roused her from absorption in her physical sensations. She raised dazed eyes then swiftly dropped them from his smiling gaze. No one could have called her a pale girl at that moment, for her face was suffused with colour. Forced to wait while her train was arranged, she struggled for composure, and it was a moment before she could overcome her confusion and smile up at him shyly.

"If you smile at me like that, I shall have to kiss you again," he murmured in her ear, but this time in the teasing tone she knew well. His return to normalcy helped her rally her forces, and she tossed him a rather impudent smile as they started down the long aisle.

"What, and shock Polite Society yet again?"

He grinned boyishly. "Don't tempt me, madam wife."

She gave a little gasp at that and decided to behave more circumspectly.

They passed along the pews filled with well-dressed, smiling people, but the only face to impress itself upon Angelica's senses was Annie's, wet with tears of joy for her nursling.

The hours of the reception passed slowly, leaving little impression on her consciousness... She smiled and received congratulations from a seemingly endless line of guests, many of them unknown to her. It was possible she ate something, and she vaguely remembered Lord Robert as groomsman proposing a toast. She remembered Jenny flitting like a pink and silver butterfly among her many distant relatives, and days later she recalled that she must speak to Lydia about allowing herself to be drawn apart for the purpose of flirtation. All the while the top of her mind and her tongue were dealing with the passing scene, the rest of her brain was re-examining the magic moment in the cathedral when Giles had kissed her. For a certainty it had been no token kiss to seal the contract publicly, but just what had it meant to him? For herself, she was honest enough to admit it had been a shattering experience and one she greatly wished repeated. But for Giles? She was not such an innocent as to be unaware that gentlemen were capable of making love to women for whom they felt no real affection, and after that kiss she had no doubts that Giles would be a charming lover. Did it mean he intended to make love to her in spite of declaring he would make no demands on her? And if it did indeed mean that, could she bear to share his favours with the woman known to be his mistress, the dashing Mrs. Marberry whom she had met briefly at an assembly?

The answer to this was a resounding "No!" Her whole being rebelled at the idea. At this stage in her unpleasant musings, it was forcibly borne in on her that the kiss may well have been merely the impulse of the moment. Somehow, she failed to derive any degree of comfort from this possibility either. What she desperately wished to believe was that he might be coming to care for her, but she was not given to self-delusion, and Giles had flatly declared he could never fall in love again.

The effort of smiling and being polite to a horde of people while her brain reeled with self-torturing conjectures was having the effect of bringing on a pounding headache. She grew more silent; the rosy glow that had lingered briefly after the ceremony had faded, leaving her paler than normal.

A group changed positions, revealing a glimpse of Lydia animatedly chattering away, looking cool and vibrant. Angelica closed her own eyes, wearily wondering from what source Lydia derived her boundless energy. Unobtrusively, she lifted a cold glass to her throbbing temple for the momentary soothing of its cool, smooth touch. Giles spotted the action and excused himself from a conversation. She did not notice his approach and jumped nervously when he spoke.

"My dear, you look utterly fatigued. I am going to insist that you rest for a couple of hours."

"Oh, but I cannot leave our guests, Giles. Don't worry about me. Surely they will not be staying much longer. I shall manage."

"Some of them will remain as long as the champagne holds out," he answered dryly. "But you will not be among them. Come." He held out an imperative hand, and after a brief hesitation she took it and allowed herself to be led upstairs to the beautiful suite which was now hers. He left her at the door to the sitting room.

"I'll leave you in Annie's capable hands. You must rest until dinner, which will be served here *à deux*." A tiny quirk of his lips held her fascinated gaze, and she was barely aware that he had raised her hand to his mouth briefly. "Until then, *ciao, cara*."

Her eyes flashed to his, then an answering gleam of mischief glinted in them, echoed by the elusive dimple as she grinned delightedly. "You are full of surprises, Giles," she murmured demurely.

His grin out-devilled hers, and she entered her apartment smiling to herself. Annie came bustling out of the bedroom and assisted in removing the lovely wedding dress. In very few minutes she was tucked into bed and fell asleep instantly.

She had to be roused by Annie in time to dress for dinner with Giles. She had slept deeply and awoke refreshed and incredibly cheerful. It must have been fatigue and nerves that had brought on that fit of depression during the reception. Giles might not love her in the romantic sense, but she was quite sure he liked her and enjoyed her company. Surely that was an adequate beginning to their marriage. If his kiss had upset her and caused her to wonder about his further intentions, she must blame her inexperience. After all, he had said he would make no demands on her, and Giles was a man of his word. Much as she loved him, she would resist any attempt to turn this marriage in name only into a real one until she could be sure he loved her also. And if he never did grow to love her? That nagging worry was pushed firmly out of her mind. This was her wedding day, and she intended to enjoy her wedding supper with her bridegroom.

She more than enjoyed it. Giles was charming company, and the chef had outdone himself in producing delectable dishes to tempt a lady's appetite. In any event, Angelica's did not need tempting — she was ravenous and made an excellent meal. Giles eyed the depredations she was making on a dish of comfits and remarked that she had certainly made a complete recovery from her indisposition of a few hours ago.

She grinned at him cheekily. "Getting married must be hungry work. I cannot recall what I ate today, but I was famished tonight."

"You ate practically nothing at the reception. It was perhaps fortunate that you drank next to nothing as well, or I fear you would have been ill."

"Well, thank heavens it is over. Now we can turn our attention to Lydia's ball. I have been meaning to ask you if you would object to it if I tried to turn the ballroom into a garden. It would be rather costly I'm afraid, but think how lovely would be the effect of flowers and small trees everywhere. It would certainly…" She broke off as she noticed his darkened expression. "If it would be too extravagant coming so soon after the wedding, you must say so, of course." She eyed him uncertainly.

He made an impatient gesture with his hand. "You may buy every flower in London if you choose. I had thought every woman looked forward to her wedding day. You sound relieved that it is over." There was a curious stillness in his regard, although face and voice were expressionless as he waited for a reply.

Angelica blinked in surprise. "Oh, but in the circumstances of course it was an ordeal for both of us surely? You must be equally relieved to have it behind you." Her eyes, more grey than green tonight, were faintly puzzled as she noted the taut line of his mouth.

"May I inquire what circumstances contributed to making your wedding an ordeal to be endured?"

And now Angelica was experiencing anger at his careful civility and embarrassment that he should pretend obtuseness.

"Well, it is no great thing to be a last-minute substitute bride in the eyes of one's acquaintances," she retorted and was instantly contrite. Once before, she had seen a flame of anger leap into his eyes and, as then, she felt utterly incapable of dealing with it.

Now he rose impetuously from the chair, but his voice was quiet, dangerously so. "Never let me hear you say that again. You are not a substitute — you are the wife I have chosen. I regret exceedingly that your wedding should have proved such an ordeal. I will do my best possible to shorten the length of the ordeal by bidding you goodnight, ma'am." He bowed stiffly and walked rapidly to the door.

Angelica recovered enough from the lash of his words to cry out penitently, "Giles, don't go. Please, my dear, do not let us have harsh words on the first day of our marriage."

She, too, rose and went toward the silent figure standing with his back to her at the door. She placed an imploring hand on his arm and continued softly, "I'm sorry, Giles. Please try to understand how I felt about the public part of our wedding, and believe I don't find it an ordeal to be married to you. We have been good friends. Don't let us start off on the wrong foot."

He turned at her touch. The anger had died out of his eyes and he regarded her sombrely. "Forgive me for losing my temper. Yes, we have been good friends and we shall continue." He took both her hands in his and raised them in turn to his lips. With an effort he summoned up a smile. "Goodnight, my dear. You are going to have a very busy time for the next few days getting Lydia launched. Get as much rest as possible."

He opened the door and was gone on her whispered, "Goodnight," leaving her relieved at the avoidance of what would have been their first quarrel, but strangely disappointed. She was totally unsuccessful in banishing speculation as to what might have happened if she had not hurt him by referring to their wedding as an ordeal.

Thankfully, Annie was not expecting to get her ready for bed on her wedding night. Walking wearily into the beautiful green and silver room, she grimaced at the sight of the sea-green cloud of diaphanous material that Annie had considered appropriate for the bride to wear. Uncaringly she pulled the pins from her hair and tossed them on the dressing table. Methodically she removed the deep rose velvet gown Giles had admired at the start of their dinner and donned the revealing nightgown, climbing tiredly into the huge bed which she would share with no one on her wedding night.

CHAPTER THIRTEEN

The remaining days to Lydia's ball passed swiftly. Angelica and Lydia were immersed in last-minute details. There were conferences with the florist, the caterer, the chef; final fittings for their gowns; a mad search for just the right shade of gloves for Lydia and innumerable lists to check kept the two girls constantly busy. Giles was not much in evidence except in the evenings, but he was friendly and cheerful. There were no more private dinners, but he seemed content in her company, and for her part her heart lurched uncomfortably each time he entered the room. True to her promise, Angelica welcomed Jenny each morning to share a cup of chocolate and all the latest happenings. Sometimes Jenny crawled into the big bed and snuggled down under the covers with her new mother, but if Angelica was dressed early, they shared their chocolate at a small table in the gold sitting room. Jenny adored this room and especially loved the beautiful collection of ivory and jade figurines. The child had a real appreciation for beauty, and Angelica delighted in the increasingly warm relationship with her. Jenny loved her; perhaps in time Jenny's father would come to do likewise.

Only in the lonely nights did she have a chance to dwell hopefully on her future as Giles's wife. The days were crammed too full for wishful thinking.

At Giles's request, Angelica's ball gown had been made up in emerald-green lace over white satin. He liked to see her in green, and Angelica was only too happy to oblige him. The admiration in his eyes when she had taken particular pains over her appearance was deeply gratifying.

On the night of the ball, as Annie was finishing with her hair, there was a knock on the door connecting her room with Giles's. It was the first time he had sought admittance to her boudoir, and it was with a voice suddenly gone shaky that she bade him enter.

He paused briefly just inside the doorway and let his eyes roam over the beautifully appointed room. They stopped at a small frame standing on the table beside the silver bed. Angelica watched in some surprise as he strode over and picked up the miniature.

"This is your mother?"

"Yes."

He studied the likeness intently, noting the radiant green eyes and the single enticing dimple near the smiling lips.

"You are very like her when you smile."

This comment brought a remarkably similar smile to the lips of the flesh and blood woman watching him in the mirror from the chair by the dressing table, but she remained silent.

Annie gave a final pat to her creation and stepped back.

"There we are. I hope the result is pleasing to your lordship," she challenged in a voice that dared him to disagree.

Angelica rose gracefully, her eyes twinkling in response to the amusement in her husband's. She swept him a deep curtsy and demanded mischievously, "And is his lordship pleased?"

"His lordship is extremely well pleased with the appearance of his lovely bride," he answered gravely, enjoying the faint colour his compliments always brought to his wife's cheeks. He brought a jeweller's box from the inside pocket of his coat and presented it with a bow as formal as Angelica's curtsy. "I had this made for you to wear tonight."

Angelica gave a startled gasp at the sheer beauty of the necklace sparkling in the box but seemed unable to move.

Only her eyes, bright with unshed tears, searched her husband's face. He smiled warmly back at her, in no way displeased by her silence, and taking the necklace from her unresisting fingers, stepped behind her, turning her to face the mirror while he proceeded to fasten it about her throat.

The emeralds and diamonds in their delicately wrought setting gleamed and sparkled back at the bemused girl staring into the mirror. As Annie exclaimed in admiration, Giles moved his hands to Angelica's shoulders, bent his head and touched his lips to the nape of her neck beneath the coils of honey-coloured hair. Angelica touched the glittering stones with one hesitant finger while her other hand covered his on her shoulder. Her voice was a mere whisper:

"I never thought I'd own anything so beautiful. Thank you, Giles."

For a moment, he pressed her back against the lean length of his body under the approving eyes of the maid, but as Angelica's colour heightened even more, he laughed and released her.

"If Madame the Viscountess permits," he drawled, offering her his arm. Angelica laughed at his nonsense, and bidding the beaming Annie good night, they proceeded to the saloon where they would be greeting their guests.

Those guests privileged to witness the formal presentation of the Honourable Lydia Weston to society that evening were agreed in the main that the new Viscountess Desmond had set a standard for other hostesses to aim for in providing a beautiful setting for a ball. From the moment one entered the hall, one had the impression of being in a garden. Huge pots of tulips and hyacinths were massed against the walls, providing a background for a lovely dogwood tree in full bloom. Upstairs, the garden spread into the ballroom and reception rooms.

Small bowers were created by white trellises covered in greenery, with flowers cunningly displayed as if growing from the vines. Several small trees in tubs brought the ballroom alive with colour. Flowers everywhere, ranging from deep reds through the shades of pink to pure white, delighted the eye.

It was a spectacular background for the sparkling daintiness that characterized Lydia Weston. Though not a beauty in the classic style, her vibrant prettiness attracted all eyes. Lydia had the gift of enjoyment, and despite her duties managed to have nearly as delightful an evening as the most carefree of guests.

Scorning the traditional white or pale blues of the debutante, she had chosen a deep rose coloured silk which enhanced her warm brunette colouring. Made in the simple style demanded by her tininess, it was ornamented only by diamond fastenings, and she wore a delicate diamond necklet that had been her mother's and a bracelet of equally fine diamonds that was a gift from Giles and Angelica. On her shining curls was a wreath of roses in a slightly paler shade than the shimmering silk of her gown.

Lydia was blessed with skin of rose-leaf perfection, sparkling dark eyes further enhanced by long, curling black lashes and a natural ease of manner stemming from her intense interest in all the people who entered her orbit. Perhaps this last characteristic was most responsible for her success. Not for her the agonies of shyness suffered by many young damsels who might be judged even prettier by an unbiased eye. She was too busy enjoying herself to spare a thought for the impression she might be making.

Watching her sister-in-law surrounded by admiring gallants, Angelica, from her position by the door where she was still greeting late arrivals, acknowledged this characteristic with pleasure not untinged with wistfulness. Would that she could as easily forget her role and cease to care whether or not she was accepted as an asset to Giles. It could certainly be said with no fear of contradiction that the Viscount Desmond's ball to introduce his sister to the ton would rank as one of the crushes of the season, but this achievement was not the source of satisfaction to Angelica that it would ordinarily be to a hostess hoping to cut a dash in society. She was nervously aware that a significant number among their guests had come primarily to assess the quality of the woman Desmond had married so quixotically. The strain of trying to concentrate on the welfare of their guests when she knew that she was being weighed, measured and judged by hundreds of eyes was draining her of energy, and it was still early. Her face felt stiff from smiling when her husband approached her suddenly and, cheerfully consigning all latecomers to the inferno, swept her, protesting feebly, into the ballroom and into a waltz.

Never had Angelica seen Giles so boyishly carefree and happy. His touch had the effect of melting her tension and bringing her alive to the sensual pleasures of the colours, scents and music. As they whirled about the beautiful room, Angelica forgot everything but the delirious joy of moving in his arms to the pulsating rhythm of a waltz. Giles attempted no conversation, but his eyes and mouth were smiling in complete physical enjoyment. In that moment she, too, ceased to worry about her role as hostess and gave herself up to sheer enchantment. She hoped devoutly that the dance would never end. Giles felt her relaxation and drew her fractionally closer.

"We may set a precedent by enjoying our own ball," he murmured, noting with amusement her guilty little start on being recalled to a sense of her duties. She protested mildly, but he laughingly insisted on finishing the dance.

After the delightful waltz with her husband at his charming best, Angelica's nervousness dissolved and she proceeded to enjoy the rest of the long evening. Her instinctive concern for the welfare of her guests made her a natural hostess, and now the quiet charm that had been masked by tension earlier reasserted itself as she circulated among the several hundred people crowding her reception rooms. With the press of social duties, she caught only brief glimpses of Giles and Lydia throughout the evening.

Giles had insisted on providing a substantial banquet in the supper room, as well as the decorative little cakes and ices favoured by some hostesses. Their guests did full justice to the tempting array of hot and cold dishes, and Angelica had the felicity of receiving several compliments from the grateful male guests.

At the end of the long, tiring evening she and Giles acknowledged a pleasant weariness, but Lydia was still bubbling with excitement. Had not Giles taken pity on his drooping wife and ordered her to bed, she would have been let in for a lengthy post-mortem with her sister-in-law. As it was, she slept the sleep of the just until Jenny bounced in to waken her.

CHAPTER FOURTEEN

Lydia's ball marked the beginning of the hectic round of social activities which followed the launching of a debutante into the life of the ton during the London season.

Her sister-in-law, soaking luxuriously in a hot tub placed in front of the fireplace where a cheerful, crackling fire burned, was thinking of her now with affection. How Lydia loved the social whirl! She was a gregarious little thing and derived almost as much pleasure from a daytime gathering of gossiping females as from the more formal activities that included the gentlemen. Her unaffected manners and vibrant good humour assured that she would be a success even with the more critical feminine element. Angelica had been in no doubt that the dancing black eyes and petite but perfect figure would draw male admirers by the score. Her prophecies had certainly been vindicated — young men buzzed around Lydia like bees round a garden. If her healthy fortune rendered her eminently eligible in the marriage mart, it was her vivacious charm that won her a coterie of admirers. She never lacked partners at Almack's or any of the private balls, and had received two offers of marriage within a fortnight of appearing on the scene.

To her credit, she refused to have her head turned by her popularity. Here the innate shrewdness Angelica had recognized as part of her makeup stood her in good stead. She had half-expected the first proposal from a titled suitor who had, in the vulgar parlance, brought an abbey to a grange and had been hanging out for a rich wife to restore his fortunes. She turned a deaf ear to his protestations of undying affection but dealt more kindly with the besotted youth who was suffering all the pangs of calf love within a month of being rusticated from Cambridge. He remained a devoted member of her train despite his chagrin at being refused.

Angelica herself could have done with a bit less of the social scene. She was of a more serious nature than Lydia and found the endless round of frivolous encounters somewhat trying, but these thoughts she kept to herself. She made all the expected responses albeit somewhat mechanically. Fortunately, one or two gentlemen had made the startling discovery that the Viscountess Desmond had an inquiring mind and appreciated being talked to as though she possessed some intelligence. Partially because she showed herself somewhat impatient with the flowery style of exaggerated compliments which passed for conversation between members of the opposite sex, she was attracting a select circle of more conversable admirers to her side. They tended to gravitate toward her at assemblies and greatly relieved the tedium she was too well-bred to show.

Giles escorted them only occasionally. He disliked Almack's and greatly preferred the company of men with similar interests in sports or politics. Angelica, soaking lazily in her scented bath, acknowledged with a small sigh that she greatly preferred her husband's company to the most brilliant social gathering. However, he had married her to provide a sponsor for Lydia's debut, and she was resolved to do her best for the girl.

Annie had been called away to settle a dispute below stairs, and Angelica had almost dozed among the bubbles. Shifting position slightly, she shivered in the now coolish water and decided hastily to bestir herself. Some of her hair pinned carelessly atop her head had come out of its pins and was clinging damply to her neck, adding to her discomfort. A huge bath towel lay folded neatly on a footstool, warming by the fire. She could just reach it by kneeling and leaning over the bath. Slightly breathless she grasped it finally and rose to her feet, releasing a cloud of lavender-scented bubbles. She was struggling to unfold the massive towel when she became aware of the opening of the sitting room door. She spoke without ceasing her activities with the towel.

"What took you so long, Annie?"

After a second or two, when no skirts rustling across the carpet proclaimed Annie's approach, she glanced over her shoulder and instantly froze with horrified embarrassment. The towel slipped from suddenly nerveless fingers. Lounging in the doorway with his arms across his chest, calmly watching her struggles with the towel, was her husband. His eyes glinted with unholy amusement as the hot colour flooded over her throat and face.

"Venus rising from the sea," he murmured, straightening up and sauntering toward her with a lazy smile on his lips. "You do rather resemble a Botticelli, my love. May I be of assistance?"

Perhaps it was his casual attitude or perhaps the arrogant little smile, but Angelica's frozen blood came rioting to flaming life. It pounded erratically through her veins and her magnificent green eyes flashed pure fury.

"No," she snapped through gritted teeth, "just go away. A gentleman would have left instantly."

This shot glanced harmlessly off the tall figure reaching for the fallen towel.

"But I am not a gentleman, my love. I am your husband, remember?"

He paused for a second before straightening up with the towel, and his eyes, dark and dangerous, met hers on a level.

She drew an involuntary breath of cold fear and snatched the towel.

Like a compass needle to north, his glance had flashed to her suddenly heaving breasts and tautened stomach muscles.

"Even lovelier than I dreamed." His insolent eyes raking her glistening form belied the soft, caressing tone.

She was struggling frantically to cover herself without letting the folds of the towel fall into the tub, greatly impeded by the anger that was causing her to tremble violently.

He misunderstood the trembling.

"You will catch your death. Get out of that tub."

"When you get out of this room," she flared, sending him a glance that should have reduced him to ashes. Reading his intentions in his eyes, she took a hasty step backward. "Don't dare touch me!"

He laughed recklessly and, gripping her around the waist with fingers that bit cruelly into her flesh beneath the damp cloth, swung her effortlessly up and out of the bath. He released her waist to encircle her dripping form with his arms while he arranged the voluminous towel around her, pinning her arms underneath it. Thus secured, she could only glare up at him in impotent fury. A little flame glowed in the black eyes staring down at her. She tried to turn her head, but he took one hand from around her back and gripped her chin roughly. Instantly his mouth covered hers with brutal pressure.

Unlike the kiss on their wedding day which she had frankly enjoyed, this one was solely a struggle for supremacy. His lips were bruising hers and she fought frantically, first to release herself and then just to get her breath. Never before had she been forcibly made aware of the tremendous strength a man possessed, and, realizing how ineffectual were her own puny efforts to combat him, she went cold with panic. The shudder that rippled through her body communicated itself to him, and she was free so suddenly that she sagged and would have fallen if he had not steadied her with his hands on her arms for a minute.

He was looking at her rather anxiously, but Angelica was too involved with her own fury to notice. Tears of rage were coursing down her cheeks. Although the towel had loosened during their struggle, she still could not free a hand to wipe them away. He made a tentative motion toward her face with a hand wanting to be gentle, but the fingers curled back as her slight figure stiffened and jerked aside. Her face whitened with fear, but it was sheer bad temper that glittered icily green in her eyes. The beautifully modelled lips drew away from clenched teeth almost in a snarl.

"I hate you!" She almost spat the words out. The anxious look in his eyes had been replaced by startled amusement as he realized he was being treated to a rather unladylike display of Italian volatility hitherto wholly unsuspected in his serene, well-bred wife. So far, her voice had been kept low, but the hint of hysteria in her manner warned him to make his escape.

Ignoring her outburst, he smiled and said coolly, "I'll leave you to compose yourself, my dear." He bowed mockingly and sauntered to the door to his apartment.

His coolness served as further fuel to her rage. Wresting one hand free from the enveloping towel, she glanced wildly around for a weapon and spotted a hairbrush on the footstool.

It cracked against the doorframe a scant three inches from his head as he opened the door.

"Temper, temper," he said soothingly, watching with amusement as she hastily re-draped the damp towel which her exertions had once more caused to fall. He hesitated in the doorway as if undecided whether to resume hostilities, but just then the sound of a door opening, followed by the rustling of petticoats in the sitting room, decided the issue.

The door closed softly behind him as Annie entered her mistress's boudoir. Her distracted apologies came to an abrupt halt once she appreciated the picture of Angelica, whose damp, dishevelled hair was streaming over a thoroughly wrinkled towel ineffectually covering her still dripping form as she stood stock-still, staring at the door leading to her husband's bedchamber. Fortunately, her infuriated expression and blazing eyes were hidden from view.

"My lady, you'll catch your death. Come over here to the fire." Putting her hands on Angelica's shoulders, she felt her quiver and led her unresisting to the warm hearth, scolding all the way. After a brisk rub with the towel, she seated her on the footstool and proceeded to dry the heavy hair. Angelica made no response to the scolding monologue, and eventually this unusual restraint slowed Annie's tongue. Covertly she studied her mistress's pale, set face and burning eyes and promptly rang for tea. Angelica gave a shuddering sigh and seemed to become aware of her surroundings. She thanked the old nurse for her efforts with a faint smile that did not reach her eyes.

Annie no longer expected her mistress to confide her problems to her as had been her invariable custom at the Court. It had soon become apparent that the young girl had changed in some subtle fashion since entering the viscount's household. That something was troubling Angelica she did not for a moment doubt, and she sighed heavily for the old days when she had always known how to comfort a frightened or distressed little girl. Now the role of comforter belonged to her husband, and no one would convince Annie that he was not in some way responsible for her mistress's present unhappiness. She knew what she knew, and Angelica betrayed none of the radiance one might expect in the adored bride of a fond husband. No one would drag one syllable from Annie's lips, but she had not been born yesterday, and she was perfectly aware that there were no signs of the viscount's having visited his wife's bedchamber on any but the one occasion. Her thoughts kept pace with her brisk movements as she tidied the room.

Angelica, gratefully drinking the sweet tea, eyed the impatient movements of her tirewoman with affection. Thank goodness she did not have to make conversation for a while. For the first time, she felt no regret that Giles was dining away from home that night. She needed time to gather her courage before seeing him again. Also, she needed to forget his abominable behaviour and her own loss of control. She was already exceedingly sorry for her childish display of temper, but Giles in one of his sardonic humours always had a disastrous effect on her own disposition. In general, she succeeded very well in concealing the hurt she felt at his occasional mocking treatment of herself, but today she had gone up in flames at the pain of being kissed as a form of punishment. If she had managed to retain her sense of humour when he first appeared in the doorway, the rest of the unfortunate scene need not have happened. After all, Giles had been most complimentary, and she had been aware for some time that he found her attractive. Why did it upset her so that Giles might desire her solely for her physical attributes? Certainly it was vastly preferable to indifference. She sighed deeply, aware that she was unreasonable in wanting nothing less than his love before surrendering to the desire she realized he sometimes felt for her. If she were really his wife, might he not come to love her in time?

At this point in her reflections, it became time to dress for dinner. She and Lydia were scheduled to spend the evening at Almack's escorted by the accommodating Lord Robert. She roused herself from her unprofitable musings to decide on the correct attire for an insipid evening.

CHAPTER FIFTEEN

Several hours later, Angelica was being readied for bed by Annie after an evening that had thoroughly fulfilled her expectations. She yawned daintily as Annie brushed out her hair and put it into one long braid for sleeping. Recognizing the sea-green confection she had worn on her wedding night, she made a wry face behind Annie's back but submitted docilely to having it put on her.

The sound of a door opening immediately followed the click of the sitting room door closing behind Annie. Standing in the middle of the room retying the ribbon binding her braided hair, she glanced in astonishment at the tall form of her husband in the doorway between their rooms, clad in a wine-coloured dressing gown.

Her first thought was that he, too, wanted to apologize for their contretemps earlier. The green eyes softened and a tentative smile hovered briefly on her lips. As he advanced silently into the room, however, she stiffened and her eyes grew wary. There was something odd about his appearance tonight. His throat was bare, as if he found his clothes restrictive, and his hair looked as if he'd been running his fingers through it.

"You don't seem particularly pleased to see your husband, madam wife." He stopped a scant two feet away from her and stared intently down into her uneasy face. There was a certain rigidity in his bearing, and his speech had seemed slightly slurred.

A little nerve started beating in her throat. Angelica had never seen Giles even slightly on the go, but suddenly the suspicion assailed her that he was more than a little foxed.

She took an involuntary step backward, but Giles's hand shot out, seizing her wrist in a merciless grip. Instantly she was imprisoned in a ruthless embrace, her arms pinioned against her sides by an arm of iron. If she had had any doubts about his condition, the dangerous glittering in his eyes and the fumes of brandy assailing her nostrils would have confirmed them. Her natural fears were secondary to a feeling of sick disappointment as she stood there silent and motionless in his arms, her accusing eyes challenging his.

"Don't look at me like that. It's more than time you learned what it means to be a wife, and I am just in the mood to enlighten you."

This time when his mouth fastened cruelly on hers, she remained passive in his grip by a great effort of will. To struggle would very likely inflame him further, and in any case, Angelica was rendered almost apathetic by unhappiness. Apart from the consciousness of being physically abused, she hated the feeling of being no more than an object to him — it diminished her in her own eyes.

The punishing kiss went on for an unconscionable time. When at last he did release her lips, it was only to jerk her head back roughly with a hand in her hair so he could assault her throat with those burning lips.

"Well, my love, why aren't you struggling as you did earlier? I'll enjoy taming you, you green-eyed witch."

His fingers were fumbling with the buttons at the front of her robe. The cold mockery in his voice and eyes finished what the brutal kisses had begun. Tears of defeat ran unchecked down her cheeks.

"Please, Giles, not like this." These, her first words since he had entered the room, were whispered brokenly, uttered in despair for the feelings he was killing.

Tears splashed onto the hands at the neck of her robe, and they ceased their movement immediately. A shudder of revulsion shook his frame. For a long moment he looked into her tear-drenched eyes, and slowly the fire burned out of his.

"Angel, forgive me for being such a brute," he muttered urgently, drawing away from her abruptly. He ran a trembling hand through his already disordered locks. "I I'm afraid I've had too much to drink, but that's no excuse. I gave my word." His voice trailed off and he swayed slightly.

Angelica sprang to his side and put a supporting arm around his waist. The huge bed was the closest piece of furniture, and she urged him backward two steps, pushing him down onto it.

Suddenly she was no longer afraid. Even drunk, Giles could not act other than as a gentleman for long, she exulted.

"Are you all right, Giles?" Her eyes and voice were anxious as she loosened the belt of his robe.

He smiled crookedly into her eyes before lying back on the pillow and closing his own. "Yes, darling, though I don't deserve to be. I'll go in a minute when my damned head stops spinning."

"Nonsense. What you need is rest. Go to sleep."

The meaning of her compassionate but ill-considered words slowly penetrated her consciousness, and she eyed him somewhat nervously for a moment or two, prepared to evade any advances on his part. As his eyes remained closed, she breathed a sigh of relief and blew out the candles on the bedside table. Using her hand to feel the way, she groped a path around to the other side of the bed. Obviously, in his condition, he had slept the second his head hit the pillow. In any event, he was her husband and she loved him, she thought fatalistically; let happen what happens.

It could not have happened much more quickly. She eased herself carefully onto the bed so as not to disturb him and settled herself comfortably on her pillow almost at the edge of the big bed. Immediately a powerful hand encircled her waist, pulling her easily to the middle of the bed.

"I never felt less sleepy in my life," he murmured in her ear with a hint of laughter in his voice.

She stiffened instinctively, but his lips on hers stifled any protest she might have been considering. All the fierceness had gone from his manner. By the time that first kiss ended, she was long past protesting anything. His warm, persuasive mouth and caressing hands were evoking a sensuous response to meet his own. She obeyed him implicitly and was grateful for his gentleness as he taught her what love between a man and a woman could mean. During the one painful moment before her body accommodated itself to his, he held her so tightly that he absorbed some of the shock that rippled through her.

"I promise it will never hurt you again, love," he whispered against her lips. Afterward he held her quietly, stroking her hair which he had undone from its plait and softly kissing her eyes and lips. His thumb traced the velvet smoothness of her cheek and jaw line.

In those wordless moments in his arms before sleep overtook them, she knew utter contentment. She was on the threshold of sleep when his hands moved lower, caressing her in a manner that aroused wholly unsuspected sensations within her. His lips became insistent again. This time she met his passion unflinchingly, glorying in the shared ecstasy of complete possession.

It was like a minor death when at last he withdrew and lay back, closing his eyes. She would have felt completely abandoned if it had not been for the arm he kept securely about her, even though he was practically asleep.

There was a rosy glow from the fireplace which gave enough light so that she could make out the huge black shapes of the wardrobes against the wall. Annie had not drawn the curtains tightly. She could tell by the faint gleam between them that the night was moonlit. She turned her head cautiously to observe her husband. She could only just make out the dark line of his eyelashes against his cheeks. A deep sense of love for this enigmatic man pervaded her being.

"Giles," she murmured, more in wonder than for the purpose of communication.

He stirred slightly and his arm tightened about her waist.

"Darling Alicia." The muttered words were almost inaudible, but his wife heard and her body jerked spasmodically, just once. She held her breath then, but except for another slight movement of his encircling arm, the man beside her remained still.

"Alicia!" The name had been little more than soundlessly breathed, but now it reverberated in her brain as if that organ were a hollow drum, and the pain of it increased in volume until she actually tasted blood where her teeth had gripped her bottom lip fiercely to prevent a wail of anguish.

She had thought he wanted her, and all along he had been pretending it was his first love he was holding in his arms.

No doubt in his condition any woman would have served the purpose. She had been so happy, but it was a false happiness based on shadow. And now reality had intruded, robbing her even of the memory of his tenderness. It had been meant for another woman.

It was sheer torture to have to lie motionless in his arms when her clamouring nerves jumped to be free of the embrace. She wanted to leap screaming from this bed and scream and scream and scream until she dropped from exhaustion. Instead, she dug her nails into her soft palms and lay rigid, feeling waves of humiliation wash over her. She was so hot she feared she would suffocate, but she must not disturb him. She would not place herself in the position of having to listen to an apology from her husband for calling her by another woman's name. She'd die first! So, feeling hot and cold by turns, Angelica lay a hairbreadth from her husband's still form but more estranged spiritually then ever in their acquaintance, until the glow had faded from the fireplace and only a faint, sizzling noise issued from across the room.

At last, very gingerly, she released herself from the weight of that arm which now repelled her and edged cautiously away from his warmth. And at last, she gave in to the bitter tears crowding her eyelids. She lay perfectly motionless and let them fall unheeded onto the pillow in an agony of regret. Giles had been angry when she had referred to herself as a substitute bride on their wedding night, she remembered. At the time she had meant a substitute for Barbara, and he had denied this. Now she knew she and Barbara and every other woman he approached were no more than substitutes for his lost love. The bitter knowledge numbed her heart. Eventually, the numbness spread to the rest of her body and she slept.

There was a persistent light behind his eyes that would not be shut out. Giles closed his eyes more tightly, and a band of pain spread around his head. Opening them to find moonlight streaming in on his face, he shifted his position irritably, but the pain inexorably followed him. He held himself very still to discourage it. Something about his surroundings penetrated the ache in his head and touched his consciousness. The position of the windows was wrong. He frowned and stopped hastily because it hurt. Raising a hand to his head, he encountered a silken strand of hair and froze for an instant. Very carefully, he eased the hand away from the hair and raised himself on one elbow, closing his eyes until his head felt steadier.

"No," he said in denial, but when he opened his eyes again, his wife's sleeping form was still there. "Dear God, I couldn't have." He concentrated on remembering his actions that evening. He had gone to Brooks's after the scene with Angelica, but her face had gotten between him and the cards so he had left early. He'd drunk rather a lot there, and he recalled taking the brandy up to his bedchamber while he waited for his wife to return home. The more he'd thought about that scene in the bath, the more irritated he'd become by her resistance to him.

He had promised himself to go slowly and try to win her love before exercising any husbandly rights. Their relationship had been deepening — he was sure of it. She had seemed so content with him. Then why such fury today? There had been no answer earlier, and there was none now. The more he dwelt on her cold rejection, the angrier he had become.

His lips tightened as his recollections ended in his room. He didn't remember coming in here. Surely he could not have forced himself on her. He was sweating profusely now, staring down at Angelica's averted face. Her hair in wild disorder streamed across both pillows. How lovely she was. Perhaps she had come to him willingly after all.

An unwelcome picture of her furious face as he had left her this afternoon rose before his eyes. She had resisted his embrace with all her strength. He wiped his forehead across his sleeve and noted absently that his hand was shaking. He certainly had the king of all hangovers, he acknowledged wryly. It took another long moment to gather the resolution to lean toward his wife, searching for something which might relieve the impending sense of dread creeping over him. As his reluctant eyes took in her appearance, he was almost overwhelmed by sheer self-loathing. Her lower lip was slightly swollen, marred by a smear of dried blood. The long, bronze-coloured lashes clung together in damp clusters on cheeks from which the tear stains had not yet faded.

At the sickening realization that he must have raped his own wife in a drunken stupor, he groaned aloud, then held his breath as she stirred slightly. He ached to take her in his arms and comfort her, but of course that solace was denied to one who had caused her distress.

Giles's exit from his wife's bed matched her entrance in caution. His eyes never left her face, gleaming pearl-like in the moon's radiance. She made not the slightest movement, scarcely seeming to breathe. He would have drawn the curtains more securely, but he needed the moon's path to guide him to his own bedchamber, for he dared not light a candle.

The curtains in his room were full open as he had pulled them on his return from Brooks's, for Giles disliked being put to bed by his valet. He crossed to the windows and stood there silhouetted in the moonlight, a tall figure, broad of shoulder but now slightly bent with his hands at his sides slowly clenching into fists. He remained untouched by the soothing beauty of the night, staring unseeingly at the moonlight with corrosive, self-loathing thoughts for company.

**

The next morning Angelica breakfasted in her room, not having sufficient resolution to face Giles across the coffeepot. She had fallen into a deep sleep of exhaustion and slept later than usual, so this deviation from her customary routine was less remarkable than it might have been.

Everything that had happened came flooding back to her with her first emergence from that friendly oblivion. Instinctively, she turned and saw that he was gone with a sense of loss but no surprise. She could not evade the bitter conviction that he had made his escape as soon as the effects of the brandy had diminished enough for him to discern that she was not his adored Alicia. After the agony of emotion endured in silence, she no longer felt the urge to scream her pain, nor did she possess the required strength.

She thought dully that she could almost hate Giles for causing her to feel so deeply before he demonstrated how little she meant to him. Billy was used to say she had the devil's own pride. Perhaps it was true. She knew she would not willingly meet her husband again until she could assume the same cold indifference he sometimes displayed toward her.

Not even Jenny's cheerful presence could lighten her mood; she felt chilled to her soul. The child chattered on of nursery happenings and displayed two paintings that would have thrilled Angelica in a more receptive frame of mind. As it was, it required a palpable effort to say all that was proper. Hopefully Jenny had not noticed anything amiss.

The rest of the day passed inevitably, and though she displayed a certain tenseness each time a door opened, she was spared a meeting with her husband.

Their first encounter took place on the following morning. She entered the library at Giles's bidding after again breakfasting in her room to learn that he was driving down to

Desmond House to attend to some pressing affairs with his bailiff.

She heard him out in unresponsive silence, never once raising her eyes above his tiepin after an initial swift glance. His erect figure and coldly remote expression did nothing to melt the ice which seemed to have formed around her heart. Immediately after he finished detailing his intentions, she rose from her chair, prepared to bid him a formal adieu.

His eyes, which had been on some papers in his hands, flashed to her face and he got quickly to his feet.

"Wait, Angelica. Before I go, I must make you my sincere apologies for ... for my behaviour the other night. I told you I would make no demands on you. It is not my custom to break my word, but I'm afraid I had drunk too much. For that, too, I apologize. You have my word of honour that you will have nothing to fear in the future."

Angelica had watched him intently during this formal speech, searching for something, some hint of emotion in his face or voice. She found none. He was paler than usual and he toyed incessantly with a letter opener on the table, but face and tone were expressionless. Another layer of ice formed within her. He had apologized, but he had offered no explanation other than the fact of being foxed. Neither had he asked for forgiveness. He left her nothing to say. To question him might lead to revelations that would only reemphasize his lack of personal feeling for her. It was sufficiently humiliating to have responded so passionately to lovemaking that was merely the result of a drunken impulse. Obviously he was embarrassed and wished to forget the episode completely. Well, so did she wish to forget, desperately!

Her clear, slightly scornful green eyes met his squarely and her small, firm chin lifted proudly.

"Goodbye, Giles. I hope your trip will be successful."

Her pride, her devilish pride, enabled her to maintain a steady, level voice and a steady, level tread to the door, which she closed ever so quietly behind her as if afraid one tiny sound might cause the whole house to explode.

The only sound in the library was the sharp, clear snapping of the ivory letter opener and the subsequent small thuds as its two pieces hit the table almost simultaneously.

CHAPTER SIXTEEN

During the three weeks that Giles was away, Angelica settled back into a tolerable routine. Acting as duenna for the lively Lydia left her little time for brooding, and she succeeded in pushing her personal problem to the back of her mind. When it threatened to emerge, she would seek out Jenny's company. The little girl, with her bubbling affection, was a constant delight to her new mother. The three lovely Weston ladies became a common sight walking or driving in the park. Even in London, spring had turned the world a tender green and gold.

Their progress during these expeditions was nearly always impeded by the fortuitous appearance of one or many of Lydia's suitors. When questioned by her sister-in-law, the young girl laughingly declared that the encounters were but fortunate coincidences.

"Do not perjure yourself, my dear," Angelica replied dryly. "I am not so green as to accept that. I must be failing in my duties as chaperone if you are managing to make assignations under my watchful eye."

Lydia dimpled unrepentantly. "You are a dear dragon, Angel, but I have my methods."

Angelica also had made conquests among the London beaux. Although she had little taste for fashionable flirtation and none at all for dalliance, there were a surprising number of gentlemen who saved their best stories and most clever quips for Lady Desmond's ears in the hopes of bringing into play that enchanting smile which started in her flowing green eyes, subsequently revealing perfect teeth and the most beguiling dimple at the corner of her mouth. Not having a frivolous nature, her smiles and kind words were bestowed rather less frequently than by the more dashing of the town's charmers, but several of the most sought-after gentlemen of fashion deemed the reward worth their best efforts. Though she would not tolerate a single cicisbeo, it was undeniably gratifying to be admired, particularly after having her self-esteem so bruised by her husband.

Whether her husband was equally gratified by the evidence of his wife's popularity that greeted him on his return to town was a question no one among his acquaintance felt competent to answer. Desmond had never worn his heart on his sleeve and he did not do so now. Certainly it was observed that his eye was often upon his wife at those events they attended together, but he made no noticeable attempts to discourage any of her admirers, nor did he appear to suffer from the smallest pangs of jealousy. He paid the usual charming compliments to the most admired females, but if he had set up a new flirt since his marriage he was discretion itself. No lady who had observed the mocking light in the viscount's eyes dared preen herself on having captured his heart, however extravagant his compliments.

Interested spectators (and there were legions following the newsworthy manner of the viscount's marriage) differed in their interpretations of the relationship between Desmond and his wife. Certainly they were seen together less frequently than before their marriage, but that was to be expected. After all, in society it was considered bourgeois to be forever in one's spouse's pocket; it simply was not done. True, Lady Desmond never appeared to be in alt when her husband graced her with his presence, but then, a lady would scorn to make a show of herself in this manner, and she was undeniably well-bred. The more romantic among their acquaintance might deem it a love match, since no one could deny that, though her birth was well enough, Angelica Wayne had been completely ineligible with respect to fortune. The less charitable (and they were decidedly in the majority) held the opinion that Desmond would have married anyone after that sordid elopement on the part of his former fiancée. As for the girl, she'd have had to be a pretty fool to whistle a title and a fortune down the wind, whatever the state of her affections.

As for the principals themselves, they treated each other with truly exemplary courtesy. If Angelica no longer found her husband's warm gaze on her when she accidentally happened to glance his way, she refused to admit disappointment even to herself. If the discovery that the polite little smiles his wife allocated him failed to reveal her elusive dimple disturbed the viscount, he concealed it admirably. In any event, they passed so little time in one another's company that it was possible these small circumstances went unnoticed. Fortunately, it escaped everyone's notice that they spent exactly no time at all in each other's exclusive company.

During Giles's absence, Angelica had gradually regained her customary serenity. She had even managed to persuade herself that she could be reasonably content with her marriage of convenience. After he returned, she avoided his company for a time, her wounded pride prompting a show of indifference. But pride is a very cold comfort, and after a while she could no longer hide from herself the bitter knowledge that she could not stop loving him simply because unrequited love was painful. Gradually her protective ice armour melted away, leaving her heart beating painfully whenever she encountered his cold look. Now she had to exercise rigid discipline to prevent her eyes from following him whenever they were in the same room. A faint wistfulness crept into her manner, adding immeasurably to her attraction, but of this she was totally unaware.

She was also unaware of her husband's eyes upon her as she made her way toward an alcove off the large ballroom in the Earl of Sussington's beautiful town house. It was the first moment she had had to herself since their arrival, and she was feeling desperately tired.

How graceful she is! the viscount was thinking as he stood within the alcove, out of range of her vision. All her movements had that grace; it was one of the first things he had noticed about her in their initial meeting...

He frowned slightly as her progress was halted by an encounter with Sir Jermyn Holloway, a noted Corinthian, whose marked attentions to his wife had not escaped the viscount's notice. He observed a mischievous smile light up her rather sober countenance, and the frown deepened.

From somewhere very close but concealed from the viscount came the murmur of feminine voices. He had not absorbed any of their conversation until his wife's name penetrated his reverie.

"Doesn't Lady Desmond look lovely this evening? Those emeralds of hers are truly magnificent, and she wears that deep green gown with such style."

"Ah, yes, the substitute bride. She is well enough I suppose, but nothing out of the ordinary after all. Not to be compared with Barbara Darlington."

"For my part," rejoined the first speaker, "I find her rather more appealing. For all Barbara's flashing beauty, she is a shallow creature. Lady Desmond has intelligence and a great deal of countenance."

"But does her husband agree with you?" This time there was no mistaking the cool malice in the other's voice. "It seems to me they are rarely seen together these days, and it is rumoured he has been rather attentive to Selina Bettincourt, not to mention that odious Marberry woman."

Giles did not linger to hear more. Angelica had apparently sent her escort for a drink and was once more approaching the alcove. He advanced to meet her, saying in an ardent — and carrying — voice, "What kept you, sweetheart? I've been waiting impatiently."

He had deliberately placed himself between his wife and the women he had overheard, or her astonished expression would have acquitted her of the social error of making an assignation with her own husband. However, she quickly realized the mocking gleam in his eyes was at variance with his voice and, moving her head slightly, she caught sight of their interested audience. Tucking her hand into the crook of his proffered arm, she gracefully leaned against him very briefly and smiled up at him intimately.

"I am so sorry, darling, but I was detained."

He grinned at the cloying sweetness in her voice and, turning, proceeded to escort her past their now enraptured audience, never once taking his eyes from her face.

"I'm afraid you will have to disappoint whomever you are promised to for this waltz that is just starting up, my love, because I am not going to relinquish possession."

By now they were safely past the two women, but true to his word, Giles swept her onto the floor and whirled her into a waltz turn. Despite the realization that he was only pretending interest, Angelica enjoyed that dance more than anything that had happened since their estrangement. Giles did not speak at all, but he held her a fraction closer than was fashionable, and she was utterly content just to move in perfect rhythm with him. They were beautifully matched in height and received more than one appreciative glance.

Angelica, floating on a cloud of rapturous physical well-being, was oblivious of anything but Giles's arms guiding her around the floor. Giles, too, was aware only of the reality of the soft, fragrant armful of femininity compliant to his touch. Neither, therefore, was in a position to appreciate the fact that their dance together was producing exactly the results they had aimed for in their earlier bit of playacting.

Inevitably, the dance came to an end and with it Angelica's glowing vitality. She felt drained of all strength as they came to a halt a few feet from Sir Jermyn Holloway, who came forward to expostulate:

"I say, Lady Desmond, that was too cruel of you to desert one for a mere husband, and your own at that. Desmond, you dog, I may call you out for this."

"What, have you been practicing at Manton's then, Jermyn?" inquired the viscount with a slight smile.

"No, dash it all. That's why I may choose to ignore the insult," he replied, grinning, well aware of the viscount's reputation with a pistol. "However, Lady Desmond must allow me to take her in to supper as a gesture of reparation."

Angelica mustered up her friendliest smile and walked away with Sir Jermyn, suppressing a wistful sigh at her husband's laughing acquiescence to the arrangement. It was with a concerted effort that she applied enough of her brain to her escort's conversation to make the required minimum of responses in the next half hour to avoid Sir Jermyn's classifying her as a dead bore. Beneath the social smile, she was conscious of extreme fatigue and a strong longing for her bed.

Her husband, glancing up from the gay party he had joined in the supper room, noticed her pallor. He also had the impression she was only pretending to eat. He looked again a few minutes later and verified this impression. Excusing himself to his friends when Angelica and her escort prepared to return to the ballroom, he managed to speak to her ear alone when he joined them in conversation with another couple.

"You look pale, my dear. Are you ill?"

"Of course not, Giles, but I am feeling wretchedly tired."

"Then let us call for the carriage and depart. What a fortunate thing Lydia went to Almack's with Mrs. Henderson and her daughter tonight. She would not thank us for leaving a ball before midnight."

Angelica smiled her gratitude, and they said their goodbyes to their hostess.

Although Giles confined his conversation to casual comments on the evening just passed and did not even mention the bit of playacting they had indulged in, Angelica felt the distance between them had narrowed somewhat for the first time since his return.

However, he bade her a formal goodnight at the door to her sitting room and she entered it, chilled once more by his manner. She had told Annie not to wait up for her and was rather relieved not to have to face her old nurse's shrewd eye. She was too tired to maintain a pretence of enjoyment for Annie's benefit. Disrobing quickly, she crawled wearily into bed, still wearing emeralds in her hair.

***

Despite a real effort to rest when possible and conserve her energy over the next few days, the overwhelming sense of fatigue persisted. She had little appetite and the odour of food, especially in the morning, brought on a wave of nausea. Angelica tried to conceal this from everyone; she refused to be sick when Lydia depended on her to accompany the parties of young people on various expeditions. It was now mid-June, and the hectic season was drawing to a close. Soon they would retire to Brighton for a time, and life would be somewhat easier. She was determined not to fall victim to some absurd complaint.

One afternoon, however, after lunching with Lydia, uncomfortably aware of that young lady's sharp eyes on her almost untouched plate, she was forced to cancel their plans.

"I'm so sorry, love, but I'm afraid I simply couldn't bear to stand through hours of fittings today. I have the headache a little and will be better for an hour's rest. Do you mind very much postponing our shopping till tomorrow?"

"Of course not, Angel, but are you sure it's a headache that is troubling you?"

"Why, what do you mean?"

"Well, I am not exactly stupid, you know. I can see that you have no appetite lately. And you seem very tired. I know that we have kept up a mad pace but I am never tired. Angel, do you think that you might be increasing? It would be the greatest thing! Jenny would love to have a baby sister or brother, and I should adore it too."

Angelica stared at Lydia's bright, eager face with blank astonishment written on her own. It had never once crossed her mind. Surely nothing could be more unlikely — barely possible of course, but no, it could not be!

Her voice was shaken as she protested, "There is nothing wrong with me, Lydia. You are mistaken; you must be mistaken. It ... it is just a headache."

She trailed off in the face of Lydia's obvious scepticism.

"Don't endanger your soul by lying, Angel," was the dry rejoinder. "Why don't you call the doctor? You are certainly not yourself these days."

"I don't need a doctor — I shall be better directly. All I need is a little rest." She rose from her chair in some agitation and advanced to the door, but her queasy stomach and swimming head betrayed her. Lydia caught her as she collapsed.

When Angelica came to her senses, she was in her own bed attended by Annie and Lydia. The latter said immediately in rather defiant tones that she had sent for the doctor. Angelica protested feebly but was hushed by Annie. She turned her head away to conceal the tears of weakness quivering on her lashes and subsided without a word. Nothing seemed to matter very much at the moment, and she was too tired to struggle against anyone.

The doctor, after his examination, was delighted to confirm Lydia's diagnosis and warmly congratulated the still unbelieving Angelica. She smiled faintly at him, avoiding her sister-in-law's triumphant glance, and sank back on the pillows with her eyes closed as soon as the door clicked shut behind them. For a few minutes, there was absolutely no movement at all from the slender figure on the huge bed, then the beautifully moulded lips trembled into a very small, secret smile.

Lydia was back almost immediately, bouncing over to the bed to kiss her sister-in-law jubilantly.

"What did I tell you, Angel? Are you not simply thrilled? Does Giles know? Oh, how foolish of me. From your very expressive face when I suggested it earlier, you had not the least suspicion, had you?"

"No, and I must confess I feel decidedly foolish at this moment."

Lydia grinned, then said more seriously, "How do you feel right now, Angel? You must not try to do so much in future. Tonight, for instance, we shall stay home and have a comfortable cose instead of going to Almack's."

"Don't be nonsensical, love. I told you all I needed was a rest and that was the truth. If I lie down upon my bed in the afternoon on occasion, I shall do splendidly in the evening. Robert is coming to escort us tonight, and I expect to enjoy myself excessively." She hesitated briefly. "I know I need not remind you to say nothing to Giles or Aunt Minerva until I have broken the news."

"Of course not, Angel. Now you have that rest. I'll join you for tea later."

After Lydia had left, Angelica found she no longer felt like resting. She was not looking forward to telling Giles. Try as she would, she could not guess whether he would be pleased or not. There was no doubt he adored his Jenny, and Aunt Minerva had indicated it was Alicia not Giles who decided against more children. But when a man had no love for his wife, would he welcome her child? She began to pace the room anxiously, trying to fight down a rising sense of panic. Suppose Giles were very displeased, what would she do, indeed what could she do? She put a shaking hand up to her forehead, which was damp with nervous perspiration, and frowned ferociously. She must gather her wits and compose herself. She owed it to herself to stay calm; she must not fret over Giles's possible reaction. Gradually, she became more tranquil. It would not do to worry about Giles's reaction until after she had told him. She would put it out of her mind until then.

Fortunately for the success of this admirable resolution, she did not have very long to wait. Lydia joined her for tea in her sitting room, and they were comfortably discussing their respective wardrobes when Giles entered abruptly. His eyes went immediately to Angelica. At the sight of her serene figure his own taut body relaxed perceptibly, and he greeted them both before taking a chair and rather absently accepting a cup of tea. His first words confirmed that the unusual honour of his presence at tea was not for social reasons. Ignoring Lydia's offer of jam tarts, he turned to his wife and said shortly:

"Chilham tells me you fainted this afternoon and the doctor was called. What is wrong?"

Angelica glanced imploringly at Lydia, who understood the unspoken message and excused herself hastily. Her brother did not take his eyes from his wife's bowed head as she busied her hands unnecessarily at the tea tray.

The silence seemed to propagate itself, spreading like smoke and stifling any sounds therein. Angelica raised a hand nervously to her tight throat but could not manage any kind of answer. The tension was becoming brittle when Giles leaned forward and seized her wrist with steely fingers.

"Well," he repeated grimly, "what was it?"

She gave an involuntary shiver at the unsympathetic tone and glued her eyes to his as though compelled to study them. She thought — she hoped they were evidencing more anxiety than sternness. Her own were softly luminous as she said gently:

"It was nothing…" At his impatient shake, she hastened on, "Nothing serious, I mean. We … I am going to have a baby."

She felt him recoil; her hand was almost flung back as he released her. His voice when it came was level. "And the happy father is myself?" he added swiftly, but it was too late. He saw dawning horror replace the radiance in her eyes, and all colour drained from her face, leaving her eyes glittering like green glass. Before he could move she was on her feet, her hands gripped together in front of her as though only thus could she keep them from his face. She spoke softly with controlled, icy anger:

"How could you? I'll never forgive you for that, never."

She was across the room and had closed the bedroom door behind her almost before he had struggled to his feet and taken an impetuous step forward.

He had laughed at her tempestuous fury over his appearance during her bath, but he had never felt further from laughter than now when faced with her cold, scornful rage. He went swiftly to the door, determined not to allow this mood to exist between them, but paused with his hand on the knob as he heard Annie's cheerful voice giving commands to her mistress.

"Damnation!" He had almost decided to get rid of Annie and force Angelica to listen to him when Chilham appeared in the sitting room entrance with a message for him, putting forward the hour at which he was to dine with friends. He glanced frowningly at the mantel clock but realized he had not time to settle this with his wife at present. With another muttered imprecation, he strode out of the gold-toned room.

CHAPTER SEVENTEEN

It was after midnight when Angelica and Lydia returned from Almack's. Lydia was in radiant good humour, having successfully escaped Angelica's chaperone's eye to engage in not one but two delicious flirtations. She chattered gaily all the way home in the carriage, needing no more encouragement than an occasional murmur from Angelica to reveal in her artless way just how successfully she had evaded her sister-in-law and to what frivolous use she had put her brief freedom.

"And he was so importunate I felt I simply had to console him by bestowing a rose from my nosegay on him. It was the kind thing to do, don't you agree, Angel?" she finished rather breathlessly, turning her piquant little face toward her companion. The demure little mouth was belied by black eyes dancing with mischief, and at last her sister-in-law's abstraction was pierced.

"Oh, Lydia, how indiscreet of you," she uttered, aghast at this latest evidence of her charge's capricious nature. "You know you don't even like Sir Julian above half either. Now we shall find him camped forever on our doorstep. If you do not take care, my girl," she continued, with unwonted severity, "you will find yourself betrothed to someone you do not care a scrap for because one of your outrageous flirtations has been taken seriously."

This appalling prospect had no appreciable effect on Miss Weston. "Oh, pooh," she said, tossing her curls airily. "I can handle Sir Julian. If he presses his advantage, I'll tell him I was carried away by his poetic compliments but that Giles considers me far too young to contemplate marriage. I do not expect he will, though. You take this too seriously, dearest Angel. Everyone flirts at parties; it is what makes them so much fun."

"You must take care not to be thought fast, my dear," returned Angelica seriously, "lest persons of sensibility take you in disgust. Someday, there will be a man for whom you will learn to cherish the warmest emotions. How terrible if he should be turned aside by a reputation as a heartless flirt."

"When I fall in love, I shall know how to convince the object of my affections of my sincerity, never fear. And of course then I shan't wish to flirt with other men, except a very little perhaps," said the unrepentant rogue, dimpling adorably. "But don't alarm yourself, dearest. I am really most discreet and do not allow gentlemen to go beyond the line."

Angelica sighed, fearing Lydia's definition of discretion would not coincide with her brother's, but as the coach was drawing up to the front door at this moment, she allowed the subject to drop.

Inside, Lydia yawned daintily. "My bed will look good to me tonight, I confess." Sweeping her sister-in-law with a discerning eye, she added, "You have been a trifle off-colour this evening. My conduct is not responsible for your pallor and depression of spirits. Are you feeling ill again?"

Angelica met her sympathetic eyes briefly. She was grateful for Lydia's affection and concern, but could not burden the younger girl with the reasons for her present unhappy mood.

"I have the headache a little tonight," she evaded. "A good night's sleep will put me to rights again. Goodnight, my dear."

But later, in the misty green boudoir that usually soothed her spirits, she admitted to herself that the restorative sleep she had spoken of so confidently was going to elude her for quite some time. She had quickly dismissed Annie and sat musing at her dressing table, abstractedly brushing her hair while unseeing eyes gazed unhappily back at her from the mirror. Her black anger at Giles's cruel words had quickly burned itself out, leaving behind humiliation that he could think such a thing of her but faint bewilderment, too. Surely he did not believe in his heart that she would be so disloyal? It occurred to her that jealousy might have prompted his remark, but her brain dismissed this forlorn hope impatiently, allowing her to derive no comfort therein.

He did not love her, so how could he be jealous? Then possessive, perhaps? Giles, with two unhappy experiences behind him, could be expected to be more sensitive about his honour than another man. Still her mind balked at accepting that he might honestly believe her capable of such treachery. She had thought he knew her better, that he had showed understanding and even respect for her in the beginning of their marriage. Even without love, she had been so happy with his companionship.

That never-to-be-sufficiently regretted night had changed everything. A flush crept up from her neck emerging creamy-white from a froth of apricot ruffles as, brush stilled, she relived for the thousandth time the experience that had meant so much to her and so little to him. Rather worse than little, because he had altered toward her directly afterward.

How could he be so tender and ardent in his love-making that night and then turn so frigid toward her at their very next meeting? It was impossible to avoid the mortifying conclusion that she had not pleased him. But he had not acted so at the time — indeed, far different.

She knew Giles to be experienced with women. Perhaps he found her deficient in some way, but how was she ever to remedy this if he never gave her any indication of what was wrong? Despairing as this thought was, it was worse to consider that very likely Giles preferred this state of affairs and had no slightest desire to come to a better understanding or forge a closer relationship than the state of cool civility under which they had dwelt for almost two months. The fierce pride that had managed to sustain her in the beginning was no longer sufficient. She was finding it increasingly difficult to pretend to a non-existent calmness and serenity of spirit in her daily routine. She felt smothered in a thick fog of depression with diminishing strength with which to battle through the mist. How was she to spend the rest of her life living with a man who treated her with the cold courtesy of a stranger without turning bitter and acidulous in her other relationships? She had married Giles knowing full well that he did not love her, but she had foolishly hoped their friendship would deepen into a real affection. Now she had even lost his friendship, and the pain of it would be her constant companion.

She sighed deeply and resumed brushing the long, silken hair. No good could come from morbidly dwelling on this state of affairs. Better to think about the baby who would need her care and love. She was indeed fortunate that she would at least have Giles's child. It must be a boy; somehow she was instinctively positive the baby would be a boy.

The eyes in the mirror, which had become narrowed and dreamy with inner seeing, suddenly widened in surprise as they met the shadowed dark ones of her husband.

"Giles! I … I did not hear you come in," she stammered, laying the brush down with meticulous care as his presence in her room set her nerves tingling. Her hand crept up to her throat in an ineffectual gesture to ease the uncomfortable tightening sensation that increased as he took two more steps forward and stopped, looking down at her soberly, his hands jammed into the pockets of his wine-coloured dressing gown. She was totally conscious of her tingling body clad only in diaphanous apricot silk, but incapable of movement of any kind.

"I was home early, waiting for you to come in so I could apologize for what I said this afternoon." His voice deepened to passionate intensity. "You must believe that I never really meant what I implied. It's just that I have no memory of that night, and at first I could not connect your news with myself. I know that is no excuse for insulting you, my dear, and I earnestly beg your forgiveness."

All colour had fled her face at his words, but she managed to echo faintly, "You — have — no memory...?"

He turned away abruptly, pulling his hands from his pockets and consciously relaxing the clenched fists.

"No," he said through clenched teeth, "and I had no desire to recall such shameful conduct." He turned and faced her, eyes black with intensity. "Good God, I never — forced a woman in my life, foxed or not. I couldn't face the thought that I'd hurt my own wife, when all I ever desired was to take care of you almost from the moment you entered my house."

"Giles!" She rose swiftly from the chair and came toward him, her pride washed away by a wave of sympathy for his self-disgust. The green eyes shimmered with unshed tears. "You didn't rape me, my dear, nor did you hurt me except for what was inevitable. Foxed you certainly were, but as soon as you realized I was frightened, you became as — as considerate a lover as any woman could wish."

"Angel!" A light flared in his eyes and he grasped her shoulders urgently, searching her face intently, then suddenly his own darkened again. "Then why did you cry, Angelica? Don't deny it —" this as she shook her head helplessly, eyes averted. "I saw your face when I awoke; it was all tearstained, and there was blood on your mouth. Why would you cry yourself to sleep if I had not been brutal?"

Angelica's courage was gone, and she could not swallow the remnants of her pride to confess the truth. She remained silent, but he shook her slightly, repeating his demand:

"Why did you cry?"

"All — all women cry on their wedding night," she assured him, trying to keep her voice from trembling "It does not mean anything." She tried desperately to meet his intent gaze, but her lashes fell before the demand in those near-black eyes. "Please, Giles, you're hurting me."

His grip on her loosened perceptibly, but that inquisitorial stare never wavered. After a moment, when she continued to evade his glance, he forced her chin up with the knuckles of one hand.

"No," he said deliberately, "not all women cry, unless they dislike their husbands intensely." His faint inflection made a question of the accusation.

Stung, she retorted hotly, "Or unless they realize they are just a substitute for another woman." She rushed on now as though a dam had broken, heedless of his dumbfounded expression. "You called me Alicia when you were falling asleep, and I knew then that you had been pretending I was your first wife all the time you had been making love to me."

The tears were running unchecked down her face now, and she was too upset to struggle as he gathered her up into his arms. He sat in the large chair, cradling her head against his shoulder and tenderly smoothing her loosened hair back from her wet face. He did not speak until she had succeeded in controlling the tears, but his arms were eloquent of comfort and protection. As she grew calmer, he murmured thoughtfully:

"I can't imagine why I would call you Alicia, because except at the very beginning I was never happy with her. It took very few weeks for me to realize that she had no love for me at all, or later, for Jenny either. The marriage was completely empty, and I never planned to marry again. However, one does grow lonely, and when I saw that Lydia really needed a chaperone for her come-out, I cynically decided to select a suitable female to serve as companion for both of us. I stupidly believed I could never love again you see, Angel, so I had no qualms about offering my name and possessions to a decorative young woman whose eyes were equally open and whose affections were, I was well aware, unengaged. I wanted no emotional demands made on me, and I thought Barbara would make none."

His arms tightened convulsively around her and he continued somewhat jerkily, due to the fact that his lips were feathering kisses along her cheekbones, sending shivers down her spine. "But I reckoned without love, my darling. You had not been in my house above a sennight when I realized I couldn't marry Barbara."

Angelica had been listening dazedly, with green eyes huge and questioning, but here she interrupted, "But you decorated this room for Barbara; you were still planning to marry her until she eloped with Sir Anthony and you asked me to substitute for her."

"My foolish child, I hate to contradict you, but do you honestly believe this misty green room, which exactly matches your eyes when you are thoughtful, was meant for anyone except yourself?" His lips were caressing the tiny hollow beside her mouth. She shivered with delight and her arms wound themselves around his neck, but still she lingered outside the gates of paradise.

"What would have happened if Barbara had not eloped?" she whispered haltingly.

"I was not pinning all my hopes on Haring's infatuation. If he had not come up to scratch, my darling, much as I would have deplored the tactic as unbecoming a gentleman, I'm afraid I should have given Barbara cause to break our engagement by flaunting my alleged mistress before her eyes in public. She had not been my mistress for some time, but no one knew that. I felt sure Barbara's pride, plus her very real indifference to me, would overcome any maidenly shrinking from scandal."

His mocking voice grew husky with feeling. "I could not lose you, Angel. I would have done any desperate thing to induce you to marry me, but I feared to ask for your love in the circumstances, so I played on your soft heart and your sense of duty. I intended to woo you slowly, because I didn't want another wife who pretended to love me. I did not want anything from you that was not freely given. Then I got drunk and ruined everything, or so I thought." Gently drawing her head back with a hand entwined in her hair, he searched her countenance probingly and said quietly, "You do love me, do you not, Angel? I haven't been wrong again?"

The tears were shining in her eyes again, but this time they were tears of joy.

"I think I have loved you since you rescued me from the lake ten years ago."

His eyes blazed triumphantly down at her. "Show me," he demanded huskily, and his mouth came down on hers in a warm, thrilling kiss to which she responded with an intensity born of all the pent-up longing of the lonely weeks since he had last caressed her. She was breathless and shaken when at last he released her lips to kiss the enticing hollow of her throat, where a pulse was beating wildly. She seized the opportunity to whisper anxiously:

"You ... you don't really wish there wasn't going to be a baby, do you, Giles?"

"Of course I don't, my foolish little love. It's high time Jenny had a brother or sister." His lips quirked in the lopsided grin that was the first thing she had learned to love about him. "But you won't mind if I hope for a son first, will you, love?"

"It will be a son," she assured him, smiling shyly into his tender, amused eyes. He continued to devour her face, and as his eyes darkened with passion, she lowered her lashes in confusion, the delicate colour fluctuating over her cheeks and the breathless sensation creeping back.

He rose from the chair abruptly, carrying the delightful burden easily.

"Come, my darling," he whispered, striding to the bed, "you are one memory ahead of me."

A NOTE TO THE READER

Dear Reader,

If you have enjoyed the novel enough to leave a review on **Amazon** and **Goodreads**, then we would be truly grateful.

Sapere Books is an exciting new publisher of brilliant fiction and popular history.

To find out more about our latest releases and our monthly bargain books visit our website:
saperebooks.com

Printed in Great Britain
by Amazon

51650278R00139